# CHASING FIRE

An I-Team/Colorado High Country Crossover
Novel

## PAMELA CLARE

www.pamelaclare.com

# CHASING
# FIRE

AN I-TEAM/COLORADO HIGH COUNTRY
CROSSOVER NOVEL

USA *Today* BESTSELLING AUTHOR

# PAMELA
# CLARE

**Chasing Fire**
An I-Team/Colorado High Country Crossover Novel

Published by Pamela Clare, 2018

Cover Design by © Jaycee DeLorenzo/Sweet 'N Spicy Designs
Image: Period Images

ISBN-10: 1733525106

ISBN-13: 9781733525107

*This book is dedicated to our courageous wildland firefighters and their families, who sacrifice so much to keep us all safe.*

## Acknowledgments

Many thanks to Russ Shumway for his insights on wildland firefighting. You helped me visualize a scenario I have (thankfully) never faced.

Thanks as always to Michelle White, Benjamin Alexander, Jackie Turner, Shell Ryan, and Pat Egan Fordyce for their support during the writing of this book.

To fans of the I-Team and Scarlet Springs series for their unwavering support. This book is for you.

## Introduction

On July 9, 2016, two transients left an illegal campfire untended on private property in the mountains above Nederland, Colo., where they had trespassed. Embers from their campfire started a wildfire that threatened 1,000 mountain homes and the entire town of Nederland. More than 1,900 people were evacuated, and eight houses were burned before the fire was contained four days later. Nederland, which has burned to the ground before, was spared this time.

I just happened to be listening to Boulder County's police and fire channel, as I often do while writing, and I heard the nightmare unfold. I was struck by the selflessness of firefighters and law enforcement officers as they did their best to protect lives. One deputy said over his radio, "We tried to evacuate the houses on this street but the entire street is engulfed!"

I couldn't imagine standing where he was standing at that moment.

Colorado had recently purchased a 747 Supertanker, and the images of the jet flying over the town to drop flame retardant on burning mountainsides were stunning. Just as amazing to me personally was the news that the fire had burned to within 36 inches of my brother's former in-laws' home before being stopped by a direct hit from a slurry bomber.

Thankfully, no lives were lost in the Cold Springs Fire. At the end of the day, Colorado isn't California. Fires here aren't as severe as fires there.

In the aftermath of the Cold Springs Fire, the idea for this story was born. I wondered what it would be like to bring my two contemporary series together—the straight contemporary Colorado High Country series and my romantic suspense I-Team series. I had other writing priorities at the time, so this had to sit on the back burner.

Since then, catastrophic fires have devastated California, causing horrendous and unprecedented loss of life. The images from those fires and the stories of survivors are both chilling and heartbreaking. Who could imagine such a thing?

It is painfully clear that big fires have become a regular occurrence. Fighting them becomes more dangerous and challenging as more people move into the wildland-urban interface (WUI), building homes in areas that used to be far outside our cities. As local governments are unlikely to halt the expansion of towns and neighborhoods into the WUI, it becomes increasingly important that individual property owners work with firefighters to minimize the risks to their property—and to lives.

If you live in the WUI—in the mountains, in the chaparral, or in heavily wooded areas—contact your local fire department to find out what they think you should do to create defensible space around your home. Fire mitigation saves property, and it saves lives.

Above Nederland, one homeowner worked hard with

the local fire department to mitigate fire risk on his land. He took the necessary steps, sacrificed some trees, made some alterations to his house—and I'm certain he's glad he did. The eight houses that burned surrounded his, but his house still stands, an island untouched by the fire.

The best time to prepare for a catastrophic wildfire is long before it's headed your way. Here in Colorado and much of the arid west, it's not a matter of *if*. It's a matter of *when*.

*Pamela Clare*
Dec. 13, 2018

## Chapter 1

A *THUNK* WOKE ERIC HAWKE.

Beside him, Vicki moaned and stretched, the sheet slipping below her bare breasts. "He's awake already?"

As much as Eric would have loved to start his day with a little sex, the toddler was loose in the house again. And that was the irony. The sex act produced children, which, in turn, made it hard to find time to have sex.

Eric glanced at his alarm clock, saw that it was just before six in the morning. "Go back to sleep. I need to get up anyway."

He didn't mind being the first one out of bed. He'd worked in search-and-rescue all his adult life and had been fire chief for the past seven years. He was used to odd hours and early mornings, and he loved this time of day. Besides, given how often he was away from home, he enjoyed the time with his son, and Vicki deserved a break.

He kissed her cheek, climbed out of bed, and pulled on a pair of boxer briefs and shorts.

Another *thunk* sent him hurrying down the hall to Caden's room, which he found empty, a wet diaper sitting in the middle of the wooden floor together with a pair of pajama bottoms. It figured. At twenty-three months, Caden was a world-class escape artist and, apparently, a budding nudist, as well.

Eric hurried downstairs past the living room with its big fireplace and cathedral ceiling toward the kitchen, his heart skipping a beat the moment he saw. "*Jesus!*"

Caden had pushed a chair over to the kitchen counter and now sat on top of the refrigerator, naked from the waist down, a box of graham crackers in his hands. "Tookie."

"Hey, little man, what are you doing up there?"

No wonder people got gray hair after having kids.

"Tookie," Caden said again.

"No cookies before breakfast." Hawke took away the box of graham crackers, lifted his son into his arms, and headed back upstairs. "We need to get you dressed."

While Caden chattered about Thomas the Tank Engine, Eric dressed him in a pair of dry training pants, shorts, and a little T-shirt that read, "I'm proof my mommy can't resist firefighters."

Eric wouldn't lie. He liked that T-shirt.

"You're all set." He tousled his son's dark hair. "Try to keep your britches on, okay?"

Back in the kitchen, he settled Caden in his high chair with some loose Cheerios and got busy scrambling eggs, making toast and coffee, and washing fruit. He enjoyed this morning routine, his life richer now than he'd imagined it could be. Vicki had entered his world, and everything had changed.

"Want some blueberries?" He put a few berries on Caden's tray and couldn't help but smile at the look of concentration on his son's face as he picked up each berry to put it into his mouth. "You like those, don't you?"

"He loves them."

Eric glanced over his shoulder to find Vicki leaning against the door jam in her white bathrobe, her shoulder-length dark hair tangled, a smile on her sweet face. "Do you know where I found him?"

"On the table?"

Eric shook his head. "On top of the *refrigerator*."

Vicki's eyes went wide. "Good grief! We have to do something. He can't have the run of the house when we're asleep. If he had fallen…"

Eric had been a paramedic for as long as he'd been a firefighter. He knew what even a short fall could do to a small child. They lived in a huge, two-million-dollar multi-level house—a wedding present from Vicki's gazillionaire father—and there were so many ways for an unsupervised toddler to hurt himself. They'd tried a dozen different kinds of baby gates, but Caden had climbed them all. They had a baby monitor, of course, but the little stinker was quiet when he got up to things he knew he shouldn't be doing.

"I'm not sure what to do. Put iron bars over his door? Install a motion detector?"

Why did children gain mobility before they acquired sense?

Vicki's eyes narrowed. "He takes after you, you know. Robin says you used to climb out of your crib, too. She says you climbed everything."

Eric's mother lived in a cabin on their property and watched Caden when he and Vicki were both at work. It was a convenient arrangement for everyone, but his mother talked too much. He opened his mouth to defend himself, but what she'd said was true. "Hey, it's all good. I turned it into a career, didn't I?"

His love of climbing had become serious when he was

a teenager, landing him a coveted spot on the Rocky Mountain Search & Rescue Team straight out of high school. Rescue work had led him to wildland firefighting and then the Scarlet Springs Fire Department. Eventually, he'd become the youngest fire chief in the history of Scarlet Springs.

He got breakfast on the table and went back for the coffee, pouring half-and-half in Vicki's and leaving his black. When he turned toward the table again, he found a small gift bag sitting beside his plate. "What's that?"

*Shit.*

Had he forgotten an anniversary or something?

Vicki smiled, an excited sparkle in her eyes. "Open it and see."

He handed Vicki her coffee, took a sip of his own, and sat. "Is it a new cam?"

Vicki laughed as if he'd said something stupid. "No. You don't trust me to buy you climbing gear, remember?"

"Oh. Right." He took the bag, reached inside, and searched through the tissue paper, his hand closing around something small and oblong that was made of hard plastic.

He drew it out—and stared.

Heart thudding, he met Vicki's gaze, saw the joy in her eyes. "This is… Are you?"

She nodded. "I'm pregnant."

A pang of tenderness filled his chest. She'd had such a rough time with Caden, twenty-six hours of labor ending with an emergency C-section. Eric wouldn't have blamed her if she'd refused even to consider having another baby and demanded he get a vasectomy.

"But … how?"

She laughed. "You know how. You were there."

That's not what he'd meant. "It took so long with

Caden, and you only went off the pill last month. I thought it would take six months, maybe a year."

"I guess we've gotten better at making babies because we nailed it on the first try."

"Well, that takes some of the fun out of it." Eric meant that as a joke, but the moment his words were out, he saw that Vicki hadn't taken it that way.

*Good job, dumb shit. Any other stupid things you'd like to say?*

"That was just a stupid joke." He reached across the table and squeezed her hand. "How are you feeling?"

She'd had terrible morning sickness with Caden.

"Fine so far." Her smile returned, but there was a hint of vulnerability in those brown eyes now. "Are you happy?"

"God, yes! I'm elated, stunned. I'm so excited that I'm acting like an idiot." Eric got out of his chair and knelt before her, taking her hands in his, and kissing them. "I love you, Vicki. Because of you, I'm the happiest man on earth. Never doubt that."

Behind him on the counter, his pager went off.

He got to his feet, crossed the room, scrolled through the message, not liking what he read, but not surprised either.

"What is it?" Vicki asked.

"Another red flag warning." They'd had red flag warnings every day for the past ten days thanks to this endless dry, hot, windy weather.

The mountains that surrounded Scarlet were in prime condition to burn.

———

MARC HUNTER TOWELED his hair dry, wrapped the towel around his waist, and stepped out of the bathroom into the bedroom. He headed to the walk-in closet he shared with Sophie and tossed a navy-blue Denver Police Department polo and a pair of dark green tactical cargo pants onto the nearby chair.

Today, he and Julian Darcangelo were heading up to Scarlet Springs, a weird little mountain town known for its good beer, to take part in a joint training exercise with the US Marshals Service and other law enforcement agencies. The exercise was intended to foster interagency cooperation or some shit, but Marc had signed on as a way to escape the heat and spend a day in the mountains with friends.

He and Darcangelo had known each other for eight years now, both of them employed by the DPD—Darcangelo as head of vice and Marc as SWAT captain. Okay, so that's not how they'd met. Marc had been an escaped convict at the time, and Darcangelo had hunted his ass down and brought him in.

It had been the start of a beautiful friendship.

The bedroom door opened and Sophie stepped in, still wearing that lavender silk robe he loved so much, her strawberry-blond hair damp. She closed the door behind her and locked it, her lips curving in a sexy smile.

She walked over to him with slow, seductive steps, took hold of his towel, and yanked it from his body, letting it fall to the floor. "The kids are still asleep."

He liked the way her mind worked. "We shouldn't let that go to waste."

GOD, he loved her—her mind, her body, her big heart. She was a wonderful mother to their two kids, Chase and Addy, and no man could ask for a better partner. She'd stood by him when the rest of the world had condemned and forsaken him, risking her career and her life to save his. Without her, he'd have rotted in prison—or died with a shank in his back.

What a damned lucky thing it was that he'd given her a ride home from that stupid high school graduation party all those years ago. He'd wanted to protect her from a group of asshole guys who'd been hopped up on meth, but in the end, it was she who had saved him.

He'd given up worrying about whether he was worthy of her and focused instead on being the man she thought he was. He'd made it his life's work to please her, both in and out of bed. He knew her moods, her fears, her dreams. He knew how to make her laugh, how to comfort her. He knew what made her scream, how to make her come fast, how to hold her on the edge until her nails dug into his back and her every exhale was a plea for release.

He watched as Sophie took his cock in hand and stroked him to readiness, desire naked on her beautiful face.

His gaze locked with hers, Marc grasped her wrist, drew her hand from his aching cock to his lips, and kissed her palm. Then he gave her a little shove, toppling her backward onto their queen-sized bed.

She gasped as she hit the mattress, her robe falling open to reveal paradise.

Without breaking eye contact, he dropped to his knees, forced her thighs wide apart, and stroked her just where she needed it most. "Mmm. You're wet."

"Get inside me already!"

Her impatience made him chuckle. "What's the rush?"

He lavished attention on her clit, watching with satisfaction as she raised one clenched hand above her head, her eyes drifting shut.

"Oh, *yes.*"

He kept up the rhythm until his fingers were drenched

and she was writhing on the bed. Then he lowered his head, drew her swollen clit into his mouth, and suckled.

Her hips jerked, her hands flying to fist in his hair. "*Marc!*"

She'd always been passionate, the most responsive woman he'd known. She'd been only sixteen the night he'd taken her virginity, and still, she'd blown his eighteen-year-old mind. Somehow, sex with her just kept getting better.

She was close now, the tension in her body building, her clenched fists pulling almost painfully at his hair, her breathing ragged.

He withdrew his mouth from her, laughing at her moan of protest, her scent filling his head, her taste in his throat. Then he settled his hips between her thighs, the breath rushing from his lungs as he entered her with a single, slow thrust. "*Sophie*."

She drew her knees up to her chest, opening herself to him fully. "Fuck me."

"Hell, yeah." There was no need to take it slow, no need for subtlety or finesse. He drove into her hard, her body gripping him like a fist, pleasure making his balls draw tight.

She bit back a cry as she came, bliss shining on her sweet face. He rode through it with her, then let himself go, his body shuddering as climax burned through him, white-hot and incandescent. They lay there together for a moment, breathing hard, hearts pounding.

Sophie smiled, laughed, her eyes still closed.

Marc pressed kisses to her bare breasts, smiling, too.

Then Chase's voice came from the hallway outside their bedroom, and the doorknob jiggled. "Mommy, are we going to the Cimarron today to see the horsies?"

Chase was seven years old now and fancied himself a cowboy, due to the influence of his Uncle Nate, who'd married Marc's younger sister, Megan. Nate and his father, Jack West, owned the Cimarron Ranch, where they ran black Angus cattle and bred champion quarter horses. They also spoiled the hell out of Chase and Addy.

The plan was for Sophie and Tessa, Darcangelo's wife and Sophie's closest friend, to take the kids up to the Cimarron for a day of fun. After the training, Marc and Darcangelo would join them for cold beer and grilled steaks.

No one could grill a steak like Jack West.

Sophie bit back a laugh. "Yes, honey. Get yourself dressed, okay? I'll be right out."

Marc pulled out, got to his feet, and drew Sophie up with him. He took her into his arms and held her close, the love he felt for her glowing inside his chest. "You sure got my day off to a good start."

She drew back, looked up at him, worry darkening her blue eyes. "You'll be safe up there, won't you?"

His wife was one of the strongest people he knew, but his last brush with death had left her grappling with post-traumatic stress. She'd watched terrorists drag him away to kill him, had heard a gunshot, and had believed him dead for long, agonizing minutes. She was doing much better now, nineteen months later, but she still worried every time he left home.

He smoothed a strand of hair from her cheek. "This is just a training exercise. We're going to run around in the forest pretending to chase bad guys—just a bunch of boys playing with toys."

What could possibly go wrong?

———

NAOMI BELCOURT STEPPED out of the women's staff

bunkhouse and walked toward the Dining Hall, rubbing the ache in her lower back. She'd never been seven months pregnant before and hadn't realized how uncomfortable it would be to sleep in a bunk. But there were only four days left before this second session ended. She could deal with it.

The day was bright and sunny, the sky overhead blue, the air fresh with the scent of ponderosa pines. Ahead of her, groups of campers ran, hopped, skipped, and jostled their way to breakfast with their counselors, their happy laughter making her smile.

This was her dream.

Naomi had grown up not knowing who she was. Abandoned in an alley as a newborn by her birth mother—a teenage white girl—she'd been adopted by a family of religious extremists who had raised her with warped ideas about women and "heathen Indians," beating her when she dared to challenge them. She'd run away from home at the age of sixteen when her adoptive father had tried to marry her off to a much older man against her wishes. She had waited tables to put herself through art school, but she hadn't known anything about her true heritage until she'd met Chaska.

Chaska and his sister Winona had saved Naomi's life after a couple of escaped cons had attacked her while she'd been camping not far from Scarlet Springs. As she'd recovered, Chaska had helped her uncover the truth about her past, finding her biological father, teaching her about Lakota traditions, and sweeping her off her feet. He'd married her in a traditional Lakota ceremony, giving her father a bride price of twenty-two horses—or rather, a 22-horsepower riding lawnmower.

She'd spent time on the reservation with Chaska, had learned to speak Lakota, and had gotten to know her blood family—her father Doug, his wife Star, and her half brothers and sisters—Mato, Chumani, Chayton, and Kimímila.

Somewhere along the way, the idea for this camp had begun to form in her mind. She had held several fundraisers and written dozens of grant applications to get the start-up money. Once she and Chaska had gathered the funds, they'd bought this old summer camp, repaired the cabins and dining hall, erected a tipi in the center, hired a crew to build an archery range and ropes course, and recruited Lakota counselors to run the day-to-day operation.

Now, Camp Mato Sapa—Camp Black Bear—was in its second year with three, two-week sessions that served 120 kids each summer. It was a place where Lakota children could come at no cost to their families to learn about their culture and traditional values, have fun in the outdoors, build their confidence, and escape the hardship that many of them faced at home.

Naomi served as the camp's director and taught art classes, while still running her shop, Tanagila's. She had never imagined that her life could be so rich and full.

She looked for Chaska but didn't see him. He was an early riser and had probably beaten her to the Dining Hall. Then Naomi spotted Kat James. Kat, a Navajo, was there with her husband, Gabe Rossiter, and their three children, Alissa, Nakai, and Noelle, who rode on her father's shoulders. They had spent the night in one of the guest cabins so that Gabe could be here to help Chaska supervise the kids on the ropes course this morning. The two men knew each other through the Rocky Mountain Search & Rescue Team—called the Team by locals—and both were world-class rock climbers. Hanging on ropes was their idea of a good time.

Naomi waved. "Was the cabin comfortable?"

"It was great. Thanks." Gabe swung little Noelle to the ground.

Kat took the toddler's hand. "It was really windy last night."

"Did it keep you awake?"

"Oh, no. I kind of like it."

Naomi and Kat talked about odds and ends as they walked the rest of the way to the Dining Hall—how Naomi was feeling, how fresh the air was high in the mountains, how vital it was for children to spend time in nature.

Naomi watched Gabe as they walked, amazed at how confidently he moved on his prosthesis. He'd lost his left leg below the knee in a desperate attempt to save Kat's life many years ago, but it hadn't slowed him down.

"I heard we've got a red flag warning again today." Gabe, who'd once been a park ranger, reached out to open the Dining Hall door for them, the mingled scents of bacon and coffee making Naomi's stomach growl.

"Let's hope we get rain soon. The land needs it." She followed Kat through the door into the Dining Hall—and stopped short.

Chaska and another camp counselor were breaking up a fight between two of the older boys, the other children watching with wide eyes from the food line.

Gabe hurried to help, stepping between the two boys.

Chaska caught hold of Dean, the bigger of the two, and held him back.

"Let me go!" Dean struggled to free himself.

Dean had been a problem since he'd arrived, breaking the rules, using rough language, and bullying the other children. Naomi could have expelled him, but she suspected that what they saw in his behavior was only a reflection of the violence he experienced at home. She didn't have the heart to send him back to that.

"He punched me!" Mervin, the smaller boy, got to his feet, fists clenched.

"*Iníla yaŋká po*! Quiet!" Grandpa Belcourt bellowed.

The room fell into startled silence.

"Let's talk about this like human beings." Grandpa looked sharp in his white shirt, beaded vest, and bolo tie, a single eagle feather in his long gray hair. "I saw you hit this boy."

Dean's face was still flushed, and he was breathing hard. "He called me stupid."

"No, I didn't!" Mervin's lip was swollen. "I said, 'Don't be stupid.'"

Grandpa held up a hand for silence and turned to Dean. "This is what you do when someone says words you don't like? You hit them?"

Dean's chin came up. He probably looked like a delinquent, a troublemaker, to most of the adults. To Naomi, he seemed like a scared little boy. "My father raised me to be a warrior."

"You think hitting another boy makes you a warrior?" Grandpa Belcourt chuckled, moving toward the center of the room. "Listen, children, all of you. Too many of our people have forgotten what it means to be a true warrior, so I will tell you."

Chaska released Dean. "Listen to Old Man now."

Naomi got a knot in her chest. God, she loved Chaska. He was a mechanical engineer who spent his workday building satellites, not a camp counselor or referee. Still, he'd jumped headlong into this whole summer camp adventure because it was important to her.

After waiting a moment to let the tension build, Grandpa spoke again. "A warrior isn't a man who hits people or fights with other men. A warrior is someone who sacrifices himself—or herself—for the well-being of others."

Dean rolled his eyes. "Yeah, right."

"Listen." Chaska rested a hand on Dean's shoulder.

Grandpa continued. "A man who protects the sick and the weak is a warrior. A woman who has a baby is a warrior because she suffers to bring life into the world. A boy who watches over his little brothers and sisters is a warrior. You want to be a warrior? Shovel snow from your grandma's sidewalk and carry her groceries without being asked. Watch over those who are younger and weaker than you are—two-legged, four-legged, and winged ones. Think of others before you think of yourself. Then you will be a true warrior and worthy of respect."

"*Aho*." Chaska nodded.

Dean's gaze dropped to the floor.

## Chapter 2

BRANDON SILVER'S heart thudded in his chest, orgasm fading into a kind of blissful stupor, his breathing beginning to slow. Libby lay limp against his chest, completely spent, her long strawberry-blond hair a tangled mass that spilled over his ribs and shoulders.

They'd been lovers for the better part of two years now and had fucked in pretty much every way and every*where* they could. In the mountains. At his place. At her place. In the stacks at the new library. In the park. At the theater. In the Scarlet Springs cemetery. At the firehouse. In the front seat of the big fire engine. On the gurney in the back of the ambulance. On the stage at Knockers, where Joe Moffat, her boss and the brewpub's owner, had caught them with their pants down. Behind the brew tanks at Knockers, where Joe *hadn't* caught them.

Libby was as creative a lover as she was a brewmaster. Maybe the two were related. Maybe the same part of her brain that came up with things like Plow Me Orange Chocolate Peppermint Cream Stout was the same part that had her asking him to tie her naked to the sawhorse in her garage.

One day, she would fuck him literally to death, but until then...

It was on the tip of his tongue to tell her he loved her, but he knew that would send her running. Libby loved sex, but she wasn't into commitment. The last time he'd slipped, she'd gotten angry, stomped off, and hadn't spoken to him for days.

But, damn, he *did* love her, from the tip of her freckled nose to the toenails she'd painted with black and green stripes. He burned for her. He'd been a firefighter for ten of his thirty years, but he had no idea how to put out this kind of blaze.

Libby was his obsession.

His pager buzzed in his cargo pants somewhere on the floor, but he couldn't do a damned thing about it. "Are you going to untie me?"

Right now, he was her prisoner, tied spread-eagle to her bed like an offering.

She stirred, raised herself, hands on his chest, her beautiful pink-tipped breasts swaying in a way that made him ache to suckle them. "I should keep you here. You have the body of a god, you know. I could play with you all day."

She slid her hands over his pecs and shoulders.

"And how many gods have you fucked?"

"That's my secret." She explored the muscles of his arms, which were stretched over his head. "What would happen if you didn't show up at work?"

"Hawke would have my balls." Brandon was Hawke's B-shift captain. It was his job to run the firehouse and respond to 911 calls—24 hours on, 48 hours off.

She sat up straighter, reached behind her, and cupped

the organs Brandon had named, her touch both gentle and teasing. "But I like your balls. He can't take them."

Brandon's pager buzzed again. "Then you'd better let me check that."

"Fine." She reached up, untied the silk cords that held him fast to the brass bars of her headboard. "I hate it when you have to go."

"We could get a place together." The words were out before he could stop them.

*Shit.*

She climbed off him to the floor, grabbed her bathrobe. "Please don't ruin this."

He sat up, flexed his fingers and reached down to untie his ankles. "How does that ruin anything? If we moved in together, we'd be together whenever I was home."

She turned to face him, slipped her arms into her robe. "Then we'd have to talk about mundane things like who cooks and who cleans and who takes out the garbage. You'd start leaving socks on the floor, expecting me to do your laundry, and asking me what's for dinner as if meals were my job. It wouldn't be fun anymore."

"What are you talking about? I'm not that kind of guy." He got out of bed, grabbed his pants, drew his pager out of the pocket.

Another red flag warning with winds expected later in the day.

"That's what they all say." She turned and disappeared out of her bedroom.

Okay, now *he* was pissed.

He dressed, jammed the pager back into his pants, and followed her. "I don't know what kind of men you met before me. They must have been assholes."

"Did you see the new study that showed that women *still* do most of the housework and childcare—even when they work outside the home and earn more than their husbands? Does that seem fair to you?"

"Hell, no, it doesn't seem fair, but I'm *not* those men." He drew a breath, tried to rein in his temper. "I don't get you, Libby. You want me, but only in bed. I'm not a sex toy, you know. I'm not a living vibrator."

She measured out coffee beans. "Do I treat you like a vibrator?"

"Well, no." They did things together besides fuck. They ate meals, went for hikes, went to the movies, had long conversations, watched TV.

"Then what's the problem? We have a *good* thing, Brandon. I don't want to ruin it by putting labels on it and making it more complicated."

"What's complicated about living together?"

She turned toward him, the bag of coffee beans still in hand. "A relationship is like a stick of gum. That first bite is amazing and tastes so good. Then a few minutes later, the taste is gone, and you want to spit it out."

He leaned against the counter, crossed his arms over his chest. "We've been seeing each other for almost two years, and no one is spitting anyone out."

She closed the grinder, pressed the button, raising her voice to be heard above the machine. "Well, you're *amazing* in bed."

The words ought to have been gratifying, but instead they hurt. "So that's all you want from me—a hard dick?"

"You say that like it's a bad thing." She probably thought she was funny, but Brandon didn't find it amusing in the least.

To *hell* with this.

He might as well come right out with it. "You know why our sex life is so good? I love you, Libby. That counts. It matters. It changes everything."

She shook her head, laughed. "How many times have you thought you loved a woman only to break up with her later?"

"Everybody has failed relationships. You can't—"

"You can't truly have loved someone if one day you *stopped* loving them."

What could he say to that?

"I'm not going to get tired of you if that's what you think. The way I feel… I can't get enough of you. It's not just sex. It's *you*. You love me, too. I know you do. You'd have moved on a long time ago if that weren't true."

She turned toward him and stared up at him like a deer caught in the headlights, blue eyes wide. But it wasn't anger he saw there. It was fear.

In a heartbeat, the emotion drained from her face. "You should probably go."

The words felt like a blow to his solar plexus.

*Shit.*

Was she breaking up with him?

Of course, not.

You couldn't break up with someone if you'd never really been together.

What the hell had just happened?

*You sure fucked this up, Silver.*

He tried to swallow his emotions the way she'd done, played it cool. "Okay. I'm going to be late anyway. Have a good day. See you later."

She showed no sign that she wanted to kiss him good-bye, so he walked past her and down the hallway toward her front door.

"Be safe!"

The sound of her voice followed him outside into the summer heat.

———

DARCANGELO OPENED the rear passenger door of Marc's SUV and shoved his backpack and rifle case onto the seat. "You're late."

Marc wasn't about to explain why he was late. His sex life was none of Darcangelo's business. "I had to give you time to make your hair pretty."

It was an old joke between the two of them. Marc kept his hair short, while Julian, who spent a lot of time on the street undercover, wore his in a ponytail.

Darcangelo chuckled, shut the door, then climbed into the passenger seat. "Hey, at least I have hair."

"My hairline is *not* receding." Marc glanced in the rearview mirror just to make sure and was relieved to see his hairline where it had always been.

They left Denver, heading west on Highway 36 toward Boulder, talking about their two favorite subjects—their families and firearms. Marc's police radio served as background noise, the mountains looming larger with each mile.

"I hear McBride set up a lunch at that brewpub, Knockers."

Zach McBride, the Chief Deputy US Marshal for the Colorado Territory, was a good friend of theirs. They'd met McBride through their wives, who had worked together at the *Denver Independent* as part of the newspaper's Investigative Team—or I-Team. The second-highest ranking lawman in the state and a former Navy SEAL with a Medal of Honor to his name, McBride clearly knew what mattered most to other LEOs at these events—food.

Darcangelo nodded. "Good. I fucking hate MREs."

"Tell me about it." Marc had served in the US Army as

a sniper, serving eighteen months in Afghanistan, where he'd eaten enough MREs to last this lifetime and the next.

"Did you have any trouble with your conversion kit?" Darcangelo asked.

They would be firing Sim rounds today — non-lethal Simunition filled with paint. The conversion kits ensured that no one could accidentally load a live round and kill someone. Not that real ammunition looked anything like Sim rounds, but safety came first.

"Piece of cake." Marc started to say something about the sweet Colt Cobra he'd shot at the range yesterday when something on his police radio caught his ear.

He turned up the volume.

"… a red flag warning for the mountains until midnight tonight with a dry cold front expected to bring gusts up to fifty-five miles an hour later in the afternoon. There is an open fire ban in effect statewide."

Marc turned it down again. "Let's hope that cold front isn't as dry as they think."

They talked police department politics most of the way to Boulder and up the canyon to Scarlet Springs. Old Man Irving was retiring in the fall, so a search was on for his replacement. The bean counters were trying to figure out how best to utilize the money the department got from taxes on legal marijuana sales. And why the hell couldn't they get decent food in the cafeteria?

"There's the turn." Darcangelo pointed to a sign that said "*Caribou.*"

"I see it."

Caribou was the site of a ghost town and an old silver mine. The landowner—a guy named Joe Moffat—had generously given them permission to use his land for today's exercise, enabling them to run around with their firearms away from the public. Seeing cops with weapons in their hands had a way of freaking people out.

Marc turned onto a dirt road and followed it uphill, stopping for a bull moose that stood in the middle of the road as if trying to remember why it had come this way. "Anytime now, buddy."

The moose looked over at them, velvet still on its massive rack, and then sauntered across the road and down the embankment.

Darcangelo clicked a photo with his smartphone. "What a beautiful animal."

"Did I ever tell you about the hunting trips I used to take up here?"

"Oh, God, here we go again. Do your kids know you killed Bambi's mother?"

Marc chuckled. "Bambi's mother was a deer. I hunted elk. You do know there's a difference, don't you?"

"Blow me, Hunter."

"No way."

They found a dozen or so law enforcement vehicles parked at the top of the road. Marc pulled in parallel to the black SUV marked MARSHALS SERVICE on the rear.

They climbed out and walked over to McBride, who was standing with several uniformed men and women in the shade of a big pine.

"Hunter, Darcangelo." He grinned, shook their hands. "Glad you two could make it. Have you met Sheriff Pella?"

Pella, a lean, middle-aged man with gray at his temples, was sheriff of Forest County, which included both Scarlet Springs and Caribou.

Marc reached out a hand. "Marc Hunter, DPD SWAT captain."

"Julian Darcangelo, DPD vice."

Pella repeated their names, then grinned, his gaze fixed on Marc. "You're that guy who broke out of prison and hid out up here, aren't you? The governor gave you a pardon."

Yeah, Marc had figured that would come up. It had been a long time ago, but people didn't forget that sort of thing. "Yes, sir, I'm that guy."

Pella chuckled. "Glad you could join us. This is one of my deputies, Julia Marcs. She's been with the department for eight years now."

Marc frowned, her name somehow familiar.

Deputy Marcs looked up at them through mirrored shades, her dark hair pulled back into a ponytail. "Pleasure to meet you both."

And then it was time to get down to business.

McBride gave a short introduction. "Since the legalization of marijuana in the state, we've seen a fifteen percent increase in criminal transients here in the mountains west of Boulder. Some of the transients we encounter are just folks down on their luck, but a significant percentage are felons—sex offenders, drug dealers, armed robbers. They came to Colorado thinking they'd become millionaires dealing legal weed, only to find out state law prevents anyone with a criminal record from participating in any aspect of the marijuana industry. Rather than leaving, they hide up here, camping illegally on county and national forest land and posing a threat to locals and tourists alike."

Pella cut in. "When you boys drove them off the streets of Denver, they came here. They've taken over a couple of campgrounds, squeezing out decent folks. I want them out of my mountains and away from my town."

Marc couldn't blame Pella for that.

McBride nodded in understanding. "It's going to take a coordinated effort from federal, state, and local law enforcement agencies to make that happen. The point of today's exercise is to explore the challenges inherent in apprehending suspects in the mountain environment."

Pella glanced over at Marc, a grin on his face. "We've got an expert here."

Marc ignored the comment, listening as McBride explained what would happen next. Several illegal campsites had been set up in the forest to the north of the old mine, away from mine shafts and other hazards. They would take turns in mixed teams of three moving in on the campsites and apprehending the DUSMs pretending to be bad guys. They would then evaluate their performance and get feedback from McBride and his crew.

"Each group of volunteers will be running their own scenario, so expect surprises," McBride said. "Remember that we're above nine thousand feet elevation here, so stay hydrated. I don't want anyone coming down with altitude sickness. After lunch, we'll head out and get a look at the kind of damage these folks do to campgrounds and wilderness areas."

Pella got specific. "You'll see the trash, erosion, piles of human excrement."

"Sounds like fun," Darcangelo said.

Deputy Marcs gave him a wry look. "You'll get to do what we do every day."

Marc's gaze shifted to the west to take in the breathtaking view of Indian Peaks.

*What the hell?*

He pointed. "Someone tell me that's supposed to be there."

In the distance, a narrow column of white smoke curled against the sky.

JESSE MORETTI RODE the chairlift toward the top of Eagle Ridge, chainsaw resting across his lap. He'd been assigned to supervise the crew that was cutting whippers from the glades today. The forest was always trying to reclaim the slopes. Clearing whippers—scrub and saplings that grew more than a foot above the ground—made up a lot of the work they did here at Ski Scarlet over the summer. If they didn't stay on top of this shit, the slopes would quickly become unskiable.

He preferred the work he did here in the winter. From November to May, he was part of Ski Patrol. He rescued people who'd gotten injured, kept stoners and drunks off the slopes, and tossed bombs—blasting powder caches with explosives so they wouldn't cause avalanches. It didn't feel like work most of the time because his feet were strapped to a pair of skis.

But as soon as the snow melted and ski season ended, his job changed to a kind of landscaping gig—clearing whippers and rocks from trails, removing invasive weeds, and reseeding grass on runs to prevent erosion. It was hot, sweaty, thirsty work.

Still, no one would catch Moretti complaining. He'd done hotter, dirtier work in Iraq when he'd been an Army Ranger.

What he'd experienced at war had brought him to Colorado in search of peace. He'd seen the mountains and had fallen head-over-heels in love, something beautiful after years of ugliness. He'd become obsessed with rock climbing, had learned to ski, and had gotten a job on Ski Patrol that following winter, volunteering with the Team in his free time.

The move to Colorado had been the best idea he'd ever had because it had led him to Ellie and the twins. Ellie, a widow and a registered nurse at Mountain Memorial Hospital, had lived next door to Jesse with her two small children, Daniel and Daisy, who hadn't yet turned three. Then a highly contagious case of strep throat had brought them together, and Jesse had fallen head-over-heels in love again.

Now, he and Ellie had a little three-month-old son—Dylan—and Jesse couldn't have been happier. The little guy was growing so fast. He could already hold up his head, roll over, and push himself up on his arms.

Yeah, fatherhood was pretty damned amazing.

Off to Jesse's left, a golden eagle soared over the tree-tops, feathers gleaming golden-black against a bright blue sky. It wheeled toward the west, its wings flat.

Jesse was so caught up in its flight that it took him a moment to notice.

Smoke.

It came from a valley to the northwest of the ski area.

He sat up straighter, squinted. "Son of a bitch."

Was there a controlled burn scheduled for today? Sometimes land managers burned piles of slash, clearing out fuels to prevent catastrophic forest fires, but Jesse hadn't heard anything about a burn being slated for today. There was a red flag warning in effect. Only an idiot would risk a burn on a red flag day.

He reached for his hand mic. "Forty-two to dispatch."

His boss, Matt Mayes, responded. "Forty-two, go ahead."

"Is there a controlled burn on the schedule for today?"

"Not that I've heard. No one would be stupid enough to burn on a red flag day."

That's what Jesse had thought. "There's smoke rising from a valley northwest of us."

"Copy, forty-two. I'll call it in."

Jesse watched the smoke column, a spindly tendril that

curled in the breeze. It hardly seemed menacing, but he'd heard the stories about the big fire that had almost wiped Scarlet Springs off the map back in 1878. Of course, they hadn't had modern firefighting equipment back then—no slurry bombers or flame retardant, no smokejumpers or hotshots or helitack crews, no helos equipped with hoses or buckets for water drops.

They hadn't had modern forecast technology either. The fire had swept down on the town from the mountains and burned most of it to the ground. Only one building had remained when the smoke cleared—the Forest Creek Inn. The Inn stood there today, still owned by the same family. But dozens had been killed by smoke and flames, most of them prospectors and miners who'd had no warning that the fire was coming.

The Scarlet Springs Town Council and the fire department had spent the past century and a half trying to prepare for the Next Big One, educating the public about wildland fire, urging homeowners to clear fuels from around their homes, and installing a reverse 911 system. So far, every fire that had started near town had been snuffed before it could do any damage.

"Dispatch to forty-two."

"Go ahead, Dispatch."

"The sheriff's department said the fire has already been called in and relayed to Scarlet FD, as well as the Rocky Mountain Control Center."

That was good news.

Hawke and his crew would be on top of it in no time.

Matt went on. "We're in the evac zone this time, so they want us to be ready to get out if necessary. I told them to feel free to use our space to fight this thing."

"Great idea."

The parking lot would make a great fire camp, and the

slopes, which were cleared of trees and vegetation, were perfect safety zones.

"In the meantime, I want someone watching that smoke column. It's much too close for comfort. The wind is going to kick up this afternoon, and it could come our way. I don't want anyone on our crew to get caught in a runaway blaze."

"Copy that." Jesse dug his smartphone out of his pocket.

He wanted to warn Ellie, to tell her to be ready just in case.

## Chapter 3

ERIC STRODE through the firehouse toward his locker shouting orders to Silver. "I want eyes on Bear. Someone locate him and bring him here until the fire is controlled. If you can't find him, I want to know."

From what Eric had gleaned from the calls, the fire was on Forest County's Haley Preserve property next to Tungsten Creek. Bear lived somewhere out there, coming into town to offer his blessing to passersby in exchange for a warm meal. He'd been part of the community for as long as Eric could remember. No one knew how old he was. He'd just always been here. Big like his namesake, Bear had the mind of a child—except when it came to the Bible, which he knew chapter and verse. The residents of Scarlet watched over him, sheltering him during blizzards, making sure he got medical care, buying him meals.

Eric would *not* lose him to a wildfire.

"You got it, chief." Silver stopped outside the locker room. "Do you need a ride to the Boulder County airport?"

"No." That would lose him an hour. "The helo is

picking me up at the hospital."

Mountain Memorial had the only helipad in the area. It was the fastest way for him to get airborne. He needed to see the fire for himself, get a look at the terrain before he put a crew out there or called for resources.

Right now, he wasn't even sure where the fire was.

Eric stepped into the locker room, opened his locker, and got into his wildland firefighting gear—brush pants, fire resistant T-shirt, brush shirt, boots—his mind running through a list of campgrounds, known transient camps, and private property west of town. All reports so far said the fire was small—a single column of white smoke. With any luck, they'd have it out in a few hours before the temperature rose, relative humidity dropped, and the winds fanned it into a threat to life and property.

Eric had spent part of every day since becoming fire chief planning for the worst-case scenario. He'd pored over maps and observed the topography around Scarlet, filing away his observations every time he went out on a call, went climbing, or drove through the mountains. He'd memorized the locations of streets, dirt roads, meadows, lakes, creeks, and trails—anything that might serve as a fire break. And he'd prayed that the next big one would never come.

Fires in Colorado's mountains could be treacherous, in part because of unpredictable weather, but also because of the terrain. Fire burned more quickly uphill than down. If the slope was steep enough, the top of the fire column could ignite fuels high above it. Eric had seen fire consume a steep mountainside in a matter of minutes, seeming to leap and roll uphill, incinerating everything in its path. Canyons, draws, and saddles—they could change a fire's behavior, funneling flames and super-heated gases.

That was the thing about fire. It wasn't evil. It didn't

have a hidden agenda. It just went where weather, topography, and fuels enabled it to go. That didn't mean fire behavior was always easy to predict, but it wasn't rocket science, either.

He finished dressing, grabbed a wildland pack, a weather kit, and a charged radio, and left through the open bay door, driving himself to the hospital and parking near the helipad. The helo itself was privately owned. It had been hired by the National Forest Service to fly over the state's vast stretches of wilderness to watch for fires.

Eric heard it before he saw it—a retired AH-1F that had seen service in Vietnam. It came into view to the east, its red and white paint a contrast to the blue sky. Eric stayed by his vehicle until the craft had touched down. He ducked down and ran through the rotor wash, then climbed through the open door into the back, settling his pack on the floor and buckling in.

He pulled on his headset, gave the pilot a thumbs-up. "Let's chase smoke."

Terry Robertson, fire chief for the Forest County fire crew, turned to look back at him, his voice sounding tinny in Eric's earphones. "We could see the smoke coming in. It doesn't look like much. A single hand crew can probably put it out by suppertime."

Robertson was a good guy, but he'd been doing this job for too long. He loved the ceremonies and pomp that came with his position, but he no longer had the belly for making tough calls. It was as if a part of him had already retired, even while he still wore the uniform.

Eric tried logic first. "Let's get a look at the terrain before we commit any crews. There's a cold front coming through this afternoon. We need to hook it before that wind hits."

As soon as they were in the air, Eric saw it—a thin

column of white smoke in the distance. Robertson was right. It didn't look like much.

It took just a few minutes to reach it.

The pilot hovered, giving Eric the GPS coordinates.

Eric looked down at the blaze. "Looks like an illegal campsite. The campfire got out of hand. Sparks ignited the duff."

Below him, fire crept along the valley, burning through the duff—the layer of pine needles, debris, and old, dried branches that covered the forest floor. The point of origin looked like an illegal campsite off a dirt access road next to Tungsten Creek. The road and the creek had kept it from spreading eastward.

That was the good news.

But there was bad news, too.

The mountainsides to the east and west of the fire were steep with dense, mixed-conifer forest, giving the fire plenty of fuel in every direction. The trees hadn't ignited yet, but when fifty-mile-an-hour winds hit those flames this afternoon, the situation would change.

"That looks like maybe fifteen acres," Robertson said. "Whoever was camping there is probably hell and gone, run off the moment they saw the fire got out of hand. I don't think this poses any risk to town. I'll get one of my crews on it."

*What the fuck?*

No risk to Scarlet?

Clearly, they weren't reading the landscape in the same way.

Eric had never claimed to be God's gift to firefighting, but fire spoke to him. He could look at the landscape, the fuels, and the weather conditions and know with some certainty what a fire was going to do. This one was not going to stay benign for long.

He tried to be diplomatic. "To be on the safe side, we ought to call for some bucket drops. If the fire is still burning when that front hits, upcanyon winds will push it to the northwest toward Ski Scarlet or send it straight eastward toward town or both."

That was the stuff of Eric's nightmares.

But Robertson was already on his radio, telling his crew to make ready.

A knot formed in Eric's stomach.

*Shit.*

This fire was primed to burn in any direction the wind decided to take it. Initial attack had to be successful, and, in this terrain, that meant using aircraft. But helicopters and single-engine air tankers, or SEATs, didn't grow on trees. They were hard to come by during a bad fire season.

Three fires were already burning in Colorado—one near Manitou Springs, another on Grand Mesa, and yet another outside of Eagle. The state had only a few rotary aircraft equipped to fight fires, and they were probably already committed. The SEATs and the lone 747 Supertanker were busy fighting the Manitou fire. That meant requesting a chopper from the Colorado National Guard or asking for federal resources through NIFC—the National Interagency Fire Center—a process that often resulted in denials.

Either way, it wasn't Eric's call. He was fire chief for Scarlet Springs, and this was county land. What happened next was up to Sheriff Pella and Robertson, who would be Incident Commander on this blaze.

But if Eric could talk to Pella first…

It would piss Robertson off, but Eric didn't give a damn. Robertson was putting lives on the line here—not just his crew, but every person who might be in the path of this fire if it burned out of control.

Eric turned off the mic on his headset and reached into his pocket for his smartphone.

SOPHIE SAT in the passenger seat of Tessa's Chevy Tahoe while Tessa drove, the two of them talking about everything and nothing, the four kids sitting in the back—Maire and Addy in the middle row and Chase and Tristan in the back.

Sophie loved the drive to the Cimarron, city giving way to foothills and finally to high mountains, buildings left behind for stands of aspen and pine. With every mile they put behind them, she felt the tension she seemed always to carry inside her fade, her heart growing lighter.

It was only an hour's drive, but that could be hard for young children.

"Mommy, Tristan kicked the back of my seat," Addy complained.

Sophie glanced over her shoulder. "I'm sure he didn't do it to pester you. Tristan, can you be more careful? We're almost there, kids."

"He did it again!" Abby wailed.

Tessa looked back at them through her rearview mirror, the sweetness of her Georgia accent underpinned by steel. "If y'all start squabbling back there, I'm going to turn this vehicle around, and you won't get to spend the day with the horses."

Silence.

Sophie fought back a laugh. "Well done."

The kids, like their parents, were best friends, but that didn't keep them from bickering now and again.

Sophie saw the big wooden gate that marked the entrance to the Cimarron Ranch. "Here we are, kids."

Jack, patriarch of the West clan, stood beside his pickup just inside the gate, waiting for them. He waved as Tessa turned off the highway and onto the dirt road that led to the ranch.

Tessa rolled down her window, a breeze catching her curly blond hair. "Hey, Jack!"

He bent down to look through the window. "I see you brought a load of surly cowpokes with you. Hi, there, kids. Are you ready to see some horses?"

"Yes!" the children squealed in near unison.

"All right, then. Let's not dillydally here. Head on down to the house. I'll lock the gate and follow you."

"God, I love this place." Sophie rolled down her window, let the fresh mountain air hit her in the face. "When we drive through that gate, it's like the weight of the world is lifted from my shoulders."

Tessa reached over, gave Sophie's hand a squeeze. "I know what you mean."

Tessa had been there for Sophie this past year and a half as only a true friend could be. She'd listened while Sophie had wept out her terror and grief in the aftermath of the terrorist attack on the Palace Hotel. She'd watched the kids so Marc could come to Sophie's therapy appointments. She'd brought meals and helped Sophie clean her house. Never once had she told Sophie to get over it the way other people had—as if a positive attitude could take away the horror and grief that had imprinted itself on her heart and mind the moment she'd heard that gunshot and believed Marc was dead.

Up here, surrounded by the warmth of hospitality and the beautiful scenery, the nightmare she'd lived through hardly seemed real or even possible.

The Cimarron sat in a high mountain valley in the shadow of white-capped peaks. In the fall, the mountainsides turned gold with the aspen. In winter, they were white with snow. Horses and cattle grazed in fields of grass and wildflowers.

The surroundings were breathtaking, and the ranch house matched it in every way. Made of stone and logs, it was a mix of Swiss chalet and western styles with a steep, multi-gabled roof, high cathedral windows, and a portico driveway accented by a colonnade of polished logs. Off to one side stood several large outbuildings, including horse barns, a bunkhouse, an enormous riding hall, and several corrals. The inside of the house was even more spectacular, like something from a magazine.

Jack's son Nate had married Marc's younger sister Megan, and the Wests had taken Megan's family and friends to be their own. No one could match the West clan when it came to hospitality and kindness. They'd done all they could to support Sophie, too, especially Megan, who had faced her own battle with PTSD after being repeatedly raped while in juvenile prison as a teenager. She'd understood what Sophie was going through better than anyone.

They came to the rise that revealed the valley in all of its beauty, the windows of the ranch house gleaming in the sun below.

"There's the house, kids. See it?"

Four heads craned to look out the windows.

"Home, sweet home." Tessa parked, and she and Sophie helped the kids climb out.

Nate and Megan were waiting for them at the house, their kids beside them. Miss Emily, as her grandpa called her, was now a big girl of eight and a half. She bounced up and down in her pink cowgirl hat, while Jackson, who had turned two in May, stood quietly holding his mother's hand, an adorable little white cowboy hat on his head.

Nate motioned Tessa to the side of the house, a big

smile on his scarred face. He'd been burned over almost half of his body in an IED explosion while serving with a Marine Special Operations Team in Afghanistan. He and Megan, each scarred in their own way, had found peace and happiness together.

"Good to see you all." Nate bent down, tugged on the brim of Chase's hat. "Are you ready to do some riding, buddy?"

Chase nodded, looking up at Nate with adoration on his face.

Megan welcomed Tessa and Sophie with hugs. "I'm so glad you came. Emily has been stir-crazy waiting for you to get here."

"I'm as excited as she is." Sophie pressed a kiss to her sister-in-law's cheek.

Jack pulled into the garage and stepped out, radio in hand, a frown on his face. "I just got a call. There's a fire burning somewhere west of Scarlet. It's pretty small now, but the weather is supposed to turn this afternoon."

"Fire?" Was it anywhere close to Marc, Julian, and the others?

Jack must have seen the fear on Sophie's face. "It's too far away to be a danger to us here. Let's have the men get every horse trailer we have hitched up in case there's an evacuation. I'll put in a call to Sheriff Pella and offer to transport livestock if need be."

Nate nodded. "They should gas up their trucks, too. We don't want anyone heading up to Scarlet on an empty fuel tank."

"Good point." Jack raised his radio.

While he made the call to his foreman, Nate motioned them inside. "Come say hello to Janet. I think she's got fresh lemonade waiting for you."

Janet, Jack's wife, was a former FBI special agent who'd

met Jack when he threw her off his land. They'd fallen in love despite the age difference—Jack had been sixty-three when they'd gotten together and Janet forty-five—and now they had a little girl, Lily, who was three weeks younger than Jackson.

As Sophie followed Nate inside, Tessa came up beside her and spoke for her ears alone. "Don't worry about Marc and Julian. They're with the sheriff. He'll make sure they're safe."

That wasn't what worried Sophie. She knew her husband—and Julian, too. They were the first to step up in any crisis, the first to put themselves on the line to help others. In Denver Police Chief Irving's words, the two of them were "shit magnets," always ending up in situations that put their lives at risk.

But Jack had said it was a small fire.

Sophie prayed it stayed that way.

———

VICKI PARKED, grabbed the diaper bag, and walked with Caden in her arms to Robin's front door. "You get to spend the day with Grandma Robin."

Her mother-in-law was waiting for them. She took Caden from Vicki and kissed his chubby cheek. "I see your daddy dressed you this morning. I think that's his favorite T-shirt."

Vicki set the diaper bag on the floor inside the door and shut the door behind her. "Did you hear about the fire?"

"Fire?" Robin's expression changed from happiness to worry. "Where?"

"It's west of town. Eric got toned out just after breakfast. He said it's a small fire, but he's worried because it's not far away and the weather is supposed to change."

Robin settled Caden on the floor with his favorite magnetic blocks. "Try not to worry about Eric. I know it's not easy, believe me, but my son has good instincts. He listens to his gut, and he always puts safety first. He loves you, and he wants to come home to you and Caden. He'll be careful."

Vicki nodded. "I know he will."

Then she remembered. "I have some happy news."

Robin's attention was on her grandson. "That's great. Let's hear it."

"I'm pregnant."

"Oh!" Robin's gaze jerked to meet Vicki's, her eyes wide.

"I just did the test this morning. I think I'm about five weeks along."

Robin drew Vicki into a hug. "Congratulations! I'm so happy for the two of you, for all of us. Another grandbaby! What does Eric think?"

"He's excited." Vicki told Robin how she'd surprised Eric with the news.

Then it was time for her to go.

She kissed Caden goodbye and drove into Scarlet, passing the roundabout where dear old Bear often stood preaching. He wasn't there, but then it was still early. She parked behind Knockers and headed toward the staff entrance, carrying a white chef's uniform on a hanger.

If someone had told her ten years ago that she'd end up married to a fireman, living in a tiny Colorado mountain town, and running a deep-dish pizza business, she'd have thought they were insane. She had loved her life in Chicago and her job in the fast-paced world of public relations and marketing—until she'd met Eric.

She'd come to Scarlet Springs to try to talk her best friend, Lexi Jewell, into dumping Austin Taylor and coming back to Chicago. Eric was Austin's best bud, so Vicki and Eric had gotten off to a bad start. But then she'd come back to be Lexi's maid of honor when Lexi and Austin had gotten married. Eric had kissed her, and that had been it.

Now she couldn't imagine living anywhere but Scarlet Springs. She'd traded her career to be part of a shared business venture with Joe Moffat, or Caribou Joe, as many of the locals called him. He owned Knockers, the brew-pub, and she operated her pizza business in his kitchen, offering authentic Chicago-style deep-dish pie to his customers and home delivery to the residents of Scarlet. She wasn't making nearly as much money, but she was happy.

She stepped through the kitchen entrance to find Rico, Joe's kitchen manager, head cook, and unofficial bouncer, already hard at work doing prep. A giant of a man with a bald head and bushy red beard, he looked intimidating, but he was a big teddy bear. He'd done time as a teen for stealing cars and had learned to cook while behind bars. Joe, big-hearted man that he was, had hired Rico, hoping to give him a fresh start.

"Hey, Rico. How's it going?"

"Can't complain." Rico looked up from the celery he was chopping, hairnet over his beard. "Hey, Vic. How's the little guy?"

"He escaped again. Eric found him on top of the refrigerator."

Rico looked as horrified as Vicki had felt when she'd heard. "Velcro jammies. That's the solution. Stick that rascal to his bed."

Vicki couldn't help but laugh. "I like that idea. You should patent it."

She made her way through the kitchen to the women's staff restroom, where she changed into her uniform. She stepped back into the hallway and was tucking her handbag and clothes into her locker when Libby walked in wearing her work coveralls, purple bandana over her head, strawberry-blond hair in braids. It was clear from her face that she was upset.

"Are you okay?"

Libby jerked her locker open, shoved her backpack inside, and slammed it again. "If men weren't stupid, I would be just fine."

*Uh-oh.*

"Did you and Brandon have a fight?"

Libby sat on the bench, misery on her face. "He said we should get a place together. Can you believe that? We have a great time, and he wants to screw it up by making it serious."

Vicki wasn't sure what to say. "I'm sorry you're having a rough day. I'm sure he didn't say that to upset you."

"You know what else he did? He told me he loves me and that I love him, too."

"And that's a bad thing because…?"

"I don't want to love anyone!" Libby's face flushed red. "When you love someone, they have the power to hurt you, to wreck your life. I don't want that. I just want good sex and good times. Is that too much to ask?"

Vicki sat down next to her. "I know Brandon pretty well because he works for my husband. He's a good guy, Libby. He's not one of the jerks, and believe me, I've known some real jerks."

That was an understatement.

Libby's face crumpled, rage turning to anguish. "I

know he is. But why did he have to go and complicate things?"

Vicki wasn't sure Brandon was the one making this complicated, but she didn't say so. "Being in love with a man who loves me is the best thing that's happened to me. Sure, love is a risk, but life isn't worth much without it."

"You really believe that?"

"Yes, and I bet Brandon does, too. You can talk it over with him when he comes off his shift. This fire is pretty small, so I doubt he'll end up working overtime."

"Fire?" Libby's eyes went wide.

Vicki recognized that fear. It was the same fear she felt every time Eric got toned out, the same fear every family member of a firefighter felt whenever their loved ones were called into action. But Vicki was the fire chief's wife. She couldn't let that fear show, not around the friends and family of Eric's crew.

She willed herself to smile. "There's a small fire west of town. Eric went up in a helicopter to get a look at it. He's worried about the weather turning, but I'm sure they'll get a handle on it. They'll be okay."

Joe stuck his head around the corner, smartphone in hand, his long hair tied up in a man bun. A handsome man of almost fifty, Joe, too, had a beard, though it was shorter now since he and Rain had gotten together. "Did either of you see Bear on your way in? Silver's calling from the firehouse. They're trying to locate him to make sure he's nowhere close to this fire."

Vicki and Libby shook their heads.

"He wasn't at the roundabout."

Joe disappeared again.

Vicki stood, gave Libby a hug. "It will work out. You'll see."

## Chapter 4

MARC DIDN'T like this at all. A little two-person tent sat on the lee side of an outcropping of rock. The rock protected the tent from wind and weather, but it also gave assholes a good place to hide. They could be up there right now, waiting for Marc and the others to get close enough for a lethal shot.

It's what Marc would have done.

Rifle at the ready, he moved forward, he and the others arrayed in a tactical L with the other two in front of the tent and Marc off to one side. The safety mask they'd made him wear was hot and annoying as hell, partially blocking his peripheral vision. Out here, he couldn't afford to miss anything. There were old prospecting pits and mounds of mine tailings that offered excellent cover, not to mention trees, boulders, and fallen logs.

If he got shot, Darcangelo would never let him live it down.

He stopped, motioned toward the boulders, bringing the others to a stop. Deputy Marcs and a Deputy US Marshal named Ali Ahmad nodded in understanding.

They took cover behind the trees, the deputy and DUSM focused on the tent while Marc watched the outcropping, finger on the trigger.

"US Marshals!" Ahmad shouted. "You are surrounded! Come out of the tent slowly with your hands over your head!"

"Don't shoot!" a woman's voice called from inside the tent. "I'm coming out, and I don't have a gun."

Marc left her to the other two and kept his attention on his scope.

Motion.

Someone *was* up there, inching closer to the edge, probably waiting for the woman in the tent to distract them and draw them into the open.

*Not a chance.*

Through his limited peripheral vision, he saw Deputy Marcs step out from behind the tree, weapon raised as she moved in on the suspect emerging from the tent.

The guy on the rock lifted his head to take his shot.

Marc fired.

*Pop!*

Yellow paint splattered on the guy's safety helmet.

*One down.*

Another pop.

Deputy Marcs had fired, too. Marc glanced over and saw the woman from the tent sink onto the ground, paint on her shoulder, a Glock in her right hand.

Motion.

The barrel of a rifle nudged through the brush at the rim of a prospecting hole behind Deputy Marcs.

With no time to think, Marc pivoted, dropped to one knee, and fired.

*Pop!*

More yellow paint.

Deputy Marcs and Ahmad spun to look behind them and saw the man who might have killed them—if he been a real crook.

"Shit." Deputy Marcs scanned the surrounding mountainside.

"Two headshots, Hunter." McBride came up behind them. "You're on a roll."

"Don't feed his ego." Darcangelo followed a step behind McBride. "He's hard enough to live with as it is."

They debriefed the action on-site as a group, sharing feedback, which was mostly positive. The DUSMs who'd played the bad guys—two men and a woman—ribbed each other about getting killed, yellow paint on their US Marshals Service T-shirts. Then, through the trees, came the sound of shouting.

Pella stood near the vehicles with two men dressed in wildland firefighter gear.

McBride glanced back over his shoulder. "Let's take a ten-minute hydration break. There's a Porta-Potty back by the vehicles if anyone needs it."

Marc shouldered his rifle and made his way with the others back toward the parking area, Darcangelo on one side, Deputy Marcs and Ahmad on the other, McBride a few paces ahead.

"Thanks for having our backs," Deputy Marcs said. "You're one hell of a good shot with that rifle."

Marc opened his mouth to respond, but Darcangelo cut him off.

"He was an Army sniper. How many confirmed kills, Hunter? Eighty-five?"

"Eighty-six."

"For a time, he held the record for long-distance kill, too. He took out a Taliban leader from three-quarters of a mile away."

Deputy Marcs gave a low whistle. "Wow."

McBride looked back at Darcangelo, grinning. "Don't feed the ego, remember?"

Marc didn't have an ego—not when it came to his job. "Can I say something?"

"No." McBride and Darcangelo said in unison.

"You know these two, sir?" Ahmad fell in beside McBride, a grin on his face.

"Only too well." McBride chuckled. "Once upon a time, they put their lives on the line to save my wife, Natalie, and me."

Ahmad nodded as if a mystery had been solved. "That's why you put up with their bullshit."

"Yeah. That's it."

Back at the row of vehicles, Marc dug into his pack for his water bottle and took a deep drink. It was easy to get dehydrated at altitude.

"A couple of hand crews can hook this thing and have it out in a matter of hours," said the older firefighter with a clipboard in his hand.

A younger firefighter stood his ground, looking furious. "If this thing isn't out before the wind hits, it will race up the slopes and make a run along the drainages that lead into town. Initial attack *has* to succeed. We need aircraft."

"We don't—"

"Enough!" Sheriff Pella looked like he could use a drink. "I've got to go with Eric on this one, Terry. I'm going to request a helo or SEAT and a team of smoke-jumpers, but I can't guarantee we'll get anything. You know how it goes. Establish a lookout, and get your hand crews up there. I want reports from *both* of you every thirty minutes."

Sometimes it sucked to be the one in charge.

The younger one turned to face them and gave Marc

and the other LEOs the once-over, his gaze landing on Deputy Marcs. "Hey, Julia. What are you doing up here? Did something happen at Joe's mine?"

"It's a training day. We're playing a serious game of paintball." Deputy Marcs pointed at Marc with a nod of her head. "This guy just saved my ass."

"Nice." Eric shook Marc's hand, then Darcangelo's and Ahmad's. "Eric Hawke, fire chief for Scarlet Springs."

No wonder the man had stood his ground when it came to that helicopter. If that fire took off, it might well make a run for his town.

Marc didn't have firefighter training, but he could use a chainsaw and dig. "If there's anything we can do…"

Hawke met Marc's gaze, worry making his jaw hard. "I appreciate the offer, but you'd better hope it doesn't come to that."

———

KENZIE MORGAN CONRAD walked the block to Aspen Wildlife Sanctuary for a quick meeting with her friend Winona Belcourt, a wildlife vet. The two of them were Team members and had volunteered to help with this year's Team fundraiser. It was their job to find restaurants to act as food sponsors for the event, which would be held in Boulder. The Team, an all-volunteer rescue organization, got all of its money through grants and donations, and the fundraiser brought in a substantial amount of their annual operating budget.

Kenzie walked through the front door and toward the back, where she found Winona taking care of a golden eagle, her eyes protected by goggles, heavy gloves on her hands to keep her safe from the raptor's talons. But the beautiful bird wasn't putting up a fight.

Kenzie stood outside the treatment room, waiting.

"Poison." Winona wiped blood from its beak with a gauze pad. "It probably picked up a rodent that had ingested an anti-coagulant and got poisoned second hand. The only thing I can do for it is euthanize it, end its suffering."

*How awful.*

Kenzie's heart broke for the beautiful creature.

Winona spoke to the eagle in Lakota, her mother tongue, then wrapped it gently in a towel and carried it to the back. When she returned ten minutes later, Kenzie was still wiping tears from her eyes.

Win gave Kenzie a hug. "It's awful, isn't it?"

Kenzie sniffed. "How do you deal with things like that?"

She'd never seen Winona lose her composure over the animals in her care.

"Sweat lodge helps. I pray. I do everything I can to help the animals that come to me and leave the rest to Creator." Win handed Kenzie a tissue. "Your job comes with some pretty tough days, too."

"That's true." Kenzie owned a dog kennel and trained search dogs, volunteering for the Team with her golden retrievers, Gizmo and Gabby, for SAR and HRD work— search and rescue and human remains detection.

When she got toned out, someone was either missing or dead.

"Let's go to my office."

Kenzie followed her to the back. "How is Shota dealing with the heat?"

Shota was Winona's wolf. Stolen from the wild with the rest of his litter by poachers who had killed his mother, he'd been the only pup Winona had been able to save. Now fully grown, Shota was fiercely protective of Winona

—and a potential danger to everyone else. He lived in a large enclosure behind the house where Winona lived with her brother, Chaska, and her sister-in-law, Naomi. Sometimes the wolf howled at night—a primal, haunting sound —and the dogs at the kennel howled back.

Kenzie wondered what they were saying to each other.

*Hey, I'm a big wolf.*

*!Hola! I'm a Chihuahua, but my ancestors were wolves.*

Kenzie loved the howling, but it probably drove their neighbors crazy.

"He sleeps a lot and stays in the shade. I've been giving him ice blocks to lick."

Kenzie and Winona talked through a list of restaurants they hoped they could talk into donating free food for the fundraiser in exchange for advertising in the program and on the Team's website.

"You know Joe will say yes, so we don't even have to wonder about Knockers."

Joe Moffat was Scarlet's homegrown philanthropist. His family had grown wealthy off the silver mine up at Caribou, where most of their ancestors had worked back in the day. He had always been one of the Team's greatest supporters.

"What about that fancy new place on Pearl Street in Boulder—what's it called?" Kenzie tried to remember. "Something like Terror."

Winona fought back a smile. "You mean 'Terroir'? Let's add them to the list."

They needed ten food sponsors, so they came up with a list of twenty restaurants. Then they divided the restaurants between the two of them to start making calls.

Getting people to do things for free for the Team wasn't difficult. It was a nonprofit, and it had the reputation of being the best search-and-rescue team in the country. People in Colorado were obsessive about outdoor sports, which made them sympathetic to the cause. They all felt safer knowing the Team was only a phone call away.

Winona's receptionist popped her head into the room. "Brandon Silver is on the line from the fire department. There's a fire west of town, and he wants to know if you've seen Bear."

Winona shook her head. "I haven't seen him for a few days."

Kenzie hadn't seen Bear, either. "I hope he's not in danger."

"Bear is wiser than any of us when it comes to survival in the mountains," Winona said. "If there's a fire nearby, he'll know to get out of its way."

Kenzie hoped Winona was right. "Harrison just got toned out with the rest of the Team—a woman with a broken leg. They're west of town, too."

Kenzie's husband, Harrison Conrad, had only recently returned from climbing Nuptse, Mt. Everest, and Lhotse by himself in just five days—the first man in history to do so. He hadn't done it for glory, but to heal emotional wounds and to claim the Khumbu Triple Crown, as some called it, for a lost friend. Kenzie had been scared to death for him every day of those five days, but she'd known it was something he had to do to find peace.

"Megs won't let them put their safety at risk," Win said.

Megs Hill, a climbing legend, was the founder of the Team. Kenzie had always thought of her as a bit of a hardass, but the kindness she'd shown Harrison during his recovery from the Everest disaster had proven to Kenzie that Megs had a soft side—one she kept well hidden.

Winona picked up the phone. "I'm going to call Brandon back and make sure he knows about Camp Mato Sapa. It's up there, too, not too far from Ski Scarlet. My brother and Naomi are up there with forty kids. That's a lot of people to evacuate in an emergency."

"Good idea."

Win dialed the number, stood with the phone to her ear, her face slowly folding into a frown. "No answer. I guess they're busy."

———

GABE TIED the top rope into his harness and climbed the ladder. Today's lesson was about trust and teamwork. His job was to provide a little humor relief and to prove to the kids that they wouldn't get hurt if they fell. If he impressed his wife in the meantime, so much the better. She would reward him in the bedroom.

Kat *was* watching. She sat on a blanket beneath a nearby pine, Noelle playing beside her, the two older kids running about near the tipi.

On the ground, Chaska was on belay and had taken up Gabe's slack. Gabe started across the high rope, twenty-five feet off the ground, using the guide ropes to steady himself, his blade prosthetic not intended for this. But he'd done his share of slacklining, and this was easier.

"See how he holds onto the guide ropes to steady himself?" Chaska looked up at him. "You know what would happen if he fell?"

That was Gabe's cue.

He pitched forward, letting himself fall—and jerked to a stop in mid-air.

Kids gasped, stared up at him, eyes wide.

Old Man Belcourt—Chaska's grandfather—chuckled.

"Nothing happened. See how the rope goes through that pulley and then down to me? I'm on belay, and that means that I'll stop him from falling. He couldn't get to the ground now if he wanted to."

Gabe stretched for the ground, flailed his arms and legs. "Let me down!"

Now the children were laughing, too.

Chaska lowered Gabe to the ground. "I know this is new and different from anything you've done before, but that's what this camp is all about, isn't it? Who wants to be the first to cross the high rope?"

One of the younger girls stepped forward, a shy smile on her face, hand raised.

"Way to go, Mona. Let's get you ready."

One of the counselors got little Mona into a child's harness.

Gabe untied himself from the rope and knelt to tie Mona in. "You don't have to worry. We won't let you get hurt. You're going to have fun."

Fearless, Mona climbed up the ladder as Gabe had done, followed by the camp counselor who stood on the platform behind her, encouraging her.

Mona took hold of the guide ropes, hesitating for a moment. The other kids watched in amazed silence as she took one step and then another. She froze out in the middle, looking down at the ground as if realizing for the first time how far away it was.

Chaska coached her through it. "Don't look down if it scares you. Look at your feet and the rope beneath them. You're doing great."

Mona shook off her nerves and moved carefully to the other side, a big smile of triumph on her face as she set foot on the platform.

"Well done, Mona!" Chaska called up to her.

The man was going to make a great dad.

Old Man Belcourt was waiting for Mona at the bottom

of the ladder. "You showed courage going first, but are you sure one of your ancestors isn't Iktomi? Spider Girl. That's what I'm gonna call you from now on."

Gabe knew a lot more about Navajo—or Diné—culture than he did Lakota culture, thanks to Kat and years of traveling back and forth between Denver and the Diné reservation. Still, he was pretty sure that Iktomi was a spider trickster spirit. Old Man Belcourt had complimented Mona.

The little girl looked delighted.

"Who's next?" Chaska called.

Hands shot up, the children's faith in themselves bolstered by Mona's example.

Gabe found himself smiling as he tied child after child into the harness and watched them confront their fear. He couldn't think of a better way to spend the day than up here in the mountains with Kat, the kids, and good friends.

More than half of the kids had successfully crossed the high rope when Gabe spotted Naomi walking toward them, a hand on her rounded belly, a worried expression on her face. She waited until the child on the ropes had reached the other side then asked to speak with Chaska.

"The phone is dead. I just tried to call Food Mart about the cake for our end-of-camp party, but I couldn't get a dial tone."

Cell phones were of no use up here—not until a person got out of the canyon and down the road to the main highway.

Kat walked up to them. "It was really windy last night. Maybe a tree fell on the lines."

Gabe nodded. "When we're done here, I can drive into town and find out what's going on. When I get down to Scarlet, I can let them know the line is dead."

Naomi looked relieved at this. "Thanks. I appreciate it. Sorry to interrupt."

She turned and walked back the way she'd come, while Chaska and Gabe got back to the kids and the ropes course.

"Who hasn't gone?" Chaska turned toward the kid who'd started the fight this morning at breakfast. "Dean?"

Dean glowered at the ground. "I don't want to do that."

"He's afraid," offered the kid with the fat lip.

Chaska nodded. "It's okay to be afraid. Do you know what courage is?"

Dean said nothing, but a few of the kids nodded.

"It means not being afraid."

Chaska shook his head. "Hey, Old Man, what is courage?"

Grandpa Belcourt stepped up to Dean, put a hand on his shoulder. "Everyone has their own ideas about things these days. But back when I was a boy, I was told by my elders that courage is doing something you need to do even though you're afraid."

Chaska knelt in front of Dean. "You can do this, buddy. I know you can."

Dean looked like he wanted to cry, then an expression of fury came over his face. "Fine. I'll do your stupid high rope."

Gabe tied him in. "You're going to do great."

Dean climbed the ladder, stood on the platform looking down like someone about to leap from a cliff. Gabe could almost feel the kid's heart pounding. But this was a leap of faith.

Dean took one step and another and…

He slipped and fell with a shriek.

Chaska stopped his fall. "It's okay. You're okay."

"I want down! Put me down!"

Chaska lowered him to the ground.

Gabe saw shame on his face. So far, he'd been the only child to fall.

It couldn't end this way.

Gabe knelt in front of him. "You're okay. You're safe. Do you want to try again? You can do this, Dean."

Dean looked up, something desperate in his brown eyes. "I'm scared."

"I know, but you don't have to let that stop you."

Dean walked back to the ladder, climbed up, his jaw hard as he looked out over the rope. He took one step and another and another.

"That's it. You've got this."

Another step. Another. Yet another.

Gabe held his breath as the boy passed the halfway mark, a look of utmost concentration on his face as he took those last few steps. When Dean stepped off the rope and onto the platform, everyone cheered, even the kid with the fat lip.

The triumph on Dean's face put a knot in Gabe's chest.

"You did it, man!" Gabe walked over to unharness him, gave him a high five.

Chaska did the same. "Way to go! You didn't give up even though it would have been easier."

Old Man tousled the boy's hair, bent down. "What you did—getting back up there after you fell—*that* was true courage."

## Chapter 5

ERIC PARKED the Type 6 brush truck across the road from the fire. "The county crew hasn't made it yet."

"They probably got lost," said Jenny Miller.

Chuckles.

Eric climbed out, Miller and four other members of his crew following. Because Scarlet Springs sat in the WUI—wildland-urban interface—Eric required every firefighter who joined his crew to have experience fighting wildland fires. He drilled them relentlessly on both structural and wildland firefighting techniques so they would be ready for anything—and so they would remember the differences between the two.

Scarlet had burned to the ground in 1878, and it was his job to make sure history didn't repeat itself.

Silver pulled up behind them with the rest of the crew in a surplus hotshot buggy that Eric had bought from the US Forest Service at auction last year. Running a small fire department meant getting creative with finances.

"Listen up!" Eric called out. "Right now, this fire is just hanging out here, waiting for the wind to catch it. We'll clear a chain length off the road and brush out the area on the east side as well. We need to work fast and smart to corral this thing before that front moves in."

"Bring it on!"

"Miller, it's your turn to be lookout. Head up that ridge. With all the spurs here, it's possible that stray embers might start spot fires elsewhere that we can't see."

"Got it."

He went over the trigger points with her. "If you see smoke or flames rising from any of the little canyons or draws coming off these spurs, warn us and get out. If this thing blows up and turns into an active crown fire, we all get out. Remember, there is no good black here. If we have to evacuate, we climb into these vehicles and get the hell down the road to that turnaround area. That's our primary safety zone. After that, we fall back to the parking lot at Ski Scarlet."

"What about the creek?"

"There's not enough water flowing now to do us any good."

Orange helmets nodded.

"I've got a dozer on its way, so cut those trees before they get here. If the fire spots to the other side of the road, we'll hit those fires with the brush truck. The county crew will join us on the line shortly, and Robertson will be Incident Commander when he gets here."

Groans.

"I don't like it either, but that's how it is. We will cooperate with the county crew and follow orders, but we will not compromise our safety. Understood?"

More nods.

"You got it, chief."

They grabbed their gear—packs, personal gear bags, Pulaskis, shovels, chainsaws, hoes, and cubies of drinking water. They did one last radio check and had just started up the road when the county crew pulled up and parked behind them.

Eric stayed to go over his plan of attack, but one look at Robertson's face told Eric he was still pissed.

*Too bad, buddy.*

Eric would never risk the success of an operation to appease anyone's ego.

Robertson pretended Eric wasn't there, not bothering to check in with him before he barked orders at his crew, sending them to cut line on the fire's flanks to keep upcanyon winds from moving it along the valley. "Let's hook this thing and go home."

When his team of twenty had moved up the road, he walked over to Eric, jabbing a finger in his direction. "The next time you go over my head, I'm going to demand yours on a platter."

"You're welcome to try." Robertson had no authority over Eric and no sway with Scarlet's Town Council. "It's not your community that will burn to the ground if this thing blows up. I'll do whatever I have to do to protect the people of Scarlet Springs. If that means contradicting you in front of the sheriff, so be it."

The roar of chainsaws told him his crew was now hard at work.

Not bothering to wait for Robertson's response, he outlined the plan for his own crew. "With the help of the dozer, we'll make the most of this roadway and try to get this thing contained before the wind carries it to the other side. We'll pump-and-roll on any spot fires that show up across the road. If that helo arrives, we've got a good chance of actually—"

"There won't be a helicopter." Was that satisfaction on

Robertson's face? "Pella just called to say none are available at the present time."

*Son of a bitch!*

"Did Pella try to rent one from the Colorado National Guard?"

"Who's going to pay for that? It's not coming out of my budget." Robertson turned and walked away, leaving Eric angry enough to spit.

"Fuck." With no other option, Eric shouldered his pack and hiked toward Miller's position on the ridge. He'd taken a few steps when he got a call on his radio.

It was Ryan, his A-shift captain, who'd been called in on his day off to manage things while Hawke and B- and C-shifts went out on the fire. "We've searched all the usual places and called around. No one has seen Bear for a few days."

*Shit.*

It wasn't unusual for Bear to disappear for days or even weeks at a time. He had a cabin up here somewhere on a piece of county property called Haley Preserve. Homesteading wasn't legal, but very few people knew the cabin was there, thanks to Austin Taylor, who, together with his boss, had turned a blind eye after Taylor had found the cabin a few years back.

"Get Taylor from County Parks on the phone. He knows where Bear's cabin is."

"Copy that."

He finished his hike up to Miller's lookout position.

"It's beautiful up here, chief."

"Yes, it is." But Eric couldn't see the beauty of the place.

All he could see as he looked around them was fuel ready to burn.

If the blaze broke out of this valley, if the wind caught

it and turned it into an active crown fire, it would run straight for everything and everyone he loved.

———

AUSTIN TAYLOR CRAWLED beneath the litter, slipped the ATV tire into its socket, and crawled out again. "We're good to go."

They started toward the parking lot, six Team members steadying the litter as it rolled down the trail with its injured cargo.

A park ranger with Forest County, Austin had been patrolling trails when the Team was toned out to help a woman who'd fallen while bouldering with friends near the Indian Peaks Trailhead. As rescues went, this one was straightforward and simple. Reach the victim. Offer first aid. Get her into the litter. Trail her out to the ambulance waiting in the parking lot.

Malachi O'Brien, an ER doc who volunteered with the Team on his rare days off, had given the victim an autoinjector of morphine, which had left her euphoric.

"Hey, Conrad, are you and Kenzie stopping by the—" Megs said, only to be cut off by a squeal.

"Conrad?" The victim sat up on her elbows, gaping at Conrad as if noticing him for the first time. "*Harrison* Conrad? Oh, my God!"

"Oh, here we go," Megs muttered.

"That's my name." Conrad didn't like the adoration.

"God, I've wanted to fuck your brains out for *years*. I have a shirtless photo of you in my work locker. Oh, man, those pecs!"

Conrad's face went blank as if he didn't know how to react or what to say and so refused to react or speak at all.

Austin found himself biting back laughter and saw that

the other Team members—O'Brien, Megs, Nicole Turner, Mitch Ahearn, and Bahir Acharya, the new guy—were almost choking in an effort not to smile or laugh. Before long, everyone on the Team would hear about this. It would be a long time before they let Conrad live it down.

The woman's boyfriend didn't seem to find it funny. "I'm right here, you know."

Yeah, that wasn't awkward at all.

The victim was too doped up to care what anyone thought. "Holy shit! I'm being rescued by Harrison Conrad. I'd have broken my leg sooner if I'd had any idea he would show up."

"Now, there's a testimonial for our website," Megs muttered.

The victim searched the litter around her. "Where's my cell phone? I need a photo, or no one will believe me."

Back at the ambulance, Conrad allowed her to take one selfie, insisting that her boyfriend be in the photo, too.

Austin was in the driver's seat of his ranger vehicle when Dispatch called for him over the radio. "Fifty-six-twenty. Go ahead."

"Fifty-six-twenty, we got a call from Scarlet FD asking you to contact the firehouse."

"Copy that."

He pulled out his smartphone, checked for signal, which was patchy up here at best, and called the firehouse.

Ryan answered. "Hey, we've got this fire west of town, and the chief is on the line up there. He wants us to find Bear and bring him in until the fire is out. We've searched town and called around but can't find him. Hawke says you know where Bear's cabin is. We're supposed to get a dry cold front this afternoon, and the chief is afraid this thing is going to blow up."

*Well, shit.*

Austin looked to the west. He couldn't see the smoke from here. "Bear could be anywhere between Scarlet and his cabin. Hell, he might have hangouts that we don't know about. I can head out that way and see if I can spot him, but it will take time. Is there any chance of getting a helo for this? It would be a lot faster."

"I have no idea. Pella put in a request for a helicopter for bucket drops, and that was rejected. Maybe you could snag a rescue chopper."

Maybe—if they weren't all out on rescues. It was the middle of the summer, the busiest time of year as far as rescues went.

"I'll check in with my boss and get back to you."

"What's up?" Megs stood at Austin's open window, eyes hidden behind mirrored shades.

"Hawke is worried that the fire west of town is going to blow up. He has his crew searching for Bear, but they can't find him. They want me to head to Bear's cabin and bring Bear to the firehouse."

Megs looked stunned. "You know where Bear lives?"

"I spotted him at his cabin once when I was out hiking."

Brow furrowed, Megs stared at him. "You sure kept that secret."

"I didn't want suits with the county to come in and throw him off the land. He's been here longer than they have."

"You're a good man, Taylor."

"Yeah, well, now I have to persuade my boss to let me leave patrolling so I can head out on a Bear hunt."

"Let us know if we can help."

"Thanks." Austin walked back to his truck and called his boss, Rick Sutherland, on his cell phone to explain the situation.

"I'm worried about Bear, too, but I need you. I just got off the phone with Pella. He wants us to close the trails and public campgrounds. It's just a precaution. I've been monitoring the fire on the radio, and I understand why it's making Hawke edgy."

"What about Bear? He's out there somewhere."

"If we don't close those trails and clear the campgrounds, he won't be the only one. Clear out the hikers and tourists, and then we'll worry about Bear."

———

BY THE TIME noon rolled around, Julian could have eaten one of Hunter's elk, antlers, hooves, and all. Pella had been called away to deal with the wildfire, so McBride finished debriefing the last scenario without the sheriff and led them back toward the parking area, where they all piled into a waiting van and drove down to Knockers in Scarlet Springs.

A tall man with a beard met them at the door, his hair in a man bun. "Hey, Zach. Good to see you again."

Hunter lowered his voice. "I think this guy goes to the same stylist you do, Dorkangelo."

"Dude, I have *never* worn my hair in a bun."

McBride clearly knew the guy. He held out a hand. "Hey, Joe. Thanks for letting us use your land today."

Joe Moffat, the landowner.

Joe brushed off McBride's thanks. "We sure appreciate the work you all do to help keep our town safe."

McBride introduced them all to Joe, who, in turn, introduced his wife and the pub's co-owner, Rain, a striking woman with roses, ivy, and skulls tattooed along her forearms. Their little daughter, Angel, rode in a carrier on her mother's back.

"We've got a table saved for you over here." Rain led them toward the far side of the pub, a stack of menus in her hands.

Julian sat, accepted a menu. "Thanks."

Hunter glanced around, saw pool tables, a bar, a stage, and … a climbing wall? "No wonder this place is popular."

"I think locals would tell you there's nowhere else to go," Rain joked, handing the last menu to McBride. "Cheyenne and Sam will be over to take your drink orders in just a moment. Let me know if you need anything."

"Chicago-style deep dish pizza." McBride sounded dubious. "Seriously?"

Rain overheard him, stopped, turned back. "You should try it. Victoria Hawke, the woman who runs the pizza part of the business, is from Chicago."

"You're on."

A tall, blond server who said her name was Cheyenne came to take their drink order. Everyone asked for water, most complaining that they were officially on duty and couldn't try any of the brews. A few minutes later, they overheard Cheyenne's voice and those of two other women talking to each other nearby.

"Have you ever seen such a group of hunks?" Cheyenne said.

"I think my ovaries just exploded," said another.

"Can I have the one with the ponytail?"

"Sure—if I can have the one sitting across from him."

*Shit.*

Julian met Hunter's gaze, spoke quietly, not wanting to embarrass anyone. "I think you have a fan club."

Hunter grinned. "I was going to say the same thing about you."

"Jesus fried chicken!" Deputy Marcs muttered to

herself. She turned toward the women. "Hey, Chey, Sam, Marcia—the *hunks* can hear you, and so can I."

Giggles.

A moment later, Cheyenne walked up to the table, the two other women with her, each carrying a tray with glasses of ice water.

"I'm Marcia, the bartender." A pretty woman with shoulder-length brown hair set a glass of water down in front of Hunter. "Let me know if there's *anything* you need."

The other woman, presumably Sam, gave Julian his water. "Here you go. Can I get you anything from the bar —a sampler of one of our brews, perhaps?"

There was no mistaking the interest in her eyes.

It was flattering to think that a woman in her early twenties found him attractive. He'd turned forty this year, and some of his whiskers had gone gray. Still, Julian hadn't been interested in another woman since the day he'd kissed Tessa in that hospital linen closet. She had loved him when he couldn't love himself. He couldn't imagine being with anyone else.

"I'm good. Thank you."

Sam gave Deputy Marcs her water without saying a word.

"Aren't you going to flirt with me or ogle my physique?" Deputy Marcs flexed a bicep.

"Sorry, Julia," Sam answered with a smile. "You're hot, but you're not my type."

Cheyenne and Sam stayed to take their orders, while Marcia turned to give McBride his water, her gaze still on Hunter. In the next instant, she tripped, dumping ice water down the back of Hunter's shirt.

He gasped, shot to his feet, caught her.

She stared at him where he held her, eyes wide. "Sorry!"

"It's okay. I was hot."

Julian wasn't sure that was the best choice of words in this situation.

"I'll get you a towel." Cheeks pink, Marcia hurried back to the bar.

Deputy Marcs seemed to find the whole thing hilarious. "She'll name a drink after you."

Julian couldn't help but grin. "You should have seen the look on your face."

"You think this is funny?" Hunter raised a brow at him.

Julian nodded. "Yeah, I do."

Marcia returned with a terry cloth towel, her cheeks still pink. "Sorry again. I'm happy to pay for your meal."

"You don't have to do that. Accidents happen." When Marcia started to dry Hunter off, he took the towel from here. "I can handle it. Thanks."

"Sorry!" She looked like she was going to say something more, then turned and hurried off, probably still feeling embarrassed.

They placed their orders—mostly burgers, but a personal pan pizza for McBride—and talked over the day's training while they ate. Deputy Marcs was eager for them to see the devastation at the county's campgrounds and along Magnolia Road.

"The fire burning west of town right now was almost certainly started by transients, so that's another danger these illegal campsites pose to those of us who live here. People who don't obey camping regulations are unlikely to respect fire bans."

Julian could see that. "Where is the nearest homeless shelter—Boulder?"

Deputy Marcs nodded. "Some are afraid to go to the

shelters because they don't feel safe there. Some refuse to stay in shelters out of fear of being picked up on outstanding warrants or because they don't want to follow the shelter's rules about drugs and booze."

"This problem isn't going to be easy to solve," McBride said. "That's why I brought you all up here. Apprehending fugitives is on the top of the Marshals Service's list. As for the rest—well, we don't want to demonize people, but public safety and resource protection take precedence."

The food arrived, Sam and Cheyenne carrying large trays covered with plates. A dark-haired young woman in a chef's uniform followed them, carrying McBride's pizza.

"I hear we have a Chicagoan at the table," she said.

McBride held up a hand. "That's me."

"I'm Victoria Hawke, owner of Victoria's Chicago-Style Deep Dish Pizza." She set the personal pizza in front of him. "Here's a taste of home. Enjoy."

McBride inhaled the scent. "It smells like the real deal."

Hell, it smelled incredible.

Victoria stood and watched while McBride took a bite. "And?"

McBride chewed, surprise and appreciation on his face. "This is just like Lou Malnati's pizza back home."

Victoria smiled. "I'll be seeing you here again."

McBride nodded, taking another bite. "You damned well better believe it."

## Chapter 6

BRANDON WATCHED his chainsaw bite its way through another lodgepole pine, sweat dripping down his face and the back of his neck, his throat parched, radio traffic buzzing in his earpiece. He gave the tree a shove, sent it toppling to bare earth, then stepped back and took a deep drink of water. The dozer crew had arrived a few minutes ago and was starting a run, stripping away anything that could burn and leaving a wide swath of bare soil.

That's how he felt—stripped bare.

He'd known that Libby would freak out if he told her how he felt, and he'd done it anyway. What the fuck had he been thinking? If he'd kept his mouth shut, he'd be looking forward to seeing her when he got off his shift tomorrow rather than wondering whether he'd just torched their relationship.

*To hell with that.*

He couldn't keep pretending that she didn't mean anything more to him than a good time. He loved her. If he'd had his way, they would move in together, maybe talk about getting married, but that was too conventional for her. Did she truly think he'd turn into a sexist man-baby the moment their relationship got serious?

No, that wasn't it.

She was afraid. She'd never talked about her past relationships, but clearly, someone had hurt her, belittled her, left her feeling used and abandoned.

Brandon would love to punch the son of a bitch in the face.

*Or maybe she doesn't love you the way you love her.*

The thought shot through him, left desolation in his chest.

He closed his eyes, drew in a breath. He shouldn't be thinking about this, not here, not now. He had a job to do. He shouldered his pack, picked up his chainsaw and moved down the line, stepping out of the way as the dozer passed.

A hand landed on his shoulder.

Hawke stood there, sweat and soot on his face. "Time for a lunch break, Silver."

"Thanks, chief." Brandon stepped off the line, walked with his chainsaw back toward the brush truck where the other members of his shift were already eating.

Brandon wasn't given to hero worship, but he would have followed Hawke into hell if Hawke had asked him to. True, the man drove his crews hard, but he never asked anything of them he wasn't willing to do himself. Most of all, he put their safety first. His standing up to that limp-dick idiot Robertson today was just one example of the way he fought for his firefighters and for the people of Scarlet.

Brandon went to sit with the others, took off his gloves, and reached with sweaty hands into his backpack. Then in his earpiece, someone started singing "Baby Love."

Whoever it was couldn't hold a tune to save his life—and didn't know the lyrics.

"Good God! Talk about ruining my appetite."

"Who the hell is that?"

"I think it's Diaz."

Brandon clicked his hand mic a few times, trying to let whoever it was know that their piss-poor singing was going out over the radio.

Then Hawke's voice cut in. "Hey, whoever is auditioning for the Supremes—your hand mic is stuck."

Diaz's voice came back. "Sorry!"

Howls of laughter.

Yeah, the crew would be giving Diaz a hard time about that for a while.

Brandon had just unwrapped his sandwich, when a gust of wind tore the napkin from his hand. All laughter and conversation stopped, heads turning as the wind carried the napkin through the air, depositing it twenty feet up the dirt road.

Then Miller's voice came over the radio. "There's a spot fire on the other side of the road, maybe fifteen feet to the south of B-shift's lunch spot."

Diaz came out of nowhere, charged across the dirt road, and beat the shit out of the flames with his fire flapper. "It's out."

But as soon as it was out, an ember ignited another one and another.

Hawke walked up to them. "Wind's picking up. Let's get rolling with the brush truck. Otherwise, we're going to be playing a losing game of whack-a-mole with these spot fires."

Brandon stood, finished his sandwich in a few bites, and washed it down with a gulp of water. "Back to work, everyone. Break's over."

They were running out of time.

———

CONRAD LAY with Kenzie on their bed, her head resting on his chest, the heat of climax cooling into contentment. "God, I love you."

"Mmm." She stirred, stretched, as languid as a kitten. "I love you, too."

Nooners were their thing, a tradition from the days when they'd first gotten together. Who needed a sandwich when you could get laid for lunch?

Conrad told her about this morning's rescue, still stuck between amusement and embarrassment. "Then she said, 'I've wanted to fuck your brains out for years. I have a shirtless photo of you in my locker at work. Oh, those pecs!' Her boyfriend was walking alongside us and heard her."

"Are you serious?" Kenzie sat up and stared down at him in surprise, laughing, her dark hair spilling over her shoulder. "She really said that?"

"Yeah, she did. If I could have made myself vanish into thin air, I would have." God, it had been awkward. "Everyone tried not to laugh, but I could see they were smiling. Bastards."

Kenzie straddled him, her palms moving over his chest. "Your pecs *are* pretty amazing, but it's weird to think of another woman staring at your body and getting all worked up."

Conrad didn't know which photo of him the woman had in her locker. His climbing career spanned more than a decade and hundreds of magazine articles. It's not like he had posed shirtless to titillate women. He'd probably been climbing, had shed his shirt because he was sweaty, and some reporter had taken a photo.

Kenzie stretched out on top of him, her breasts pressing against his ribs, her head resting on his sternum. "The Team is going to tease you about this forever, you know."

"Yeah. Like I said—bastards." Conrad trailed his fingers along the graceful curve of Kenzie's spine. "How was your morning?"

She told him how she'd gone to Winona's clinic to talk with her about the Team fundraiser. "She was treating a golden eagle. She had to euthanize it. She said it must have eaten a poisoned rodent. It was such a beautiful bird. I got all choked up."

"Sorry to hear that." He could hear in Kenzie's voice that she was still upset.

She had a big heart. It was one of the things that Conrad had always loved about her. That big heart had saved him.

He'd come back from Nepal almost two years ago a broken man. A serac had collapsed on Everest's Khumbu Icefall, killing everyone on his climbing team, including his best friend, Bruce. Conrad had been knocked into a crevasse and had survived. Grief and guilt had all but consumed him until Kenzie showed up at his door with a little golden retriever puppy. She'd made up a story about how Gizmo wasn't being good to little Gabby and had begged him to foster the puppy.

Kenzie had known what Conrad hadn't—that caring for helpless little Gabby would bring him back into the world of the living.

He was a lucky man.

They talked about other things after that—the Team fundraiser, the relentless summer heat, the chance that

Kenzie might be pregnant even now. They'd been trying for a baby for a little more than a month, the fulfillment of a promise Conrad had made before leaving for Nepal to attempt the Khumbu Triple Crown. Conrad hadn't been sure how he'd feel about being a father, but now he couldn't wait.

They snuggled, savoring the minutes, but all too soon, it was time to get up, get dressed, grab something from the fridge for lunch, and go back to the real world.

"Back to picking up dog poop," Kenzie said at the back door. "I live such a glamorous life. What are you doing this afternoon?"

"I'm heading over to the Cave." That was the name Team members gave the old firehouse that served as their headquarters. "Megs wants help washing and inspecting ropes. I think she wants to check drugs in the med kits, too, and make sure nothing has expired. I figure it's my turn. I want to stay on Megs' good side."

Kenzie slipped into his arms, a smile on her face. "Megs adores you."

It was strange but true. After the Everest catastrophe, Megs had flown all the way to Nepal, trekked to the Buddhist monastery at Tengboche where he'd taken emotional refuge, and dragged his ass back to the United States. She, too, had lost friends to mountains. More than anyone, she had understood.

"I should be home around six." Kenzie opened the door. "Gizmo, Gabby—come."

The two dogs, who'd been dozing on their beds near the woodstove, hopped up and followed at her heel, their golden tails wagging.

Conrad watched as the three of them made their way out the back gate, amazed by the turn of fate that had brought them into his life.

Yeah, he was a lucky man.

———

LEXI TAYLOR LOCKED the front door to her office, an old Victorian cottage she'd remodeled, and walked to her silver Lexus IS convertible to pick up her three-year-old daughter, Emily, from the Inn. Emily was in a half-day preschool program that gave Lexi time in the morning to meet with clients, but today's meeting with Marley, the owner of Nature's Meds, a marijuana dispensary, had gone on longer than usual. Lexi had had no choice but to call her dad and step-mom and ask them to pick up Emily and feed her lunch, something they were happy to do.

"What do you think I am—her grandpa or something?" her dad had joked.

The drive to the Forest Creek Inn took only a couple of minutes. She turned onto First Street to find her father standing with Rose in the middle of the street, both of them looking west. They must be talking about the fire. Lexi could just make out the pillar of smoke.

Austin had said it was a small blaze, but he'd been asked to shut down county trails and campgrounds just in case. Unfortunately, some people didn't appreciate the effort the county was making to keep them safe and had taken their anger out on Austin. As a park ranger, he was used to it, but it wasn't his favorite part of the job.

Lexi pulled into the long driveway that led to the family parking area in back. Her father had just had the Inn repainted, its walls a bright, lemony yellow, the Victorian fretwork a crisp white again. The place had been in Lexi's family since the first days of Scarlet Springs and was the only building in town to have survived the big fire of 1878. Though she'd sworn as a teenager not to have anything to do with the Inn when she grew up, it would belong to her and her younger sister Britta one day, and she hoped to pass it on to Emily.

She parked, walked to the back door, and knocked.

Kendra opened it. "Your mommy's here, Emily."

Lexi stepped inside the air-conditioned coolness to find Emily eating orange sherbet.

"Hey, Emily. That looks yummy. Can Mommy have some?"

Emily, mouth full, held out her spoon with the innocent generosity of a child.

"Thank you, sweetie, but it's yours. You can finish it."

"She ate all of her peanut butter sandwich and her carrot sticks, so I gave her a treat. I hope that's okay."

"Of course."

Kendra had married Lexi's father after her mother had been killed in a car accident. Lexi had been four, while Britta, who lived in California now, had been only three. But Kendra had never wanted to be a mother, and her relationship with Lexi and her sister had been rocky at best until recently. But whatever her failings as a stepmom, Kendra was a wonderful grandma. She adored Emily—and spoiled her rotten.

"Why are Dad and Rose standing in the middle of the street?"

"I think they're watching the fire."

"There's not much to see."

"Thank God for that." Kendra took Emily's empty dish to the sink. "You know your father. If he thinks the Inn is at risk, he can't quit worrying."

"It's not like staring at the fire will put it out."

"Maybe you could explain that to him."

Lexi left Emily with Kendra and went out the front door to find her father, wearing shorts, sandals and a

Hawaiian shirt he hadn't buttoned, arguing with Rose, owner of Rose's New Age Emporium, which sat across the street from the Inn.

"If you keep coming out here to look at it, you're going to draw the fire to us," Rose said, her long silver hair tied up in a messy bun.

"What the hell kind of bullshit is that? My eyeballs aren't magic."

"It's the law of attraction. Whatever you fear, you bring about."

Lexi's father snorted, rubbed his protruding beer belly. "Like I said—bullshit."

He and Rose had known each other all their lives and lived across the street from each other for the better part of fifty years. They bickered the way siblings might. Both were stubborn, and both were experts on everything—at least in their own minds.

"Hey, Dad, Rose. What's going on?"

"Hey, Lexi girl." Her father reached out, wrapped an arm around her shoulders.

"Your dad is out here obsessing about a little bit of smoke."

"I'm telling you, the fire is bigger than it was a little while ago."

Was it? Lexi couldn't tell. "Well, you can't put it out by staring at it, Dad."

Her father glanced down at her. "Is Austin up there?"

She nodded. "He's staffing a roadblock. He had to close the parks and campgrounds."

Her father chuckled. "I bet all the tourists love him for that."

"Yeah, not so much."

"Don't worry about Austin, Lexi, dear," Rose said. "He'll be fine."

But Lexi hadn't been worried—not till that moment. Her irritation sparked. How like Rose to put a worry in her head that hadn't been there. "Of course, he'll be fine."

⸺

NATE WEST LEANED against the wooden fence, watching while his nephew, Chase, rode Buckwheat around the corral, the sun beating down on them, wind kicking up clouds of dust. "You're doing great. Now bring him to a trot."

Chase clicked with his tongue, squeezed his legs, and Buckwheat responded, moving easily into a trot. "Good job, Buckwheat."

Buckwheat was Emily's horse—or he'd become Emily's horse after she and Megan had moved to the ranch. He was the gentlest gelding Nate had ever known, as mild as he was beautiful, his palomino coloring gleaming in the sun.

"Good job, Chase!" Nate called out.

All the kids had ridden twice this morning already. Then they'd had lunch out on the deck—burgers and homemade French fries. This was Chase's third turn on Buckwheat, while Addy and Maire played horses in the yard behind the house and little Tristan played with Jackson and Lily in the playroom.

"I want to ride Buckwheat." Emily stood at Nate's elbow kicking the dirt with her boots, impatient to have another turn.

"Your cousins don't get to ride all that often. You get to ride every day. I know it's hard, but try to be patient."

Sophie met Nate's gaze and leaned down. "Thanks for letting Chase ride Buckwheat. It's awfully sweet of you, and it makes Chase so happy."

"Why doesn't Chase have his own horse?"

"We live in a house in the city," Sophie explained. "There isn't room for a horse."

"Oh." Emily clearly thought that was the most disappointing news ever.

Out in the corral, Chase was having the time of his life. Nate gave him a few more minutes, knowing that the kid lived for this.

"You know, Sophie, if he and Addy want to come up and stay here for a week or so, we'd be happy to have them. They could ride every day. I would work with them myself. They're both good with horses."

"Are you sure? They can be a handful."

"What kid isn't? We've got plenty of room, and you know my old man loves nothing more than a full house and spoiling other people's kids."

Sophie laughed. "It's true."

Nate climbed over the fence. "Okay, buddy, bring him back to a walk. That's right. Just like that. Now, when you're ready, bring him to a halt. Good job, buddy."

Nate walked over to horse and rider and lifted Chase to the ground, adjusting his little cowboy hat. "You're getting to be a real cowboy."

Chase reached up, petted Buckwheat's muzzle. "I love you."

Buckwheat whickered.

"I think he loves you, too." Nate led boy and horse to the fence. "Thanks for being patient, Emily. You can ride again, and then we'll unsaddle Buckwheat and let him out into the field so he can graze, okay?"

Emily smiled bright as sunshine, clambered over the fence, and waited for Nate to lift her into the saddle. He adjusted the stirrups and then gave her the reins.

"You're all set.

Emily had been riding since she was four and didn't need his help. She moved Buckwheat smoothly into a walk and then a trot, her laughter making his heart constrict. It was one of the most beautiful sounds in his world.

Emily and her mother had accepted him despite the terrible scars that disfigured half his face and body. They'd brought him back to life when he'd thought he had no reason to live. No, Emily wasn't his biological child. He had adopted her when he and Megan had gotten married, and he loved her every bit as much as he loved his son.

Her biological father had been a drug dealer who had used and abused Megan, fueling her heroin addiction, getting her pregnant, then abandoning her and her unborn baby to prison. Emily had seen that bastard only once, though she'd had no idea who he was. He'd broken into Megan's home demanding money. Emily had seen him hurt Megan. She'd also witnessed his death. Nate had found him about to rape Megan and had ended the son of a bitch's life with a double tap. One day, when Emily was older, Nate would have to explain to her that the man he'd killed that terrible night was her biological father.

But not today.

Chase climbed up on the fence beside him to watch his cousin ride, a big smile on his face. He looked so much like his father—a mini-Marc.

"Uncle Nate said you could stay here for a week if you want to," Sophie said. "Do you think you'd like that?"

Chase gaped at his mother. "Hell, yes!"

Nate tried not to laugh. "He's been spending too much time with my old man."

Sophie shook her head. "I think he may have gotten that from his father."

Then Nate saw Chuck, the foreman, hurrying toward them.

"What's up?"

"The fire—it's grown a lot in the past few minutes. It's not a column of smoke now. Looks to me like it's turned into the real thing."

"Shit." Nate followed Chuck to the other side of the corral where buildings wouldn't block his view of the mountains.

Chuck pointed, but Nate didn't need help finding it.

"Holy hell."

What had been a wispy column of smoke had grown into a wall.

"Get on the radio and get the men moving. My father will want us to head up to Scarlet with every horse trailer we have before they close the highways. They'll be evacuating the areas west of town, I'm sure, and some folks won't be home to move their horses. They'll need our help to save their animals."

"On it."

Nate turned back toward the corral to give his daughter the bad news that her ride was being cut short. He would be driving one of the trailers.

But Sophie stood behind him, her gaze fixed on the smoke, fear in her eyes. "Marc and Julian are still up there."

Nate knew what Sophie had been through this past year and a half. He'd grappled with PTSD himself thanks to an IED and third-degree burns. He knew how it felt when your mind believed you were just another breath away from some new terror.

He rested a hand on her shoulder. "They're with McBride and Sheriff Pella. They'll be safe."

## Chapter 7

BRANDON WORKED THE HOSE, dousing spot fires, while Hawke drove the brush truck. The air was choked with smoke now, the heat intense as upcanyon winds breathed life into the blaze.

He heard in his earpiece when Hawke again pushed Robertson and Sheriff Pella for state and federal support.

"We're losing any hope of containing this thing. Initial attack is going to fail. We need a couple of type-one crews and aircraft now!"

This time Roberson agreed. "We've got ladder fuels igniting, spot fires popping up across the road and—"

Jenny Miller's voice cut in. "A tree just ignited about ten yards upslope from the fire. It's spotting up the mountainside heading west."

Hawke answered immediately. "Get out of there, Miller! Now!"

Brandon looked to the west, saw another tree go up and another, flames rising into the forest canopy, trees becoming torches, the fire moving in Miller's direction.

The wind had it. The fire was about to run.

Another spot fire.

Brandon hosed it down as Hawke drove slowly forward. The brush truck held only three hundred gallons. It wouldn't last long.

They went on like this for another few minutes, smoke at times making it hard for Brandon to see.

Hawke spoke into his mic. "Miller, are you down yet?"

Silence.

"Miller, do you copy?"

The area where she'd stood lookout was engulfed.

*Son of a bitch.*

A burst of static.

"Sorry, chief. I was using my hands to downclimb. I'm almost out."

Brandon let out a relieved breath, aimed the jet of water through the smoke toward the glowing orange of open flame. The water slowed to a trickle … and stopped.

He reached for his hand mic. "Hey, chief, we're empty."

It was the deafening sound that turned his head, the jet-engine roar of a fire blowing up.

He watched, unable to do anything, as the mountainside to the west of the creek went up in flame, the fire seeming to roll and leap uphill, a living thing, bathing the scene in an eerie orange glow. For a moment, all work ceased, the raw force of the fire turning firefighters into powerless spectators.

What the hell good were forty men and women with hand tools against this?

Hawke's voice sounded in Brandon's earpiece, breaking the spell. "We've got a blowup. This thing is making a run up Tungsten Peak and spotting to the east of the creek and north up the valley. We need air support now! Miller, where the *hell* are you?"

A human form in yellow and green moved toward them through the smoke, waving. "Here, chief."

Brandon closed the dump valve, disconnected the hose, Miller joining him to help fold and stow it.

Her gaze met his for just a moment, and he could tell she was shaken. "I've never seen anything move that fast."

"You did great. Way to haul ass."

They listened to the radio traffic as they worked. Hawke ordered his crews to grab their gear and get the hell off the line. Robertson called his crew off the fire's flanks and asked the sheriff to order a mandatory evacuation via reverse 911 of Ski Scarlet and all areas to the west of town up to the highway, including Camp Mato Sapa.

But Brandon's mind went to one person.

*Libby.*

She was safe at Knockers, but her house was inside the mandatory evac zone. When she heard about the evacuation order, she would probably rush home to rescue her vinyl collection. She was impulsive like that.

He finished stowing the hose and climbed into the brush truck, coughing at the smoke that filled the little valley. He searched for his cell phone to warn her not to do anything crazy. The phone wasn't in any of his pockets or his PG bag. He'd probably left the damned thing at the firehouse when he'd been making calls trying to find Bear.

*Shit.*

He probably wouldn't have gotten any signal here anyway.

"What's the plan now, chief?" Miller asked.

Hawke started up the engine, glowing embers blowing past the vehicle's windows and skittering across the hood to land on the east side of the road where they ignited grass and shrub and stump and tree.

"We head back to the station, refill the truck, and move

with everything we've got to the parking lot at Ski Scarlet to set up fire camp. Then we'll try to get a backburn going off Piñon Road. We are *not* letting this thing take our town." He called for Taylor over the radio. "Have you found Bear?"

"Negative. I've been ordered to close county parks and…" Static made the rest of Taylor's words unintelligible.

"Damn it!" Hawke drove through thick smoke back the way they'd come.

Brandon watched out the window as the landscape they'd tried to save quickly succumbed to flames.

———

JESSE HAD his earplugs in and his chainsaw running when the call to evacuate went out over the radio, so he didn't hear it. He only knew something was up when Kevin, one of the senior patrollers, rode up on an ATV and motioned to Jesse's radio.

Jesse cut the saw, pulled out his earplugs. "What's up?"

"The fire is headed our way. We've been ordered to evacuate."

"Shit." Jesse put his saw on the back of the ATV, grabbed his gear bag, and took a seat next to Kevin. "Who else is still out here?"

"Travis hasn't replied either. He's our lookout."

They found Travis playing air guitar on top of a rock on the west side of Eagle Ridge, earbuds in his ears.

"Travis!" Jesse bellowed in the voice he'd used to terrify E4s in the army.

Travis whirled to face them, jerked the earbuds off his head. "Shit! You scared me."

Kevin wasn't happy. "Be glad Moretti and I found you

and not the boss. You're supposed to be watching our backs."

Travis motioned toward the west. "I've been watching. The fire—"

Jesse pointed. "If you'd been paying attention, you'd have noticed that the little wisp of white smoke is now a dark mushroom cloud."

Travis turned to look, the wind blowing off his baseball cap. "Whoa."

Kevin pointed to the ATV with his thumb. "We've been ordered to evacuate. Get your shit, and get on."

Travis jumped off the rock, ran after his hat, grabbed his gear, and piled on.

On skis, they'd have been back down to the ski patrol office in ten minutes. Riding a damned ATV over bumpy ground took much longer. By the time they reached the lodge, trucks from Scarlet FD, the county, and the National Forest Service were rolling into the parking lot—brush trucks, a couple of Type 3 wildland apparatus, a big pumper tanker with a ladder, and a mobile command center.

The sight of so much hardware had Jesse looking over his shoulder.

"Jesus."

Thick gray smoke filled the sky to the northwest of Eagle Ridge.

Jesse stowed his gear while Kevin parked the ATV and then jogged out to the parking lot in search of Hawke. Jesse spotted him near the command vehicle.

He was covered with sweat and soot and shouting into his cell phone. "What about Colorado National Guard? They've got helos that can be outfitted with buckets and tanks. I don't give a goddamn how much they cost!"

Hawke made eye contact. "We're talking about homes *and* human lives here."

Jesse held up his red card—his wildland firefighting certification.

Hawke nodded, pointed to Brandon Silver, who stood about twenty yards to Jesse's left, drinking from a water bottle.

Jesse showed his red card again. "Got any gear I can borrow?"

Brandon nodded, sweat making rivulets in the soot on his face. "You look like you're about my size. I've got a spare brush shirt in my bag."

Jesse put the brush shirt over his T-shirt, grabbed his helmet and a Pulaski, and stood with Silver. "This thing as bad as it looks?"

Brandon nodded. "It went from six-inch flame lengths to crown fire in a matter of minutes. Hawke called it first thing this morning. He was afraid this was going to happen. He's been trying to get ahold of air assets all day and keeps running into bureaucratic bullshit. Hey, which way to the latrines?"

"Bottom floor, main lodge." Jesse pulled out his cell phone and called Ellie as Brandon headed in the direction he'd pointed.

"Are you on your way home? I heard the ski resort is being evacuated."

"I'm going to stay and do what I can to help. Brandon Silver had an extra brush shirt, and they've got plenty of tools."

"Oh."

He could tell Ellie wasn't happy about this. "Don't worry about me. I'm not going to do anything crazy."

"You? Do anything crazy?" She laughed. "Why would I ever think that?"

"You should take the kids and head with your parents down to Boulder for the afternoon, maybe visit your sister or go swimming or something."

For a moment, she said nothing.

"You think it's that serious?"

Well, she'd read between his lines, hadn't she?

"With this wind and as dry as it's been … It might be."

"I should stay to help in case the hospital has to evacuate. They'll need every hand they can get."

"Ellie…" What could he say?

He wanted to help, and so did she. But if she stayed, so did Dylan. He was only three months old and breastfed. He couldn't be away from his mother for long.

"*Please* go, Ellie. I'll be able to concentrate on doing my job if I know you and the kids are away from this and safe."

"Okay. I'll call my parents and Claire and see if they mind us invading this afternoon."

Claire, Ellie's sister, lived with her husband, Cedar, in Boulder.

"Good."

"You truly believe we could be in danger?"

"It's happened before, right? Scarlet burned to the ground once before."

"Right."

"How are the kids?" Jesse missed them when he was at work. There was nothing better than stepping through that door at the end of the day and having the twins shout, "Daddy!"

"Dylan is sleeping. Daniel and Daisy are in the yard playing dinosaurs. I hear lots of scary roars."

"Kiss them for me."

"I will. I love you, Jesse. Be safe. We need you."

"I love you, too."

Ellie had lost one husband already, and Jesse would do his damned best to make sure she wasn't widowed a second time.

———

JOAQUIN RAMIREZ REMOVED the lawnmower's dirty air filter and took the new one out of its packaging. "I like Matías."

"What about Alejandro?" Mia sat on a reclining patio chair, scrolling through baby names on her smartphone and looking sexy as hell—and very round—in a bikini top and sarong, her red hair piled on top of her head.

"Nah, man. My cousin would think we named the baby after him."

Mia was thirty-six weeks pregnant now, so it was time for them to get serious about this naming business. They'd known it was a boy since their 20-weeks scan, and they still hadn't settled on a name. Then again, Joaquin still couldn't wrap his mind around the fact that he was about to become a father.

He'd met Mia almost a year and a half ago while shooting a crime scene. She'd been a person of interest in the case, but he'd looked into her angry blue eyes and had known she was innocent. He'd been in over his head from that moment, and now…

A wife who loved him, a son—that was something that happened to other guys.

"But I *like* Alejandro."

"The name or my cousin?"

Mia laughed. "Both."

Joaquin fit the new air filter into its cover, slipped the tabs into place, and screwed the cover back on. "Now try to stall on me, *cabrón*."

"How about Rafael?"

*Rafael Ramirez.*

"It has a ring to it, but it makes me think of ninja turtles." Joaquin put away his tools and got to his feet.

"Sebastián?"

"Maybe." He pushed the lawnmower out to the spot on the lawn where it had stalled on him and yanked on the starter cord, gratified when it started.

"Oh, come on! Sebastián is a nice name."

He finished the back yard, which Mia had transformed from a big rectangle of shitty soil to a lush garden. Okay, so Joaquin had helped, but she was the horticulturalist in the family. She had forgotten more about plants and flowers than Joaquin would ever know.

That chore done, he pushed the mower into the shed and had just locked the door when he heard Mia call for him. He turned to find her holding up his cell phone.

"It's Tom."

*Shit.*

So much for a relaxing weekend.

He walked back to the patio and took his phone from Mia, who had that "I'm going to kill your boss" look on her face. "Ramirez here."

"Hey, I need you in the field today." Tom Trent, the editor-in-chief of the Denver Independent, was the best editor Joaquin had ever known.

He was also a pain in the ass.

"What's up?" As the paper's senior photographer, Joaquin was no longer expected to be on call on weekends —unless something major happened.

"There's a wildfire burning out of control west of Scarlet Springs. There's a mandatory evacuation in effect for the ski resort and the mountains up to the highway. I need someone up there—now. This might be the fire that burns Scarlet Springs off the map."

"Who are you assigning to the story?"

"I tried reaching Alton and James. They share the environmental beat. James isn't answering, and Alton has her kids. I guess her husband is already up there doing some kind of damned police exercise."

Alton was Sophie's maiden name, but Tom still used it as if she'd never married. As for Kat James, she and Gabe often went to visit Kat's family on the Navajo Reservation.

"Marc Hunter is already up there?" He and Joaquin were good friends.

"That's what I said. I'm sending Leah Tanaka, a rookie from the news side, to report on this. She'll meet you at the municipal airport in ten. I cut a deal with Channel Twelve. You're flying up in their helicopter with their news crew."

It wouldn't be Joaquin's first time in a helicopter.

"Got it." Joaquin ended the call, turned to Mia, saw the disappointment on her face. "Sorry, but there's a big fire west of Scarlet Springs."

"That's not good. Isn't the Cimarron up that way?"

"It is, but it sounds like this fire is burning west of town. The ranch is north of Scarlet. He drew her into his arms. "I'll be back as soon as I can."

"Be safe up there, okay? Don't take any risks."

He kissed her hair. "I won't."

He hurried inside, changed into a clean pair of jeans and a T-shirt, and grabbed his camera bag, which he kept ready to go at all times.

Mia met him at the door with a filled water bottle and a bag of snacks—an apple, a couple of energy bars, some trail mix, a cheese stick. "You might need these."

"Thanks." He stuck the bag and the bottle into the

outside pocket of his camera bag, kissed his wife, and grabbed his keys. "Sorry about this."

"It's not your fault."

"I'll keep in touch."

"Cell coverage is probably spotty up there."

"Right. See you tonight."

She watched from the door as he climbed into his truck.

Before backing out of the driveway, he sent a text message to Hunter.

On my way up to Scarlet Springs to cover the fire. Are you up there?

He waved to Mia and headed down the road.

━━━

MARC and the others had removed the conversion kits from their firearms after lunch and were now carrying live anti-personnel rounds. The reason for this was apparent in the garbage strewn around the abandoned campsite Deputy Marcs had found last week.

Food wrappers and plastic soda bottles lay everywhere. Next to the blackened fire ring sat a face mask. Twenty yards away, flies buzzed around a pit of human excrement mixed with wads of used toilet paper. Spent shotgun shells littered the forest floor.

Marc kept his distance. "They were cooking meth."

"Shake-and-bake." Darcangelo surveyed the piles of plastic bottles and propane tanks. "They didn't just leave a mess. They left a toxic mess."

McBride walked up to them. "Come on, guys. We've

got to go. That fire is burning out of control. Pella has ordered us to evacuate."

They climbed into the van and headed back down the dirt access road.

"I should have gone with Pella this morning." Deputy Marcs was clearly upset. "I could be evacuating people now rather than evacuating myself."

Marc didn't want her blaming herself. "Hey, you couldn't have known."

"How many people live in the evac zone?" Darcangelo asked.

"A few hundred." Deputy Marcs took a drink from her water bottle. "We've got a reverse 911 system, but some of them live off the grid and don't have phones. I don't know if we can get to all of them in the next half hour."

Marc didn't need to think about it. "I'll help."

Darcangelo nodded. "Count me in."

"I'd be happy to help, too," McBride said.

The offers of help didn't ease the look of worry on Deputy Marcs' face. "Some of the people who live up there are 'sovereign citizens,' which means they don't recognize any authority beyond the county sheriff. They're likely to meet you at the door with a shotgun—and they won't be bluffing."

Marc had the solution for that. "Pella can deputize us, turn us into his posse."

Darcangelo grinned. "Trying to build up your resume, Hunter?"

Deputy Marcs was smiling now. "I'm sure Sheriff Pella would be grateful for your help. I don't know the legal requirements for deputizing people, but he will."

She reached for her hand mic, waited for radio traffic to clear, and then spoke with Pella, who was, indeed, grateful for the extra help. All he had to do to deputize them was to put it down in writing.

"Meet me at the parking lot of Ski Scarlet," Pella said. "I'll have someone get the documentation ready and email it to the mobile command center."

They returned to the Caribou site and got into their vehicles. Ten minutes later, Marc pulled into the parking lot and got his first unobstructed look at the cloud of gray smoke. It dominated the horizon now, reaching high into the sky. "Look at that."

"Son of a bitch." Then Darcangelo pointed. "There's Pella."

They parked, climbed out, and made their way over to the sheriff, who was poring over a map with Eric Hawke and the county fire chief.

Pella looked up. "Great. Here you are. Consider yourselves deputized. Sorry, I don't have a box of spare badges in my car. We've got roadblocks on all the roads leading into the evac areas. Deputy Marcs, you put them to work clearing houses."

"You got it."

Marc listened with the others while Deputy Marcs went over the map and briefed them. His cell phone buzzed—a message from Ramirez.

On my way up to Scarlet Springs to cover the fire. Are you up there?

Marc replied, telling Ramirez that he, Darcangelo, and McBride would be helping with evacuations.

"You paying attention, Hunter?" Darcangelo asked.

"Ramirez is on his way up."

"Does he want to ride along with us?"

"If I were him, I'd focus on the action here. Besides, we don't have time to wait."

They set out, Marc and Julian in Marc's SUV and Zach in his own, a Channel 12 news helicopter passing overhead as they headed down the mountain.

They had discussed the situation from a tactical point of view and had decided to work opposite sides of the road, Marc and Julian on one side and Zach on the other. That way, they would have immediate backup in case they met armed resistance—which was a completely fucked-up thing to worry about in the middle of a wildfire evacuation.

Then again, this was Scarlet Springs.

They passed through the roadblock and made their way toward the most distant street in the evac zone, Darcangelo holding the map and giving directions.

"There should be a right turn just ahead."

"Are you sure you're holding the map right side up?"

"I know how to read a map."

Marc turned onto the road, Zach right behind them. The road was narrower than Marc had expected and heavily forested on both sides—lots of fuel for the fire. Long, narrow driveways marked with reflectors led to cabins that were built at a distance from the road. Most had NO TRESPASSING signs nailed to trees and fence posts.

Darcangelo looked around them. "Remind me not to bring the kids trick-or-treating in this neighborhood."

"Yeah. No kidding."

Marc turned up the first driveway—nothing more than a rutted single-lane dirt road. Signs warning trespassers were nailed to trees and tied to barbed wire. One threatened the use of lethal force. The cabin itself was built into the side of a hill—a sod house with a cabin front. A yellow

"Don't Tread on Me" flag flew from a log flag pole not far from the front door.

"I take it these people won't be happy to see us."

"I think you're right."

Julian stayed to the side, firearm ready, while Marc walked up to the door and knocked.

"Sheriff's deputy!" It felt strange to say that. "A big fire is headed this way. We're here to help you evacuate."

An older woman's voice came from the other side of the door. "You ain't no sheriff's deputy. You're marshals. I seen it on your vehicle. I got no time for you federal buzzards."

What could Marc say? "That wasn't my vehicle, ma'am. I'm Marc Hunter from DPD SWAT. I was deputized by Sheriff Pella to help bring people to safety."

"Where's your badge?"

"I don't have a badge because he didn't have time to give me one."

"You listen here, mister! I can't leave. This cabin is all I got in the world since my man passed on." The door opened just a crack, one brown eye peeking through. "Oh!"

Then the door opened all the way to reveal a heavyset woman wearing jeans and a flannel shirt, large breasts sagging almost to her waist, her short gray hair in curlers. In her hands was a Mossberg 12-gauge shotgun.

The woman stepped outside, spotted Darcangelo, and smiled. "Aren't you two handsome? Can you help me get out to my pickup? My knees ain't what they used to be. I got to get my social security card, a bra, and my pet rat first."

Yeah. This was going to be an interesting afternoon.

## Chapter 8

ERIC WILLED himself not to raise his voice, did his best to spell it out for Robertson. "Even if we create a backburn and stop the blaze there, upcanyon winds are going to funnel the flames around the mountain, up the river valleys, and into town."

Robertson wasn't being decisive at a time when minutes counted, and he couldn't seem to grasp the big picture.

Robertson glared at him. "Let's hear your big plan, then."

"Move the line farther from Scarlet." Eric pointed to an access road on the map. "Start the backburn here on Piñon Road far away from Scarlet. Burn out the west side of the road. The distance between the two rivers that come into town is shortest here. The forest was thinned and cleared of slash last year, and the valleys are at their narrowest. We turn as much of that as we can into good black, stand ready to put out spot fires across the road— and then we pray."

Even if they burned out a hundred yards, it might not

be enough, not when the wind was carrying embers distances of a quarter mile. The fire could spot beyond the black and ignite fuels across the road. It could finger off in other directions, pushed by those damned upcanyon winds. Or they could lose control of the backburn and start a second fire.

"You'll be putting our crews uphill from this beast."

"We'll be making good black as we move, and we'll have the road as our escape route. Without air assets, what other choice do we have?"

"You mean besides stepping back and letting the town burn?" Sheriff Pella asked.

"None that I can see." Jacob Malheur, superintendent of the US Forest Service crew, hadn't said much before now. "Hawke's plan also protects homes we would otherwise sacrifice, and if it fails, you've still got time to fall back, regroup, and try again."

Robertson looked at the map, sweat beading on his forehead. "All right, damn it. Move! We don't have much time. Hawke, this is your idea, so I'm making you Incident Commander."

Relief washed through Eric.

*It's about fucking time.*

He shouted out his orders. "From this moment, I'll be going as Scarlet Command. We'll leave some volunteers and the Forest Service crew here with the pumper tanker to protect the ski lodge, the lifts, and the outbuildings. Everyone else goes with me. On the double, people! Robertson, call the county public information officer. We've got media here, and none of us has time right now to answer questions."

He turned to Sheriff Pella. "You're sure that the reverse 911 evacuation order reached everyone—residents, businesses, Camp Mato Sapa?"

Sheriff Pella nodded. "We sent it out twice. I can ask one of my officers to check the campgrounds if you like."

"Thanks. I'd appreciate that." But there was one other thing.

He glanced around, found Moretti. "Hey, Moretti, where do you store the explosives?"

Moretti jogged over, pointed to a small building a couple hundred yards from the lodge. "If that thing blows, it will take out this parking lot and all of your pretty trucks, too."

Eric pointed to the building, shouting for the Forest Service superintendent. "See that building? It's full of explosives. If it even *looks* like the fire is going to reach it, you'll need to evacuate down the road beyond the first switchback. It's not likely to burn surrounded by bare slopes and this parking lot, but watch it all the same."

Malheur nodded. "Got it."

Eric called for all volunteer and rural fire companies to meet his crew at the top of Piñon Road with every chainsaw, drip torch, and fusee they had. Then he called his mother and asked her to take Caden to her old house in Boulder for the day.

"Are we in the evacuation zone, too?" she asked.

"No, but I'd feel safer knowing the two of you are out of town. If this thing gets away from us again, it could get ugly."

"Okay, then. This little man and I will pack up and head out. What about Vicki?"

"I called, but she didn't answer. She's probably busy. I left her a message." He doubted she'd leave the restaurant unless all of Scarlet was evacuated.

"She told me the good news this morning. I'm thrilled for you—and for me. Another grandbaby. I can't wait! You must be so happy."

He was. "Vicki surprised me at breakfast. I got toned out for the fire not long after, so I don't think it's had time to sink in yet."

"I bet. You be careful, son."

"I promise. Give Caden a kiss from his daddy. I love you, Mom."

"I love you, too."

Eric ended the call and shouted for his crew to mount up. "Let's roll!"

"You really think we can pull this off, chief?"

"We don't have a choice."

⸺

LIBBY DASHED AROUND HER HOUSE, grabbing things she wanted to save and shoving them in plastic garbage bags, unable to stop her tears. Nothing was going right today. First, she'd hurt Brandon's feelings, made him think she didn't care about him. Then some idiots had started a fire that wanted to burn down her house and her whole town.

What next—freaking bubonic plague?

She'd ducked out of work the moment she'd gotten the reverse 911 call and had driven up to her house, just making it through before the sheriff's department put up the roadblock. She'd worked hard for the few things she had. She couldn't let some damned forest fire take everything from her.

So far, she'd gotten all of her vinyl and her important papers—Brandon had made her put them all together in one folder—out to the car. She put the collection of beer bottles representing every brew she'd ever made at Knockers into a big garbage bag and set it next to the door. She couldn't let fire destroy that. Then she grabbed her camera bag, her favorite clothes, all her crazy colors of fingernail polish, her TV, her sex toys, and her laptop.

She picked up the heavy bag of beer bottles and carried it out to her Jeep, settling it in the back on the floor and hurrying back inside for the next bag. The wind was sharp with the scent of smoke now, a wall of gray rising to the west.

Brandon was out there somewhere.

She'd tried to reach him, but her call had gone to voicemail. He was probably too busy to talk. Or maybe he didn't want to talk to *her*. She couldn't blame him.

*Way to fuck up the best relationship you've ever had.*

She grabbed her camera bag next, turned toward the door, and stopped.

Her music box.

She set the camera bag down, picked up the music box, opened it. A tiny plastic ballerina in a pink tutu pirouetted to a song Libby didn't know. The music box had been a birthday gift from her father before unemployment and alcohol had made him mean. He'd turned his fists on her and her mother, and her mother had thrown him out of the house. The music box was a piece of junk, but it was the last thing he'd given her before he'd disappeared from her life.

She swallowed the lump in her throat—and nearly jumped out of her skin when a knock came at the door.

"US Marshals! I'm here to help you evacuate."

A tall man in mirrored shades stood on her front steps, a duty badge on his hip, his dark hair ruffled by the wind.

She shouldered her camera bag and, still holding the music box, stepped outside. "I'm getting stuff together as fast as I can."

"I'm Chief Deputy US Marshal Zach McBride. We

need to move quickly. There's not much time. What can I carry?"

She pointed to the bags inside the door. "That's most of it. I'm Libby, by the way."

"Sorry to meet you under these circumstances, Libby." He grabbed four bags at once— of course, he did—and followed her toward her Jeep.

Okay, yes, she'd noticed his biceps. Any straight chick or gay guy would. But she also noticed the wedding band. It didn't matter anyway. She had Brandon.

*Do you? Or did you chase him away?*

She was walking down the flagstone path to her Jeep when she heard a bunch of somethings hit the concrete. She turned to find her sex toys scattered on her front steps.

"I apologize, Libby. The bag tore open."

For one agonizing moment, she stood there in mortified silence, heat rushing into her face, her cheeks burning hotter than any fire. "Uh … God, I'm sorry. I'll pick it up."

Holy freaking shit! Could anything go right today?

She ran into the house, dragged her suitcase out of her closet, threw more clothes in it for good measure, then hurried outside and picked up her sex toys—her purple veiny dick vibrator, her rabbit vibrator, her silicone G-spot vibrator, a couple of vibrating cock rings, the pink vibrator, her fuzzy handcuffs, the silk cords she'd used to tie Brandon to her bed this morning, and two bottles of flavored lube.

Face still burning, she packed them all into her suitcase and closed it—just as two other men walked up.

"The other side of the road is cleared," said one, a big man with short, dark hair.

"Need help there, McBride?" asked the other, also tall but with a dark ponytail.

"We've got it." McBride took the suitcase from her. "I

put your TV and laptop in the back seat. I think that's the last of it. Do you want to take one last walk-through?"

She nodded. "Thank you."

He glanced at his watch. "No more than two minutes."

She walked back inside, grabbed her phone and computer chargers, and glanced around at everything she couldn't take. Would it still be here tonight?

Tears running down her cheeks, she stepped onto her deck. A gray wall of smoke filled most of the horizon, rising high in the sky, an orange glow emanating from beneath it.

Flames. Fire.

Chills skittered down her spine.

The deputy US marshal's voice came from the door-way. "Time to go!"

*Be careful, Brandon!*

She turned and walked away from her home, from most of the things she owned, not bothering to lock the front door.

———

JOAQUIN WRANGLED with the county's PIO—public information officer—until she finally agreed to let him follow the firefighting crews to wherever they were going.

Leah looked like she was about to panic at the thought of being left on her own. "What am I supposed to do? Shouldn't I go with you?"

A woman with a notepad—obviously another jour-nalist—walked up to them and offered Joaquin her hand. "I'm Wendy Hall with the Scarlet Springs Gazette."

"I'm—"

"You're Joaquin Ramirez—I know. I've admired your

work for years. The photo series that won you the Pulitzer was incredible."

"Thanks." Joaquin didn't want to be rude, but they didn't really have time for this now.

"I've got an idea." Wendy shook Leah's hand. "You're new to this, aren't you?"

Leah nodded. "It's that obvious?"

"Don't worry. We've all been there." Wendy turned back to Joaquin. "I'll take your new reporter under my wing. I know all the officials in this area and most of the firefighters, too. I'll make sure she gets the story. In return, you'll let us run one of your photos—something your editor doesn't want."

That was an unusual offer, but Joaquin didn't need to think about it. "Done."

Joaquin left Leah with Wendy and jogged to where the PIO stood having a heated conversation about him with the fire chief, a big guy with dark hair and a sooty face.

"I can't guarantee his safety, and if he doesn't listen to me…"

"I'll listen." Joaquin held out his hand. "I won't get in your way."

The man seemed to size him up, took his hand, shook. "I'm Eric Hawke, fire chief for Scarlet Springs FD."

"Joaquin Ramirez, Denver Independent."

Hawke frowned. "Why does your name sound familiar?"

"Maybe because I won a Pulitzer for—"

Recognition dawned on Hawke's face. "You're a friend of Gabe Rossiter's."

"Yeah. I am. How do you know Gabe?"

"He and I volunteer together on the Rocky Mountain Search and Rescue Team."

"Small world."

"All right. You can come, but know that I can't guarantee your safety. Have you ever trained in the use of a fire shelter?"

A fire shelter?

Hell. "No."

"Then you'd better hope we don't need them."

Joaquin climbed into the truck, buckled himself into one of the back seats beside sooty, sweaty firefighters. They didn't make eye contact with him, their minds on what lay ahead. They had already battled this thing—and lost.

He kept quiet, listening as Hawke directed operations via radio as they left the ski resort and drove toward the smoke-filled horizon.

That's why Joaquin had so much respect for everyone who worked in emergency services. They ran toward the danger while everyone else fled. They were true heroes.

One of the firefighters—a woman—spoke to Joaquin. "If I'd known someone was going to take our pictures, I'd have put on a little makeup."

The others laughed.

The woman, whose face was lined with sweat and soot, smiled. "I'm Jenny Miller."

"Joaquin Ramirez, Denver Independent."

The man in the passenger seat looked back at him. "Brandon Silver. You have any idea what you're going into here, Ramirez?"

Joaquin shook his head. "No, but I've been in some pretty tight spots before. I was in the Palace Hotel during the terrorist attack, and I was shot when a lunatic tried to kill my wife."

Eyebrows rose.

Silver frowned. "Sorry to hear that."

For a time, no one spoke as Hawke drove upward along a series of dirt roads. Then off on his right, Joaquin saw them—McBride, Hunter, and Darcangelo. He caught only a glimpse of them, dust from the road obscuring his view.

Hawke drove them upward until they crested a ridge. To the northwest was Ski Scarlet and ahead of them…

"Jesus," someone muttered.

Smoke filled the sky, gray and angry.

Hawke parked at the top of the ridge, the other trucks parking in a long row behind him. Joaquin piled out with the firefighters, moved to the east side of the road out of the way, and got his camera ready, Hawke shouting out orders to the others.

"The fire is below us. The wind is strong. There's a lot of unburned fuel between us and an active crown fire. It doesn't take a genius to know the blaze will cross that valley and run up this mountainside faster than we want it to. Stay aware of the fire's behavior at all times. One person with their eyes open could save all our lives. Silver, you're our lookout. I want you up there." Hawke pointed to an outcropping of rock. "You'll have an uphill run to safety, so leave sooner rather than later when that thing heads our way."

A group of firefighters huddled together, holding what looked like gas cans with long wands. They ignited the wands, spread out along the length of the road, some disappearing out of sight, and went to work.

"Let's show this bitch who's boss."

"Yeah!"

It was one of the most interesting things Joaquin had witnessed—like some strange kind of dance involving firefighters, wind, and fire.

Hawke's crew drizzled live flame onto the dried grasses and shrubs, then let the wind blow it toward the road. When the fire reached the gravel, it went out, leaving a three-foot-wide stretch of blackened land behind it.

The firefighters went forward again, drizzled more flame. Once more, the fire flared up and was carried toward the road. This time it went out when it hit the blackened strip—or "the black," as they called it.

And Joaquin understood.

They were burning away the fuel that lay in the fire's path, fighting fire with fire, hoping to stop it in its tracks here before it could reach Scarlet Springs.

He raised his camera and went to work.

⸻

"*PLEASE* LET ME THROUGH." Kenzie fought not to raise her voice or cry. "I promise, I'll come straight back."

She'd gotten a panicked call a few minutes ago from Chip about Crank. Crank, the sweetest pit bull in the world, was home in the evacuation zone while his daddies were at work in Boulder and unable to get to him. She'd promised to get Crank, together with their kitty, Kahlo, and keep them both at the kennel until the men could get off work and make it back to Scarlet. But Julia Marcs wouldn't let Kenzie through.

"I'm sorry, Kenzie. If I make an exception for you, I've got to make an exception for everyone. This fire isn't a joke."

"But that's just it!" Didn't Julia understand? "If that fire burns their house down, Crank and Kahlo will die."

The thought sickened Kenzie, fed a growing sense of desperation.

"I'm really sorry, Kenzie. I don't want that to happen any more than you do, but I really can't let you put yourself in harm's way."

Kenzie nodded, tears spilling down her cheeks. "I know you're doing your job."

She loved Crank. He was one of her favorite pooches —a big, silly boy who only wanted to play and be loved. She'd never met Kahlo, the kitty, but she didn't have to know or love an animal to be concerned for its life.

Julia seemed pensive for a moment, then something in her expression changed. "There are some cops from Denver helping us to clear houses in the evac zone. If you give me Crank's address, maybe they can make it there in time. I can ask them to bring the animals to the kennel."

"Thank you!" Kenzie had the address written down on a sticky note and handed it to Julia, who reached into her pocket for her cell phone and called someone named Hunter.

"Thank, man. I appreciate it. Yes, a pit bull named Crank and a kitty named …" Julia looked up at Kenzie.

"Kahlo."

Julia repeated the name. "Thanks. If you could bring them down to the main roadblock, Kenzie Morgan will be waiting for them. Crank will recognize her."

"Thanks, Julia. I couldn't stand it if anything happened to them." Kenzie stepped back, made way for others who wanted to talk to Julia.

One man shouted in Julia's face, angry that his camping plans were canceled. "Listen here, little girl, I reserved a camping spot and drove all the way here from—"

Julia cut him off, stood her ground. "There won't be a campground by tonight, sir, so I suggest you find another place to camp. Colorado is a big state, and there are plenty of options."

Five big Ford F-150s pulled up to the roadblock, hauling horse trailers. The trucks stopped, and Nate West stepped out of the first one. Kenzie had gone to school with him, though they hadn't been in the same class. The

Wests were one of the wealthiest families in the state and owned the biggest ranch in Forest County.

The tourist went back to shouting. "I want your badge number. I'm going to call your—"

"Is this guy giving you a hard time?" Nate walked up to Julia, cowboy hat on his head, jeans slung low on his hips.

"No. He was just leaving."

"Bitch." The man turned to go, his face red with rage.

Nate stopped him with a palm to the chest. "Apologize to Deputy Marcs."

Kenzie found herself holding her breath as the tourist turned a brighter shade of red.

Perhaps sensing Nate's resolve or intimidated by his height or his scarred face, the jerk backed down. "Sorry."

Nate stepped aside, his gaze meeting Kenzie's. "Hey, Kenzie. Are you okay?"

"I will be. I have some clients whose pets are trapped at home in the evacuation zone. Julia sent some officers to get them."

"We've got some extra help today from some Denver cops and a couple of guys from the US Marshals Service," Julia explained.

Nate grinned. "I know those guys. They're good people. They won't let you down. I'm here to evacuate horses."

"Sheriff Pella told me you'd be coming." Julia reached into her pocket and pulled out a folded sheet of paper. "Here are the addresses of the horse owners who called in."

"Thanks. We'll find them and bring them to safety at the Boulder County Fair Grounds."

"Thanks, Nate—and be careful up there."

"No thanks are necessary. We're happy to help." Nate

gave Kenzie a nod. "Take care, Kenzie. I hope you get those pets to safety."

"You stay safe, too. Good luck with the horses." Kenzie watched him climb behind the wheel of his truck.

After what had happened to him, how could he stand to be near fire?

*Some people are just brave.*

## Chapter 9

GABE HELPED Chaska put away the ropes, harnesses, and other gear. All of it would have to be inspected before the next camp session began, but they didn't need to deal with that today.

Gabe zipped a gear bag. "Are you excited about becoming a father?"

Chaska got a worried look on his face. "Yes, though it doesn't feel *real* yet."

"It will feel real enough soon." Gabe couldn't help but grin at the worried frown on Chaska's face. "The moment you see that newborn in Naomi's arms, the first time you hold your baby, you'll feel a kind of love you've never felt before, like your heart just grew."

"Yeah?"

"You'll see."

That's how it had been for Gabe. He had never planned on getting married or having kids—not until he'd met Kat. He'd been a closed-off and angry man, but she had broken through all of the barriers he had erected around himself and set him free. Now, he couldn't imagine his life without her or their three children.

The men walked together to the Dining Hall, where the kids were finishing their lunch of grilled cheese sandwiches, watermelon, and carrot sticks, and filled their plates. He walked past Dean, the kid who'd fallen and gotten into a fight this morning, and held out his fist. "Way to crush the ropes course, buddy."

Dean, who was sweeping the floor, looked surprised by the praise, but gave Gabe a fist bump, a smile tugging at the corners of his mouth.

Gabe and Chaska sat at one of the tables and dug in. Mountain air had a way of making a person hungry, at least in Gabe's experience.

Alissa bounded up to him, a happy smile on her face. "Mama says we can stay a while longer. Can we, Daddy?"

"Are you having a good time?"

She nodded, her face as bright as the sun. "I've been playing horses around the tipi. It's not like a *hogaan*, but I like it."

Kat spoke almost exclusively Diné to the kids, while Gabe spoke English. Both Alissa and Nakai were more or less bilingual at this point and spent a few months each year at their grandmother's home in Kaibito on the Navajo reservation.

Kat walked up, Noelle on her hip, Nakai hopping along a few feet behind her. "We can stay here while you go into town to tell them about the phone lines—unless you had planned on going straight home from Scarlet Springs."

"If the kids want to keep playing, I don't mind coming back for you."

Alissa jumped up and down and then ran out of the Dining Hall with her little brother, the two of them chattering to each other in Diné, Kat watching, a smile on her face.

Gabe took Noelle and fed her bits of his watermelon while Kat went to the restroom. By the time Kat returned, he was ready to head into town.

He sought out Naomi. "I'm supposed to check on a cake at Food Mart and then let someone know that the phone line is dead."

Naomi nodded. "If you can bring back a few ten-pound bags of ice that would be great, too. The ice maker just quit working."

"You got it."

He walked to his vehicle, caught the scent of smoke on the breeze, and wondered who'd been stupid enough to ignore the county-wide fire ban to start a campfire. He'd been a ranger for too many years not to feel irritated by this. Leave it to idiots to put other people's lives and property at risk.

He drove out of the canyon toward the dirt road that led to the highway. It was a thirty- or forty-minute drive to Scarlet, so he turned the radio to a classic rock station, singing along to Boston. After about ten minutes, he spotted an old spruce that had fallen and taken the phone lines down with it.

*Well, shit.*

That would take a while to repair.

As he rounded the next bend, a herd of elk bolted across the road in front of him, running as if spooked, forcing him to slam on his brakes.

Strange.

It wasn't like them to be active during the heat of the day.

He watched them pass then drove on until he came around another bend.

A sheriff's vehicle raced toward him, overhead lights flashing.

He pulled over, giving the officer room to pass on the narrow road.

To his surprise, the vehicle stopped.

A deputy rolled down the window, and he recognized Deputy Marcs. "We've got an active crown fire burning west of town. There's a mandatory evacuation in place for this area. You can't be here."

Gabe's heart gave a hard knock. "Mandatory evacuation?"

He had worked as a park ranger for years. He knew what an active crown fire could do. He needed to get back to the camp and warn Chaska, Naomi, and the others. "I just came from Camp Mato Sapa. Nobody told us about this."

"Don't tell me you guys didn't get the reverse 911 calls."

"We didn't. The phone lines are dead about a half mile up the road—a fallen tree branch. That's why I'm coming into town—to let people know the camp has no phone service."

Okay, there was the bit about the cake and the ice, but that didn't matter now. All that mattered was getting everyone to safety.

"Thank God Hawke sent me to check."

Deputy Marcs reached for her hand mic. "Eight sixty-five to Scarlet Command."

She released the mic. "How many kids are up there?"

"Forty-three kids and maybe fifteen to twenty adults."

"Hell." She clicked her mic again. "The phone lines at Camp Mato Sapa are down. They did *not* get the evacuation order. Break."

She paused for a moment and then went on. "There

are forty-three children and perhaps twenty adults still at the camp. They have no idea there's a fire coming their way. I'm heading there now."

Gabe slammed his vehicle into reverse, used the shoulder to make a U-turn, and hit the gas, tires spitting gravel as he sped back toward the camp and everything he loved, Deputy Marcs following closely behind him.

———

JULIAN WATCHED THE GPS, giving Hunter directions, as they sped with overheads flashing toward the address Deputy Marcs had given them. "Take the first left."

"Look at all that smoke. The fire must be close."

"Unless the house is actually engulfed, I'm going in." Julian couldn't stomach the thought of pets burning in a fire.

Hunter shook his head. "I'm not sure we're going to be able to reach the house."

The smoke thickened, until it was like fog, obscuring their view, giving Hunter no choice but to slow down.

"Damn it."

They reached the top of a ridge—and the smoke cleared to reveal firefighters at work.

"A backburn."

Crews moved along the length of the road to their right lighting fires, letting the wind blow the flames onto charred earth. Their heads turned as Julian and Hunter passed, but they didn't try to stop them.

"Gee-zus." Hunter whistled. "Have you ever seen anything like this?"

Julian's gaze shifted to the view in front of him. "Son of a …"

Across the valley, a wall of flames churned its way

toward a cluster of remote mountain homes. Built ten miles west of Scarlet's western town limits, they were clearly expensive custom homes. And they were doomed.

Hunter pushed on the gas, sent the vehicle speeding downhill toward the fire. "This is going to be close."

"Left here."

"I see it." Hunter slowed, made the turn.

Already embers rained down on the tall pines around them, four houses set back from the dirt road, all doomed to burn.

Julian pointed toward the tall Mediterranean-style house at the end of the road, the one farthest from them. "It's that one."

"Of course, it is." Hunter sped toward it, pulling to a stop in the driveway just as a large ponderosa pine in the front yard ignited. "Let's move!"

But Julian was already on his way. He took the front steps two by two, smoke stinging his eyes and making him cough. He jerked open the screen door.

Hunter coughed, too. "Use your Aikido master key."

Julian stepped back, turned to the side, did his best to focus. Then he spun and kicked the door, breaking the lock and forcing it open.

Hunter was the first inside. "You grab the dog. I'll find the cat."

The poor dog stood in the hallway, whimpering, its body trembling.

Julian approached slowly, held out a hand. "Hey, Crank, buddy. It's going to be okay. Let's get you out of here."

Julian scratched behind the dog's ears, got a little wag of the tail. "You're okay."

He yanked off his shirt, wrapped Crank inside it to

protect him from embers, and carried the big dog out to the vehicle.

Embers rained down on them, sharp needles of flame burning Julian's back and shoulders, radiant heat intense against his skin.

Julian sucked in a breath through clenched teeth. "Shit!"

He opened the rear passenger door, pushed Crank into the back seat, then shook off the embers and climbed into the driver's seat.

Fuck, that hurt.

Hunter had left the keys in the ignition—a smart move, as losing them right now would have been fatal—so Julian started the SUV and turned it around, ready to hit the gas the moment Hunter returned.

Trees and shrubs on both sides of the road were in flames now, the roar of the fire unreal, the air dense with smoke.

If Hunter didn't find the cat soon, they would have no choice but to leave it. It wasn't what Julian wanted to do, but dying in a fire wasn't big on his list either.

Somewhere nearby a propane tank exploded, making Crank yelp.

Julian reached back, petted the terrified animal. "It's okay, boy."

Where the hell was Hunter?

Then in the rearview mirror Julian saw.

The house was on fire.

Flames lapped at its walls, rose up from its roof, raced along the wooden deck.

"Son of a bitch." Julian pressed on the horn, a warning to Hunter.

Another thirty seconds passed.

Julian was about to jump out of the vehicle and run

inside to get Hunter when Hunter ran down the front steps holding a squirming something in a towel.

Julian threw open the passenger side door, and Hunter climbed in, coughing, something furry and pissed off writhing and hissing in his arms.

"Ouch!"

The cat flew from the towel, evaded Hunter's grasp, and jumped into the back seat.

Julian slammed on the gas. "I don't think the kitty likes you."

Hunter rubbed a bloody scratch on one hand. "Shut up and drive."

From behind him came another *BOOM*—probably another propane tank—and one more house was engulfed, the street now bathed in a haunting orange glow as the expensive homes and belongings of four families went up in flames.

Julian sped toward the end of the street and turned right, heading away from the destruction, the wall of flame they'd seen a few minutes ago closer than he had imagined. He floored it, speeding up the hill toward the line of fire-fighters, who were still hard at work on the backburn, their heads turning once again as Julian and Hunter sped over the crest of the hill and down the other side, overheads still flashing.

Out of the corner of his eye, he saw Hunter pull something out from beneath his DPD T-shirt. It was a wedding photo of two men, happy smiles on their faces, both dressed in white.

"I thought they might want this."

"Yeah" Julian slowed down, the smoke from the back-burn making it hard to see. "You should call the sheriff's department, let them know we got the animals."

After Hunter made the call, neither of them spoke, the

rest of the drive back toward Scarlet Springs passing in silence.

A deputy they didn't recognize stopped them.

Julian held up his badge. "We're working with Sheriff Pella. We're looking for someone named Kenzie."

"Ah. Okay. Great." The deputy pointed to a dark-haired woman who stood off to one side. "That's Kenzie there."

Julian parked and reached into the back seat for his shirt, tugging it gently from beneath Crank, who no longer seemed afraid. He slipped it over his head, wincing as fabric rubbed against what where probably second-degree burns.

Hunter frowned, leaned over to look at Julian's back. "You're burned."

"What of it?"

"You need medical attention."

"I'm fine."

"Okay. You stay here with Crank and Catzilla, while I go get Kenzie."

"I'll go." Julian stepped out, careful not to let the cat escape, and walked over to Kenzie. She was speaking with two men in expensive suits—the men from the wedding portrait.

"Kenzie?"

She stopped talking, looked over at Julian, tearstains on her cheeks. "Yes."

"I'm Julian Darcangelo, Denver Police SWAT. Sheriff Pella sent us to get Crank and Kahlo. They're in our vehicle."

Relief lit up her face. "Oh, thank God!"

One of the men pressed a hand to his heart, his eyes going shut, his head falling back on an exhale.

The other reached out to shake Julian's hand. "Thank

you so much, officer. I'm Chip. This is my husband, Charles."

"Good to meet you, and you're welcome." Julian led them back to the SUV and watched as Crank was reunited with his people and with Kenzie, his tail wagging.

Hunter joined him. "I'm not sure how you're going to get the cat out of the vehicle without getting sliced up."

"I'll go get a carrier." Kenzie dashed off.

Chip saw the scratches on Hunter's hands. "Did our Kahlo do that to you? I'm so sorry."

"Don't worry about it." Hunter grinned. "I've had worse."

Julian snorted. "That's the truth."

A few minutes later, Kenzie returned with a pet carrier. "Here you go."

Charles extracted Kahlo from beneath the driver's seat and tucked her safely inside. "Aw, baby. Have you had a scary day?"

Kahlo gave a pitiful meow.

Then Hunter reached inside the SUV again and pulled out the portrait. "I managed to take this on the way out the door. I'm afraid the rest is gone by now."

Chip and Charles took the portrait from him, stared in astonishment first at it and then at each other. Then they turned to Julian and Hunter, tears in their eyes.

Chip held the portrait against his chest. "How can we ever thank you?"

"You saved what was important. The rest is just stuff." Charles smiled through his tears. "Thank you so much."

"We're just doing our job," Hunter said.

"You're welcome. I wish we could have done more." Julian turned and walked around the passenger side of the vehicle, got in, and buckled up, the two men's joy at being reunited with their pets taking some of the pain out of his burns.

Hunter climbed into the driver's seat beside him and wiped his eyes. "Smoke."

"Yeah." Julian sniffed. "Me, too."

———

HAWKE WALKED DOWN THE LINE, his crew working hard, charred fuels crunching beneath blackened boots. They'd burned out a good hundred yards now, stretching from one drainage to the other. It was the biggest backburn he'd ever set.

Would it be enough?

He'd made a half dozen calls to NIFC and the Rocky Mountain Control Center, demanding air assets. He'd been approved for a Type 1 crew, a couple of SEATs, and a Skycrane helicopter for water drops, but the pilots had to refuel and fly up from Manitou Springs.

Yeah, any damned minute now would be great.

Several homes had already been lost, their demise hidden behind smoke and flame. Marc Hunter and his buddy Julian Darcangelo had been lucky to get out of there alive. They didn't have radios, so Hawke had no idea why they'd gone in. Someone must have been trapped. If so, it had been a close call.

Hawke hoped the people of Scarlet Springs were paying attention. Residents had fought him and the county every time they'd tried to thin the fuels around town. He loved the forest as much as any of them, but he understood something they didn't.

Forests burned.

Fire was part of the natural cycle of life up here. For the better part of a century, people had been suppressing all fires. Now, the forests were unnaturally dense, the fuel load critically high. And after a dry summer like this one…

*Shit.*

Why couldn't they understand that by opposing fire mitigation they were endangering their own lives and property and putting firefighters at risk?

A call came over his radio. "Scarlet Command, eight sixty-five."

Deputy Marcs.

Hawke reached for his hand mic to answer her. "Scarlet Command. Go ahead."

"The phone lines at Camp Mato Sapa are down. They did *not* get the evacuation order. Break."

Hawke's heart gave a hard knock. "Eight sixty-five, I'm listening."

"There are forty-three children and perhaps twenty adults still at the camp. They have no idea there's a fire coming their way. I'm heading there now."

*Fucking hell.*

Though he couldn't see the camp from here, he knew the fire had to be close.

"I'm about to lose radio… I don't think … hear me once … in the canyon." A burst of static ended contact.

*Son of a bitch!*

Forty-three kids and twenty adults were trapped in a canyon in a fast-moving crown fire.

How the *hell* had this happened?

Eric would have ordered Dispatch to call for a Chinook helicopter, but there was no way it would arrive on time. To assemble a crew, do pre-flight checks, get airborne, and fly to the camp would take an hour, if not two. Everyone there would be dead of smoke inhalation or thermal injuries long before then.

Hawke had one option. "Scarlet Command to

Dispatch. Tone out the Team, emergent. Tell them to take every vehicle they have and head up to Camp Mato Sapa to evacuate sixty-three people. Make sure they know the fire is moving fast. They *cannot* delay or linger."

Would Megs and the Team make it? Were they already too late? If they made it to the camp, would the road burn over, entrapping them all on the way out?

The thought dropped like lead into Hawke's stomach.

It was *his* job to keep people safe, *his* job to make sure no lives were lost to fire. Had he failed already?

*Fuck.*

There had to be a way out of this.

Hawke heard the tone for the Team go out over his radio. He turned to face the fire, its roar like the engines of a dozen jet fighters.

Silver's voice cut in. "Here it comes."

"Get out of there, Silver!"

"Already on my way back."

"This is it, folks." Timing was everything. "Silver, confirm when you're out."

Seconds ticked by.

Silver's voice came over the radio. "In the black!"

Hawke gave the command. "Light it up!"

He watched as his men ran forward, lighting everything they could on fire before retreating into the black and walking back to the road with their tools and drip torches to watch the spectacle unfold.

Hawke stood his ground. "Come and get it, bitch."

The flames from the backburn spread, rose up, dark smoke billowing skyward. But instead of being caught by the wind and running eastward into the black, the flames of the backburn were sucked toward the hundred-foot-tall wall of the main fire, pulled in by the bigger fire's greed for oxygen, burning away all the fuel in the fire's path as they went.

Hawke watched, barely able to breathe as the two walls of flame drew closer together, one like a tidal wave of orange, the other smaller. The heat was almost unbearable, forcing him back. He heard the whirring sound of a camera.

*Ramirez.*

The guy was a friend of Rossiter's, so Hawke tried not to be irritated.

"You should evacuate back to the road," he called out.

Ramirez nodded, turned, and jogged back to where Hawke's crew stood.

He heard a shout, and then a call came in over the radio.

"Scarlet Command, the fire has fingered off to the south! It's making a run up the south side of that drainage toward Ski Scarlet."

*Goddamn it!*

That's *exactly* what Hawke hadn't wanted to hear.

It was getting away from them again. It was making an end-run around the backburn. It could jump back across at any time, ignite the forest and the homes behind them, making it impossible for them to get back to town.

If only that fucking Skycrane or the SEATs were here. A few thousand gallons of water in the right place at *this precise* moment would have been their game-changer.

Hawke didn't hesitate. "Everyone fall back to Ski Scarlet!"

"You got it."

But Hawke barely heard the reply, the fire moving toward him with the force of a hurricane. It sucked the backburn into itself, the two walls of flame merging. Then the main head of the fire sputtered, shrank, went out.

It was like someone had flicked a switch, the silence deafening, dark smoke hanging like a curtain in the air, twisting in the wind.

Cheers.

Jenny Miller's voice came over his radio. "It jumped the river to the north! There's a finger headed straight east toward town."

Hawke's stomach sank.

God help them.

He reached for his mic, gritted his teeth in helpless rage. "Dispatch, Scarlet Command."

"Scarlet Command, go ahead."

"Close Boulder Canyon to westbound traffic, and order the immediate evacuation of Scarlet Springs."

## Chapter 10

AUSTIN PARKED on the access road beneath Pinnacles a hundred yards west of Azure Lake. Smoke filled the sky to the west, flames making its underbelly glow orange. He shouldered his pack and ran toward the isolated cabin as fast as he safely could in the terrain. He'd finally gotten Sutherland's permission to leave the barricade to another ranger and head to Haley Preserve to evacuate Bear.

There wasn't much time.

Austin had been able to see the fire from the access road, and it looked ugly. He'd lost radio contact the moment he'd stepped away from his truck, as his handheld radio didn't get signal up here. He had no idea whether Hawke and his crew had been successful with the back-burn. If they hadn't, the fire would be heading his way.

"Bear!" He called out as he neared the cabin, not wanting to startle the big man. "Hey, Bear! It's Austin Taylor. You home?"

He stopped, glanced around the clearing, saw seven small wooden crosses standing side by side on the edge of the forest. A little cemetery.

Still no sign of Bear.

*Shit.*

"Bear, are you here?" Austin made his way around the outhouse and cabin.

The cabin looked old, logs that had long ago been stripped of their bark polished by wind and weather, the chinking a mixture of mud and grass that was as hard as brick. Some of the chinking looked new, proof that Bear maintained the place.

Austin found a neat stack of firewood next to the front steps. In front of the cabin stood an old-fashioned well pump with a tin bucket below. That must be where Bear got his drinking water—a better option than Azure Lake.

"Bear? It's Taylor." Austin walked up creaking stairs to a door of split planks.

Its string was out.

He knocked.

No answer.

Austin hesitated, not wanting to violate Bear's privacy, but concern got the better of him. What if Bear were hurt or sick—or dead?

Austin pulled the string and stepped through the door —and back in time.

A rough-hewn table stood in the middle of the main room, eight hand-made chairs around it, a worn, hand-braided rug beneath it, a kerosene lantern sitting in its center. Wooden shelves held antique enameled dishes and cast-iron cookware, big milk jugs sitting beneath an iron sink that emptied into a large tin bucket. A wooden washtub sat there, too, complete with an old washboard.

It was like something out of a history book.

Austin crossed to the soot-blackened hearth, held his outstretched palm above gray ash. It was cold. Then again, it was the middle of the summer.

A small chest of drawers stood against the wall, crocheted doilies sitting beneath an old book and a faded photo of a man, a woman, and six children—four boys and two girls.

Eight family members.

Seven crosses outside.

Was one of those little boys Bear? Did the graves outside belong to his family?

Austin picked up the photograph, tried to recognize the man he knew. Yeah, there was no chance of that. He'd never seen Bear without his bushy beard.

Austin set the photo down, picked up the book. On the inside of the front cover, were written the words, "Diary of Rebecca Fletcher." The first entry was dated May 5, 1959.

Did this journal belong to Bear's mother or someone else in his family? That would be something if it did. No one in Scarlet knew anything about his background.

*"Today, Abel and I begin our new life in the mountains of Colorado, where, by God's grace, we will raise our family away from the temptations and licentiousness of the world. Matthew and little Luke have already made themselves at home, playing in the meadow as young boys should, while Mary, who is not yet weaned, stays with me near the tent. Abel has promised to have our cabin built before the end of the month, and I shall make do without complaint. Abel has often told me of his ancestors, who came over on the Mayflower. I can only imagine what the young mothers onboard went through trying to survive their first days on new shores. Compared to the hardships and privations they surely endured, my life is easy."*

Smoke.

*Shit.*

Austin set the book down beside the photo, glanced into two small bedrooms. There were six small beds and one large bedstead, but no Bear.

"Bear, where are you?" Austin walked to the front door, stepped outside—and froze.

The sky rained embers, the forest to the west in flames.

"Holy shit."

Austin ought to have run straightaway for his truck, but something stopped him.

*The photograph. The diary.*

If this cabin was doomed to burn, he couldn't leave them.

He pushed his way back inside, grabbed the photo and the diary, and stuck them in his pack. He wished he had time to search the place. This cabin held everything Bear owned, but Austin didn't have time to do more. If he didn't get his ass out of here now…

He bolted out the door, stunned by what he saw.

"Son of a bitch."

The fire was moving faster than he'd imagined.

He set out at a run, heading south toward his truck, wind dropping embers in the dried grass around him, igniting small fires that swelled and grew.

Several mule deer with fawns ran out of the trees and across the meadow. They were running for their lives, too.

Austin glanced over his shoulder, saw Bear's cabin go up in flames.

*You're not going to make it back.*

The thought struck him in the solar plexus, sent adrenaline surging through his veins. Then his training kicked in, his mind racing through his options. He didn't have a fire shelter or a magic wand or a helicopter or…

*Azure Lake.*

He turned and ran as fast as he could toward the lake, heart slamming, thighs burning as he pushed himself to his physical limit.

A bull moose.

It paid no attention to him but ran past him and kept going.

Austin could see a glimmer of blue through the trees, the fire close enough now to feel hot against his skin. If he didn't make it to the water, if he couldn't push himself harder, he would never see Lexi or Emily again.

A tree to his left went up in flame, the fire roaring behind him.

He threw himself forward, away from the searing heat, stumbling down the embankment and into the chilly water, not far behind the moose. The big animal stopped out in the middle and laid down, not seeming to notice Austin.

*I hope you don't mind sharing, big guy.*

But now the fire was here, the roar of it horrific, the heat unbearable, smoke choking the air. Flames leaped from tree top to tree top, engulfing the forest around him. It was the most terrifying and the most amazing thing he'd ever seen.

Heart thudding, Austin dropped to his knees, raised his backpack to cover his head, and sank down in the water up to his neck, the water cold against his skin. The lake was a few feet below the level of the forest, protecting him from the worst of the smoke and gases. He would probably become hypothermic, but that beat the hell out of burning alive. Breathing hard, he kept his mouth close to the water's surface where the air was cooler and less smoky, embers landing with a *hiss* in the water around him. If he could keep from inhaling too much smoke or heated air, he could survive.

CHASKA STEPPED outside the Dining Hall, made his way

to the tool shed, hoping to fix the broken ice maker. He'd taken just a few steps when he heard a bawling sound.

He turned, looked behind him.

Three bear cubs ran out of the forest, followed by their mother.

They didn't stop. They didn't seem even to notice the children playing dodgeball nearby. They ran through camp, headed out of the canyon.

Chills skittered down Chaska's spine.

What would make a mother bear run like that?

He caught the scent of smoke on the breeze, ran to the nearest tall ponderosa pine, and climbed its branches to get a better view.

*Son of a...*

Fire stretched across the horizon, orange flames rising above the tops of the trees. A crown fire. It looked like it was directly below Pinnacles now, a massive cliff of eroded rock. It was burning through Haley Preserve and headed straight for them.

"What do you see?" Old Man asked from below.

Naomi stood there, too, along with a dozen or so children.

"Why is he climbing the tree?"

"I don't know," Naomi answered. "I guess he wants to see something."

He answered his grandfather in Lakota to keep from alarming the kids. "*Peta.*"

*Fire.*

He downclimbed as fast as he could. "We need to leave camp—now. There's a forest fire headed this way."

Naomi's eyes went wide. "What?"

Chaska hurried toward the front porch of the Dining Hall, Naomi a step behind him. "There's an active crown fire headed this way. Did you see the family of bears that ran out of the forest just now? They were fleeing a fire."

"What are we going to do? We only have three vehicles."

Naomi had picked up most of the camp counselors from the airport with the camp's 12-passenger van, while the kids had arrived by chartered bus. The van couldn't hold all forty-three kids, let alone the camp counselors, and the chartered bus wouldn't be coming for them again until the last day of camp.

"We use what we have, pack as many kids into the van and into the two other vehicles as possible." Chaska rang the dinner bell.

Counselors and kids alike stopped their activities— some were still watching the fleeing bears—and turned to look at Chaska.

"Everyone, listen!" He raised his voice to be heard. "We need to evacuate camp now. There's no time to gather your belongings. Counselors, get your kids to the vehicles now. We'll load as many children as we can. No time to get your things. No time for discussion. Move!"

Kat stepped onto the porch, holding one of her kids on her hip, the other two following behind her. "What's wrong?"

Naomi lowered her voice, but Chaska could hear her fear. "There's a forest fire headed this way."

Kat's eyes went wide. "Gabe took our car into town. He doesn't know. I have no way of getting me or the kids out."

"We'll find a way." Chaska set off toward the vehicles. "Naomi, do you have the keys to the van?"

"They're inside."

"Get them now. You're driving. Hurry!"

Smoke hung in the air over camp now, the fire getting nearer.

How much time did they have?

Chaska called out to the counselors. "Naomi will drive the van, and the owners of the two other vehicles will drive their own cars. We pack as many kids in as we can, and then you drive."

"What about the rest of us?" asked one of the counselors.

"I don't have an answer for that yet."

Naomi returned with the keys, clicked the fob, opening the sliding door.

"Come on, kids." He helped Mona into the van. "Go all the way to the back, Spider Girl. Keep moving. Hurry now."

He picked children up, one after the other. "Big kids, hold a smaller child on your lap. That's right. Squeeze in as tight as you can."

One of the counselors got in his face. "You can't pack so many kids in here. There aren't enough seatbelts."

Chaska fought to keep the irritation out of his voice. Did people not get it? "Seatbelts don't matter right now."

All that mattered was survival.

He saw Old Man helping children into one of the counselor's SUVs, while Naomi did a head count amid the chaos.

They managed to cram twenty kids in the van—not even standing room left. Another eleven fit in the SUV. Eight fit in the little blue Prius. That left Kat and her three children, together with fourteen camp counselors, Old Man, and Chaska.

Naomi got into the driver's seat, tears in her eyes. "I can't just leave you here."

"It's going to be okay." He cupped her cheek. "You

need to take care of yourself and the baby—and all of these children."

He gave her a quick kiss, helped her into the driver's seat, shut the door. "Don't stop for anything. You need to be gone before the fire reaches the road. Go!"

She started the engine, backed up, and turned, driving down the dirt road toward safety, the Prius and the Ford Explorer following.

Chaska exhaled in relief.

The sound of a siren.

Flashing overheads.

Old Man grinned. "It's the cavalry."

A sheriff's vehicle sped toward them, passing the van and the other vehicles. In front of it was a familiar SUV.

"Gabe!" Kat ran forward.

Rossiter pulled to a stop, jumped out. "Kat, you and the kids are leaving—now."

"You're going, too, right?"

Gabe shook his head. "We've got room for the kids plus a couple of adults in there. I'll stay here and wait for the next sheriff's vehicle. Deputy Marcs got a call off to Dispatch. They know we're here."

But Kat didn't budge. "Are you sure they're coming?"

The hard set of Rossiter's jaw told Chaska he knew there wasn't time.

"I'll be fine." Rossiter took the car seats out of the car to make more room. "Alissa, Nakai, come on. Get in. You're going to sit on someone's lap."

Deputy Marcs called out to them. "I've got room for five adults, maybe six, but we have to move *now*."

"We can fit four or five in here." Rossiter met Chaska's gaze, understanding passing between them. "I volunteer to stay. Anyone else?"

Chaska nodded. "I'll stay."

Old Man raised a hand. "I'm staying, too. This old man has had a good life."

The remaining counselors glanced at each other, one in tears, some clearly on the brink of panic, some calm and focused. One of the women and most of the men volunteered to remain behind. In the end, Deputy Marcs packed six in her vehicle, while Kat fit five, leaving three counselors, Rossiter, Old Man, and Chaska.

There was no time for goodbyes.

"Go!" Rossiter slammed his hand on the roof of his own vehicle.

"There is no sheriff's vehicle coming, is there?" asked one of the younger men.

"Probably not." Rossiter's gaze was fixed on his vehicle as it drove away.

The fire was dangerously close now, embers floating on the wind.

Chaska glanced around, at the camp. After all the hard work he and Naomi had put into this place, it was all going to burn. But he didn't intend to burn with it.

"Now what?" asked one of the counselors.

Old Man turned and walked toward the tipi. "I gotta get the drum."

"The drum?"

"It's the heartbeat of our ancestors. I won't leave it behind."

"We're not going anywhere, Grandfather," said one of the counselors.

Chaska glanced up at the rock walls that surrounded them to the east and north, looking for a way out. It wouldn't do them any good to climb the canyon wall because the fire would spread to the trees up there, too.

Then Rossiter pointed upward. "Is that what I think it is?"

Concealed behind an arete and a hundred feet above the ground, Chaska saw it.

A cave.

"Let go of me!"

A child's voice.

*What the hell?*

Chaska turned to see Old Man carrying the drum—and pulling Dean along with him. "How the hell did this happen?"

He'd thought all the children were safe.

Rossiter stared. "Holy shit."

"I found him hiding in the tipi."

Dean glared defiantly up at Chaska, tears on his cheeks. "I don't want to go home."

Chaska's heart broke for the boy. He would rather face the unknown horrors of a wildfire than go home. "Okay, you're with us. But you have to do exactly what we tell you to do."

Dean nodded.

Rossiter took off at a run.

"What's he doing?" Old Man asked.

Chaska was pretty sure he knew. "Getting ropes."

━━━

FIGHTING TEARS, Lexi fastened Emily into her car seat and then lifted their black Lab, Mack, who was inside his crate, into the back of her Lexus. She'd called Austin and texted him, but he hadn't answered. Last she'd heard, he was staffing a roadblock.

He had told her this day might come. He'd said it was the risk they took by choosing to live in the wildland-urban interface. He'd warned her not to be sentimental but to grab the basics and get out. But no warning could prepare her for the reality of leaving her home like this.

She ran through a quick mental checklist, her thoughts scattered by adrenaline. She had all the important papers—passports, birth certificates, professional certifications, Emily's and Mack's immunization records. She'd packed her duplicate hard drive with all of her client records. She'd grabbed their computers and flash drives, including the one with the video that Eric and Vic had made for their wedding. She'd packed clothes and toiletries. She'd taken Emily's and Mack's favorite toys, as well as dog food and people snacks. She'd also grabbed the album of old family photos from before her mother's death.

That was the important stuff.

She tried not to think of what she was leaving behind, but couldn't help it. The quilt she'd had since she was four. Framed photos. Her romance novels. All of their Christmas decorations. Her wedding dress. Austin's climbing gear—itself worth thousands of dollars.

Tears streaming down her cheeks, she sent her father a quick text message to ask whether he needed help evacuating. Then she backed out of the garage and drove down the road toward the highway into town, Emily humming to herself in the backseat, blissfully unaware of what was unfolding in her life.

Lexi focused on the drive to Boulder. It was going to be chaos. Three highways converged in Scarlet, but two were already closed because they followed the rivers up into the mountains toward the fire. That left only one way out of the mountains for almost fifteen hundred residents.

She reached the highway, found bumper-to-bumper traffic, waited to merge.

Herb, who'd been the town's pharmacist since before

Lexi was born, stopped for her, flashed his brights, and waved for her to merge.

She waved back, joining her neighbors as they moved slowly downhill away from danger. It was bumper-to-bumper traffic down into Scarlet proper, cars, trucks hauling horse trailers, and SUVs inching along.

Then ahead she saw flashing lights—firefighters trying to get through.

Almost as one, the column of traffic pulled over, driving onto sidewalks and front lawns to make room for the men and women who were trying to save their town.

A hotshot crew.

It headed up the canyon in the opposite direction from everyone else, the words IHC PINE RIDGE HOTSHOTS on the side.

"Stay safe." Lexi knew they couldn't hear her, but it felt good to say something.

A helicopter rose off the reservoir and flew over town, hose dangling beneath it.

Her cell phone buzzed—a message from Kendra.

Your dad refuses to go. He wants to go down with the ship. Stubborn S.O.B!

Lexi let out an exasperated groan. "Dad!"

She knew Austin would want her to keep going and let the sheriff deal with her father, but she couldn't just leave him. She had to at least try to talk some sense into his head. For all of his failings—and he had many—he was her father, and she loved him.

She flipped on her turn signal, waited until she reached First Street, and made a left. There, standing in front of the Inn, was her father, garden hose in hand, spraying down the building.

She drove up, pulled over, climbed out. "What are you doing?"

"What does it look like I'm doing?"

Kendra charged out of the front door. "Thank God, you're here! I loaded up the car, but I can't get him to go."

"I'm not leaving. You two head on down the canyon."

Kendra stamped her foot. "If you stay, I stay."

Across the street, Rose hurried out of her shop, ran down the stairs with a box in her arms, and shoved the box into her white Chevy Tahoe. Next to her, Marley was rolling a dolly loaded merchandise—medical and recreational marijuana—out to a small truck.

He waved to Lexi, shouting to be heard. "I don't want this all going up in smoke!"

She knew he was trying to be funny, but she couldn't laugh. She walked up to her father, jerked the hose from him. "Dad, why are you doing this?"

He took the hose back, pressed his thumb against the nozzle, sending a jet of water onto the roof. "It didn't burn in 1878, and I can't let it burn now."

"Dad, you could be hurt—or killed. How do you think Kendra, Britta, and I would feel if the Inn survived, but we lost you?"

He kept spraying. "I promised your mama when they lowered her into her grave that I would pass the Inn onto you and your sister or die trying."

"You stubborn bastard!" Kendra looked both angry —and hurt.

She had always been jealous of Lexi's mother's memory.

"I owe this to my daughters."

Tears filling her eyes, Lexi touched a hand to her father's arm. "No, you don't. Mom wouldn't want this either. She'd want you to be safe."

"You go on, Lexi. Take that sweet baby girl with you. I'll be fine."

"Hey, Bob!" Rose called from across the street. "I'm about to take off. Since you're staying, can you spray down my shop, too, make sure it doesn't burn?"

Lexi's father turned around and sprayed Rose with the hose, soaking her while she screamed. "You want to save your shop? Stay, and spray it yourself!"

"Come on, Dad. Let's go. I can't just leave—" Lexi's phone buzzed.

It was Rick Sutherland, Austin's boss.

"Hey, Lexi, have you heard from Austin?"

"No. I sent a few texts but haven't heard back. He told me he was staffing a barricade."

Silence.

Lexi's pulse skipped. "Is something wrong?"

"He asked for permission to head out to Bear's place on Haley Preserve. Radio contact out there isn't good. We lost touch with him a while ago."

Across the street, a furious Rose was shouting at Lexi's father.

"I'm sure he'll contact you as soon as he can."

"Haley Preserve burned over ten minutes ago. We don't know for certain he was there when it did. That's why we're calling around."

"Wh-what?" Lexi's heart seemed to stop, her mind struggling to understand what Rick had just told her.

"I hate to say it, but the fire moved through there ten minutes ago."

She managed a single word. "N-no."

## Chapter 11

VICKI HELPED Rico put a day's worth of prep into the walk-in fridge, her thoughts on Eric. He'd texted her not long ago, so she knew he was safe. Still, her heart hurt for him.

Today was turning out to be the worst day of his life.

He had warned people this might happen. He had tried to thin the forest west of town. He had tried to get mountain homeowners to create defensible spaces around their homes. Very few had listened. And now it looked like the worst might come to pass.

Every house that burned, every person who was injured, every pet that was lost or killed, even dead wildlife —it would weigh on him.

Rico put a big hand on her shoulder. "He's going to be okay."

Vicki nodded. "I know."

She stripped off her apron, tossed it in the laundry basket, and walked out to the dining room to see whether Rain or Joe needed help closing. Cheyenne and Sam were already gone, along with most of their customers.

Hank still sat at the bar. A regular, he had served time in jail for blowing up his own home while trying to extract hash oil from marijuana. Vicki had watched Eric try to save the house, had watched while he'd shepherded Hank through a mess of his own making. She hadn't been able to help loving Eric after that.

"What are you goin' to do with the booze?" Hank asked Joe, who was packing receipts into a bank deposit bag. "I could take some in my car, drive it to safety."

"No, thanks, Hank," Joe answered. "The booze stays here."

Hank looked horrified. "You're going to let all that fine alcohol burn up?"

"If it comes to it, yes. It's just booze."

"Just booze?"

"Come on, Hank." Rain walked to the front door, Angel still on her back, and held the door open. "Time to go, buddy. Stay safe, okay?"

"Do you need anything else?" Vicki asked Joe.

Joe shook his head. "You take care of you. Don't risk going home, okay?"

"I won't." She had no reason to go home.

Robin and Caden were already safe in Boulder, and Eric kept the originals of their important documents in a fireproof safe for precisely this reason. He'd put copies in a safe deposit box at the bank.

Libby stormed out of the brewery, visibly upset. "I've turned everything off. That entire batch is going to be lost. That's thousands of dollars literally down the drain. I'm so sorry, Joe."

"Don't apologize. It's not your fault. It's just grain and hops. It will be okay."

"No, it won't." Libby's chin quivered, tears spilling

down her cheeks. "My house is gone. My street. They said it was engulfed."

Joe rested a hand on her shoulder. "Hey, listen to me, Libby. We're not going to leave you without a home. You're not alone in this."

"Oh, honey." Vicki hugged her close. "Do you want to follow me down the canyon? We can go together, wait it out at the fairgrounds."

Libby sniffed, nodded. "I would like that."

"We'll meet you down there," Rain said. "Lark is already there. She says it has turned into a party. Some of the guys from the Timberline Mudbugs who had to evacuate are apparently putting on an acoustic show."

That made Vicki smile. Only in Scarlet.

She was about to head out to her vehicle when her phone buzzed.

Lexi.

"Hey, Lex, are you—"

"Austin—he went to get Bear, but the fire burned through there more than ten minutes ago." Lexi's voice was thick with tears, her words coming out in a rush. "They don't know if either of them are still alive."

*Oh, God!*

Vicki's stomach turned. "Where are you?"

"I'm at the Inn. My dad won't go, and I can't leave, not without knowing."

Vicki didn't think Lexi would be able to drive now anyway. "I'm coming for you. I'll be right there, Lexi. Hang on, okay? We'll figure this out."

Vicki ended the call, found the others watching her. "Austin went after Bear. The fire burned through there about ten minutes ago, and no one knows whether either of them are alive."

"Oh, God." Rain raised a hand to her mouth, her eyes wide.

Joe rarely seemed surprised by anything, but he gaped at Vicki. "Jesus."

Vicki turned to Libby. "I've got to go to her. Are you good to drive?"

Libby nodded. "I'll follow you."

Vicki went to her locker, grabbed her clothes, and, not bothering to change, hurried out to her vehicle, her thoughts running in a loop.

Austin couldn't be dead—or badly burned or hurt. He was the love of Lexi's life. He was Eric's best friend. He couldn't be dead. He couldn't be.

With Libby close behind her, Vicki drove as fast as she could through traffic, crossing the main highway only after some kind person let them through. She floored it down First Street, smoke making the air hazy, a wall of angry gray stretching to the sky just to the west of town.

She parked in the back and, not bothering to knock, stepped with Libby through the Inn's private entrance into the kitchen. "Lexi?"

Lexi looked up at Vicki through haunted blue eyes, her face pinched by fear, Emily playing with blocks on the floor beside her. "Still nothing. They don't have a helicopter to check on him. They're trying to find a helo to rescue the people trapped at Naomi's camp."

God in heaven. Were the kids trapped, too?

Fear filled her belly—for the children, for Naomi and Chaska, for Eric, who would blame himself for anything that happened to any of them.

She sat, took Lexi's hand. "I'll call Eric. I'll ask him to—"

Lexi shook her head, tears spilling down her cheeks,

her hand holding tightly to Vicki's. "There's nothing he can do. No one can get back there except by air. I've already called Dispatch twice. They'll call me if there's news."

Vicki knew this had to be unbearable for Lexi. If Eric were missing in a fire…

God, she couldn't even think about that.

But they couldn't stay here.

Vicki knew Lexi didn't want to leave, but she didn't have a choice. "It's not safe here, Lexi. I'll leave my car here. We can take your vehicle down to the fairgrounds and wait for news there. Your dad, Kendra, Emily—we'll all go together."

She looked up, met Bob's gaze, defied him to disagree.

———

KENZIE COULDN'T LET herself panic. She had twenty dogs to evacuate, plus Gizmo and Gabby. She didn't have time to fall apart.

*Megs won't let Harrison take unnecessary risks.*

Harrison had been toned out with the Team to rescue people trapped at a camp—that's all he'd told her—and that meant he was headed straight *toward* the fire.

He was always the first one to volunteer for tough rescues. Kenzie loved him for it—but it also scared the shit out of her.

*Be safe!*

The office phone rang—again. Kenzie ignored it, let it go to voicemail. She didn't have time to talk right now. She had recorded a message for her clients explaining that she was evacuating their dogs to the Boulder County Fairgrounds and that she would update them as the situation unfolded.

She put the dogs in their crates. "Come on, Loki. We're going for a little drive."

The Jack Russell terrier whined, no doubt able to sense her fear.

Behind her, the door opened.

She turned to see Chip and Charles.

"Need help?" Charles asked.

Kenzie let out a breath of relief. "Oh, God, do I ever."

"You helped save our fur babies," Chip said. "We're here to return the favor."

They finished crating all of the dogs and managed to fit four in Charles' vehicle and three in with Crank and Kahlo in Chip's vehicle. Kenzie loaded Gabby and Gizmo into her truck without their crates, which left her room for three more pooches.

That left ten dogs.

"I'm going to see what Winona's doing. Maybe she knows about someone who can help." Kenzie sent a quick text message to Winona.

How are you getting your animals down?

Winona replied right away.

I'm staying. I don't have any way to transport them all. I won't leave Shota. Chase, Naomi, and Grandpa are still up there with the kids. I'm afraid something awful has happened. I can't reach them.

Kenzie's stomach sank. "Oh, God."

Was that who Harrison had gone to rescue?

"What is it?" Chip asked.

"Winona says her brother and the rest of her family

are still at their kids' camp. She's staying with the animals. She won't leave them—or Shota."

Chip's jaw tightened. "Where are those two ripped and handsome boys who rescued Crank and Kahlo?"

Kenzie didn't know. "Last I saw them, they were near the roadblock."

Chip shot out the door, disappearing around the corner at a run.

"So, the point of this is to get the dogs to safety, right?" Charles asked.

Kenzie nodded.

"Come on." He motioned toward the door. "I have an idea."

She followed him to the roundabout, where traffic was inching along. What in the world was he doing? She didn't have time to mess around.

He stepped into traffic, raised his voice. "Can anyone drive a dog to the fairgrounds?"

Kenzie understood now.

She stepped up beside him, her voice all but drowned out by car engines and a helicopter that passed overhead. "Does anyone have room for a dog?"

Traffic kept moving, heads shaking.

Then Hank stopped. He was the last person Kenzie would have expected to help. "You can fit a couple of dogs in my backseat. My house already burned down once, so I don't have much stuff. Besides, I need the good karma."

"Can you pull in behind the kennel?"

Horns honked, people angry at Hank for stopping.

He flipped them the bird out the window. "Sure thing."

With Charles helping, Kenzie loaded Slate, an Australian cattle dog, and Loki, the little Jack Russell terrier, into Hank's backseat.

"Drive them to Boulder County Fairgrounds and wait

for me there. Don't go anywhere else, and don't let them out of their crates. Don't leave them in the car, either. It's too hot."

"Yes, ma'am."

Kenzie watched him pull back into traffic and head toward the canyon.

Charles was at it again, flagging down drivers, asking for help.

Herb, the pharmacist, said he could fit a small crate in his front seat.

Kenzie gave him Trixie, the toy poodle, and told him where to meet her.

Seven dogs to go.

Then a familiar pickup truck pulled up, towing a horse trailer behind it.

Nate West looked down at her. "You need some help there, Kenzie?"

Kenzie explained as quickly as she could both her situation and Winona's. "I don't know how many animals she has, but one of them is an adult wolf."

"Right." Nate nodded. "I'm going to pull over."

Kenzie followed him as he drove into the kennel's parking lot, catching a glimpse of Rose as she passed through the roundabout. She looked like she'd just stepped out of the shower.

Nate stepped out of his truck, talking on the phone to someone. "That's right—a wolf. Okay. I'm at the kennel now. I'll ask."

He turned to Kenzie. "How many dogs?"

"Seven."

Nate repeated the number into the phone. "See you in a few."

"My old man's on his way." He opened the door to the front of the trailer to reveal a living area complete with a television. "How many dog crates can we fit here if we get creative?"

The answer was all seven, Kenzie, Charles, and Nate working together to load the dogs quickly. They had just closed the door when Charles returned, Marc Hunter and Julian Darcangelo beside him.

Nate grinned, hugged Marc and then Julian. "I figured I'd run into you sooner or later."

They knew each other?

Nate told Marc and Julian what was happening. "I'm heading down the canyon with a couple of horses and the rest of the dogs, but the wildlife clinic still needs help."

Marc looked at Julian. "I told you we ought to stick around."

Julian rolled his eyes. "No, I told you."

Nate chuckled, climbed into his truck. "I'm leaving you in good hands, Kenzie."

"I can't thank you enough, Nate. I'll see you at the fairgrounds."

As Nate pulled out, his father, Jack West, pulled in, hauling a similar trailer. He leaned out of his window. "I hear there are some critters who need a ride."

<hr />

CONRAD FOLLOWED Megs in his SUV, smoke and dust from her tires all but obscuring his view of her pickup. Ahearn brought up the rear in his SUV, the three of them rushing to reach Camp Mato Sapa before the fire did. It didn't look good. A dark wall of smoke hung over them, flames turning its underside orange, creating a strange twilight. Deer and elk fled, heading down the road and away from the danger.

Forty-three children and twenty adults.

*Son of a bitch!*

Would they be able to rescue everyone if they packed people in like sardines? The kids would have to be their first priority. After that…

*Fuck!*

Usually when the Team got toned out, Conrad knew they were going to make a difference. This time, he wasn't sure any of them would make it back.

Megs had left it up to Team members to decide whether they wanted to take the risk. Not many Team members had been available. Hawke, Taylor, and Moretti were already fighting the fire. Nicole, Sasha, and O'Brien lived in the initial evacuation zone and had their hands full. Acharya rode a motorcycle, which was useless in this situation. Everyone else was scattered—at work, too far from Scarlet to make it, on a climbing vacation somewhere. That had left the three of them—Conrad, Megs, and Ahearn.

The last thing Conrad had wanted to do was drive *toward* the fire, but he couldn't let those kids die.

Ahead of him, Megs suddenly stopped, her brake lights flashing red, the color visible through smoke and dust. Conrad slammed on his brakes, stopping a few inches short of her back bumper. He half expected Ahearn to rear-end him, but he managed to stop on time.

Headlights.

On the other side of the road, a van and two other vehicles drew to a stop.

Conrad put his SUV in park and climbed out, engine still running, to find out what the hell was going on.

Naomi sat in the driver's seat of the van, young children packed in behind her, fear on their little faces.

Conrad's first reaction was relief. They'd found a way to get themselves out.

*Thank God.*

Then he heard what Naomi was saying.

"We've got all of the children except for Kat and Gabe's kids. I don't know how many adults are still there. Deputy Marcs and Gabe Rossiter pulled in after I left. I doubt they could fit everyone."

"Chaska's still there?" Megs asked.

Naomi nodded, her expression crumpling. "Grandpa Belcourt, Gabe Rossiter, Kat, and their kids, and several camp counselors and are with him."

*Shit.*

"Get these kids out of here," Megs said. "Scarlet Springs has been evacuated, so you head through the roundabout and straight down the canyon to the Boulder County Fairgrounds. We'll get everyone we can and meet you there."

"Thank you!" Naomi reached out, took Megs' hand, gave it a squeeze.

"Go!" Megs turned and ran back to her own vehicle, shouting over her shoulder to Conrad and Ahearn. "Let's get the rest of them!"

Conrad climbed behind the wheel again and followed Megs. The smoke was so thick now that it came in through his ventilation system, making him cough, burning his eyes. How were they going to spot the turnoff to the camp when they couldn't see five feet in front of them?

Embers drifted through the air now like orange snowflakes, landing on his hood and windshield.

Flashing red and blue lights.

It was a Forest County sheriff's vehicle, and it didn't stop. Behind it followed an SUV, Rossiter's wife, Kat, at the wheel, adults and children in the back.

Was that everyone?

They pressed on, embers falling thick and hard now.

Yeah, this couldn't be safe.

Ahead of him, Megs stopped again, but this time she put her truck in reverse.

And then he saw.

Ahead, in what should have been the mouth of the canyon, was nothing but flame, and it was moving toward them. If they didn't get the fuck out of here *right now*, they were going to roast on the road.

"Damn it!"

In tandem, the three of them backed up, turned around, and headed back toward Scarlet with Ahearn in the lead this time, the fire running toward them.

"Fuck!"

Conrad looked down, saw that he was going almost forty miles an hour. If they'd been driving on a straight road, they would have been able to get away with no problem. Instead, the road curved, while the head of the fire was making a run straight eastward.

It was gaining on them.

Another curve.

The trees on both sides of the road went up in flames.

*Keep going. Keep going. Faster!*

A flaming branch fell onto the rocky shoulder of the road, sending up a shower of embers. Conrad drove straight through it without slowing.

Another curve.

Spot fires flared up ahead of them, heat radiating through his vehicle. There was nothing he could do but drive.

"Keep going," he said aloud this time.

All of Conrad's near-death experiences had come in the Himalayas in ice and snow. How ironic it would be if he ended up being barbequed right here, just outside his hometown.

*Kenzie.*

He couldn't do that to her.

He glanced in his rearview mirror, saw Megs riding his bumper, embers dancing off her truck, nothing visible behind her but flame.

The road sloped sharply downhill now, and the fire seemed to fall back. Conrad remembered Hawke telling him something about fire burning uphill faster than downhill.

"Woohoo!"

The smoke began to clear, and ahead he saw it—the highway.

Ahearn slowed but didn't stop at the stop sign, fish-tailing as he turned right and heading toward Scarlet at sixty miles an hour, Conrad and Megs following.

They didn't stop till they got back to The Cave.

It was only after he'd turned off his engine that the full force of what had just happened hit him, uncertainty gnawing at him. "Shit!"

Had everyone gotten away, or had they just abandoned friends to die?

## Chapter 12

GABE REACHED for the last hold as he neared the entrance to the cave. He'd done some hairy free soloing in his life, but he'd never had to free solo to save lives. Every person here was depending on him for their survival. It didn't matter that he wasn't wearing a climbing prosthetic or that he was on-sighting what was a solid 5.12—no practicing while roped in, no time to examine the route, no beta from someone who'd climbed it already.

*Don't think about it.*

He hauled himself upward, caught the lip of the cave, pulled himself over the edge. He got to his feet, glanced inside the dark space, relief rushing through him.

The cave was big enough to hold all of them.

He shouted down to Belcourt. "We're good!"

He fixed a pulley in the rock with a rusty piton, set up a kind of assisted belay, and lowered the rope to Belcourt, who already had everyone in climbing harnesses. "Hurry!"

The fire had already engulfed the camp buildings and was now burning through the grass and brush toward them.

Gabe hauled little Dean and the lightest of the camp counselors up, the two of them harnessed together, Dean in tears despite the counselor's attempts to reassure him.

"We're going to burn to death down here if you don't hurry!" another counselor shouted.

That wasn't going to help.

Gabe ignored that, tried to comfort the boy. "It's okay, buddy. You're safe up here. Go back and find a good place for Grandpa Belcourt to sit, okay?"

Dean sniffed, nodded.

Gabe sent down the rope again, and, with the help of the first camp counselor, hoisted up the other two counselors, their dead weight supported in part by the pulley, until only Belcourt and his grandfather remained on the ground.

"You next," he heard Belcourt say.

"You go. I can wait."

"No, Grandpa. I can climb this without the rope. I'll be right behind you."

Gabe lowered the rope, his hands blistered from the friction.

Grandpa was a bit heavier than the others.

"Pull!" Gabe shouted over his shoulder to the counselors.

The fire was almost below them now, its roar deafening.

Belcourt had done as he'd said, following his grandfather up, climbing without the security of a belay as Gabe had done. If he fell...

As soon as Old Man Belcourt was up, Gabe tossed down the rope, shouting to be heard. "Hold on!"

Belcourt took hold of the rope, letting Gabe and the others pull him the rest of the way up to the cave.

The fire had reached the cliff now, smoke thick in the air, the heat rising up from below almost unbearable.

Coughing, Belcourt hauled himself over the edge and into the cave.

Gabe took his hand, pulled him to his feet. "Are you okay?"

That had been awfully damned close.

Belcourt nodded, still coughing. "A bit toasted ... You are ... one hell of a climber, man. I'm not sure ... I could have done that."

"You almost did."

It had been a calculated risk.

If Gabe had fallen, he'd have been killed, and they would have wasted precious minutes that probably would have cost the rest of them their lives. If the cave hadn't been big enough to hold them all ...

Yeah, that would have been a clusterfuck.

Smoke was blowing into the cave now, carried by the wind, making everyone cough. If they didn't stop it, they might end up dying of smoke inhalation anyway.

Belcourt gestured toward the cave's entrance. "We ... should try ... to cover it."

Gabe glanced around for something that could span the five-foot-tall and two-foot-wide opening. "Anyone have a ... tarp stuffed in their underwear?"

Grandpa Belcourt turned over the big drum he cradled in his arms. Strapped to the underside was some kind of blanket roll. "I have this old ... Pendleton blanket. It was a gift... from your Grandma's parents."

Gabe didn't want to take that. Embers would scorch it. It might even catch fire. He opened his mouth to say so, inhaled smoke, coughed.

*Shit.*

They didn't have a choice.

155

Grandpa untied it, handed it to Belcourt, who unrolled it, his expression grave. "*Pilamayaye, Tunkasila.*"

Gabe had spent enough time with the Lakota, who had a special relationship with the Navajo, to understand that Belcourt was thanking the old man.

Smoke stinging his throat and eyes, Gabe walked with Chaska to the entrance, fumbling through the camp's rack of climbing gear in search of something to hold the blanket in place.

Belcourt used the flashlight on his cell phone to examine the rock, coughing hard. "There's a … crack here. Any … small cams?"

Gabe handed him the smallest cam he could find, then held the blanket in place, shutting out light and smoke, while Belcourt jammed the device into the small crack as far as he could.

One of the camp counselors held something on an outstretched palm. "I've got a carabiner on my keychain."

"That just might work." Gabe took it, held the blanket in place while Chaska searched for another fissure in the rock.

Gabe saw it—a narrow crack. "Here."

Belcourt took the carabiner, picked up a rock, and beat the metal loop into the crack. "If this doesn't hold…"

"It won't—not for long." Gabe turned to face inward, pressed his back against the blanket where it overlapped with rock, then stepped carefully onto the bottom of the blanket to keep out as much smoke as he could.

Belcourt put away his cell phone and did the same, leaving them in the dark, the two of them standing only two feet apart, the fire raging below, drowning out the sound of coughing.

"We don't have to stay long!" Gabe shouted. "Just till the fire passes!"

That's when it hit him, like a fist to the stomach.

Fear.

Kat. Alissa. Nakai. Noelle.

He loved them more than life itself.

Had they made it back to Scarlet? Was the fire about to catch them on the road?

Gabe closed his eyes, sent up a silent prayer.

*Creator, keep them safe.*

Then, in the darkness … a drum beat.

The deep thrum of the drum was audible above the roar from outside. Gabe could almost feel it in his chest, like a heartbeat—strong, steady, sure.

Then the old man started to sing.

"*Wakan Tanka, Tunkasila/Wakan Tanka, Tunkasila/Pila-mayayelo he…*"

Grandpa was thanking the Great Mystery for providing this cave, for giving them the skills to reach it, for keeping them safe.

Belcourt began to sing along with his grandfather. The camp counselors joined in, too, their voices stronger together, rising in the darkness, chasing away death, banishing fear. Then above the other, deeper voices, Gabe heard it.

Little Dean was singing, too.

———

JOAQUIN RODE in the back of the truck, the mood somber since Hawke had gotten the call on the radio about the kids' camp—and his missing friend. Brandon Silver had explained the situation to Joaquin quietly.

Hawke had asked his best friend, a park ranger named Austin Taylor, to search for someone named Bear. The fire had burned through the area where Taylor had gone, and no one had heard from him since. The fire had also burned through a canyon where more than sixty people, most of them children, had been trapped. The people Hawke had sent to rescue the kids hadn't been heard from either.

*Madre de Dios.*

Joaquin didn't want to imagine what might have just happened—people, including children, dying of smoke inhalation or being burned to death. The thought put a knot in his stomach, the mental images it conjured too horrible even to consider.

He turned his mind back to his work, scrolling through the images on his camera. Firefighters using drip torches to start the backburn, the sky beyond them gray with smoke. An exhausted firefighter taking a drink, sweat beading on her soot-blackened face. Firefighters looking up at the helicopter as it arrived for its first water drop.

Then Joaquin came to it—the shot that told the story.

Hawke stood with his boots planted firmly in the black, sunglasses in hand, glaring at the hundred-foot-tall wall of fire as it raced toward the backburn, as if trying to put out the blaze through force of will alone.

The exposure was perfect. The contrast in colors—the yellow of his shirt and green of his pants against the black beneath his feet and the orange wall of flame—made it pop. The composition was pretty solid, too.

It was his pick for the front page—so far.

"Great shot."

Joaquin looked up from the camera to find Silver looking over his shoulder. "Thanks."

Silver kept his voice low. "So, you're friends with Gabe Rossiter?"

Joaquin nodded. "Good friends."

"Is he as crazy as he seems when it comes to the climbing shit?"

Joaquin couldn't help but smile. "Crazier."

"I believe it."

Now it was Joaquin's turn to ask a question. "Do you have family in town, people trying to evacuate while you're up here?"

Silver's brows drew together in a frown. "A girlfriend—or maybe she's not my girlfriend. Hell, I don't know. It's complicated. Her house is gone. I want to call her to see how she's doing and make sure she's safe, but I left my phone at the firehouse."

Joaquin held out his. "You can borrow mine."

"Thanks, man." Silver took the phone, typed in a number, left a short message. "She didn't answer."

"She probably didn't recognize the number."

"Yeah." But there was worry on Silver's face.

What a terrible thing to be split between duty and the desire to protect loved ones.

In the front passenger seat, Hawke was speaking to someone with his hand mic.

"He's talking with the super of the hotshot crew," Silver explained. "They're meeting us at Ski Scarlet."

*Any word about the kids or Taylor?*

Joaquin wanted to ask but couldn't. He didn't want to distract anyone, least of all Hawke, who had the weight of the world on his shoulders right now.

They drove up the switchbacks toward the ski resort, the sun dimmed by smoke. The firefighters climbed out, most of them heading toward thermos barrels of water. Joaquin was last, but he followed Hawke toward a group of firefighters standing around a turquoise buggy with the words IHC PINE RIDGE HOTSHOTS painted on the side.

A Native hotshot crew. How cool was that?

Hawke shook hands with the group's superintendent, Aaron Tall Bull, and the two men got down to details. Joaquin didn't get all the firefighter jargon, but he did understand the basic discussion. The fire had outflanked the initial backburn, so they were trying to decide where to start again—on the ridge just above Scarlet Springs or in the canyon below it. The ridge would be riskier for firefighters, but falling back to the canyon below town meant letting Scarlet Springs burn.

Hawke turned away from the conversation, spoke into his hand mic. "Eight-sixty-five, Scarlet Command, go ahead."

*Eight-sixty-five.*

Those were the call numbers of the person Hawke had spoken to when he'd gotten the news about the kids' camp.

"Are you certain?" The man's expression gave away nothing, but his jaw tightened. "Who stayed behind?"

Hawke squeezed his eyes shut, breath leaving his lungs in a tight exhale. "Any word on Taylor? Okay. Eight-sixty-five, copy."

He released the mic. "Fuck."

His head fell forward and for a moment he stood there, silent and still. Then he drew in a breath, lifted his head, and raised his hand mic. "Dispatch, Scarlet Command. Have the rescue helicopters continue to Haley Preserve and Camp Mato Sapa to search for survivors."

Joaquin supposed another photographer might have tried to capture that moment—the stress, the despair—but he couldn't.

Hawke turned to him, shadows in his eyes. "Our buddy Rossiter was at Camp Mato Sapa when the fire burned through. He and a handful of others voluntarily stayed behind because there wasn't enough room in the vehicles for everyone."

It took a moment for Hawke's words to sink in, but when they did, they were like a blow to the gut, knocked the breath from Joaquin's lungs.

*Rossiter.*

That son of a bitch.

Joaquin's next thought was for Kat and the kids— Alissa, Nakai, little Noelle.

*Mierda.*

He swallowed the lump in his throat. "Has anyone contacted Kat—his wife?"

Hawke shook his head. "She was driving one of the vehicles and knows he stayed behind. I'd rather wait to call her until we have some final word."

"Yeah. Right." Joaquin felt sick.

How much courage had it taken for Kat to drive away and leave the man she loved behind, knowing he might not survive?

"Is there any chance he might have made it?"

"Knowing Rossiter, there's always a chance." Hawke rested a hand on Joaquin's shoulder and then went back to his discussion with the hotshot crew.

NAOMI SANG, the kids singing with her.

"The wheels on the bus go 'round and 'round, 'round and 'round, 'round and 'round. The wheels on the bus go 'round and 'round all through the town."

Ironically, the van's wheels were barely moving. They were stuck on the highway just outside town, traffic slowed to a crawl.

"The wipers on the bus go swish, swish, swish…"

She kept the song going, doing her best to make this less scary for the children, but it had been terrifying for her, too.

Leaving Chaska behind like that, seeing the fire coming toward them…

Thank God the sheriff's deputy and Gabe had arrived when they had, Megs, Conrad and Ahearn not far behind them. They would make sure Chaska and the others got to safety.

The camp would burn, all the work they'd put into restoring the buildings lost. But the buildings and everything in them could be replaced.

If she had lost Chaska…

*God, no.*

She couldn't go there.

She would have to come up with an evacuation plan so this never happened again. She'd never imagined having to drive everyone from camp at once. They'd been extremely lucky this time, no thanks to that fallen tree.

"The horn on the bus goes beep, beep, beep…"

A horn honked outside, making the children laugh.

Naomi laughed with them and went back to singing. "The horn on the bus goes beep, beep, beep, all through the town."

Then in her side-view mirror, she saw the sheriff's deputy and Kat and Gabe's SUV slow to a stop. They'd made it out.

*Thank God.*

"Mona stepped on my toe!" a little voice called out.

"I didn't mean to," Mona answered.

"I'm sure it was an accident. Can you say 'excuse me,' Mona?"

"'Scuse me."

"I know you're all crowded in here. Try to be patient

and understanding with each other. We need to pull together like true Lakota. As soon as we get to the fair-grounds, you'll be able to get out and play."

What they would do after that, Naomi didn't know. They needed safe lodging for the counselors and the kids, or they needed to send the kids home a few days early. None of that was going to be easy to arrange.

"What should we sing next?" she asked the kids, moving forward a couple of car lengths.

"Row Your Boat!"

"No, that's for babies."

"Twinkle, Twinkle Little Star!"

In her side-view mirror, Ahearn, Conrad, and Megs pulled up, making up the rear of the long line of traffic.

Conrad jumped out of his SUV, ran up to the sheriff's vehicle, and talked with the deputy—it looked like Julia Marcs—through the window. His head fell forward, his fists clenching. He kicked the dirt.

Naomi's pulse skipped.

She watched as he walked to Kat's vehicle, bent down, his head shaking.

Kat climbed out, ran to the side of the road, and threw up.

*Oh, God.*

Ice slid down Naomi's spine, fear making her throat tight.

Megs leaped out of her truck, joined Conrad and Kat, taking Kat into her arms.

Naomi pulled over, parked. "Stay in the van, kids. No fighting!"

She ran to where the others stood. "What is it? What happened?"

Conrad met her gaze, a sheen of tears in his eyes,

regret like pain on his face. "We didn't get to the camp. The fire … We barely made it out ourselves."

His words didn't make sense to Naomi, a rushing sound in her ears.

She shook her head, backed away, ran to the sheriff's vehicle, hand on her heavy belly. "Is Chaska in there?"

Julia shook her head. "I'm sorry, Naomi. There wasn't room. He, his grandfather, Gabe Rossiter, and three camp counselors volunteered to stay behind. There's a rescue helicopter on the way, but the fire burned through the camp not long after we left."

Naomi staggered back, shaking her head. "No."

Chaska couldn't be gone. He couldn't be.

*Chaska!*

Strong arms caught her as her knees buckled.

Conrad drew her to her feet, held her close. "We don't know anything for certain yet. There's still hope."

*The children.*

The thought cut through Naomi's shock and anguish. She pulled away from Conrad, turned toward the van. "I have to get back to the kids. They need me. I have to—"

Conrad caught her with a hand on her shoulder. "I don't think you should drive."

"Saint Barbara's has a bus we can borrow for the kids," Deputy Marcs called out to them. "Let's get everyone together there."

"You can ride with me," Conrad said. "One of the counselors can drive the van to the church. We'll regroup there and get you all to safety at the fairgrounds."

Naomi nodded, barely aware of what was happening around her as Conrad led her toward his SUV. Then Kat was there.

There were tears on Kat's cheeks, but she smiled and

hugged Naomi tight. "We'll get through this together, no matter what. You won't be alone."

In that moment, Kat's words meant everything to Naomi.

Her eyes filled with tears, her throat tight. "Thanks."

It took what seemed like an eternity to reach the parking lot at St. Barbara's, where the priest, Father Pemberthy, stood waiting for them beside a big yellow school bus.

Naomi fought to pull herself together, fear making her feel sick. But she didn't know anything for certain yet, and right now, the children needed her. She couldn't fall apart.

*Chaska!*

Conrad parked his vehicle, the hollow look in his eyes telling Naomi that he was suffering, too. What had Chaska said to her about getting through the *inipi* when she'd freaked out over the darkness and the heat?

*When it gets tough and you don't think you can take it, pray for the person next to you. They're having a hard time of it, too.*

Naomi sent up a prayer for Conrad, for Megs and Ahearn, for Kat, for Chaska and Gabe and Grandpa and all the camp counselors and the kids. It didn't take her pain away, but praying seemed to bring her back to herself.

She reached out, touched Conrad's arm. "Please don't blame yourself. I know you did everything you could."

Conrad squeezed his eyes shut. "We weren't even sure anyone was still at the camp, not after Julia and Kat passed us on the road. The fire got ahead of us on the way out. If I had known they were still there … But even then … *Shit.* I'm so sorry."

"There's nothing more you could have done. Like you say, there's still hope."

Naomi clung to that hope, somehow managing to walk

to where the kids stood in a neat line to board the bus. "Settle down, everyone."

She took a quick headcount to reassure herself.

Thirty-nine children, not counting Kat and Gabe's kids.

No, that couldn't be right. She wasn't thinking clearly. She'd gotten it wrong.

They couldn't have left a child behind. They couldn't have.

Fighting to keep calm, she started counting again.

Tina, one of the counselors, ran up to her. "Dean is missing. One of the kids saw him run and hide in the tipi when we were loading the van."

Naomi's heart seemed to shatter.

## Chapter 13

TEETH CHATTERING, Austin waded on stiff legs to the water's edge, treading on blackened reeds and tripping on charred, fallen branches until he stepped on dry, scorched earth. The fire had passed to the northeast, rolling onward like a tsunami, the roar distant, gray smoke blotting out sunlight.

*Holy fuck.*

He was alive. Apart from hypothermia and a touch of smoke inhalation, he was fine.

He glanced around at the changed landscape, charred trunks standing where there had once been forest, scrub and duff burned down to the soil. Flames lapped at smoldering logs, smoke twisting in the wind, the air still acrid. Out in the middle of the lake, the moose was now grazing, the fire already forgotten. Apart from that, there was no sign of life—no birds singing, no animals, no Bear.

Austin trudged along in wet clothing and boots, making his way toward his truck, slowed by bone-deep cold. It had to be eighty degrees outside today. If he kept moving, he'd warm up.

Okay, so that's not how hypothermia worked.

He needed help.

Once he reached his truck, he would check in with Dispatch and head back to town. He'd drowned both his handheld radio and cell phone in the lake—not that either of them worked up here anyway.

Yeah, Sutherland wasn't going to like his losing a radio. He'd probably take money out of Austin's paycheck to replace it.

*Shit.*

Then again, a few thousand bucks wasn't a bad price to pay for being alive—and saving the journal and photograph from destruction.

God, it had been close.

If he had tripped, if he had kept running for his truck instead of the lake…

The thought made him shiver—or maybe that was the hypothermia.

He knew more about wildfire now than he'd ever wanted to know—the unbearable heat, the deafening roar, the way the trees seemed to scream and groan as flames consumed them. When heat radiating off the blaze had become too hot for him, he'd ducked all the way under, only to inhale smoke when he'd come back up for air.

In that moment, he'd thought it was over, that he was a goner. He'd coughed his lungs out, thoughts of Lexi and Emily racing through his mind. How much he was going to hurt them by leaving them like this. How Emily was almost the same age as Lexi had been when her mother had died. How he'd always thought that he and Lexi would have more children.

What a lucky son of a bitch he was. Lexi still had a husband. Emily still had her father. And he and Lexi could still have more children. Unless he collapsed out here and went into a fucking hypothermic coma.

He found himself grinning at the idiotic thought of freezing to death on a hot summer day because of a fire, except that it wasn't funny.

*Keep moving.*

His legs were sluggish, his feet clumsy as he stumbled over the blackened ground like a drunk. If he stopped now, he might not get moving again. He needed to get to his truck, call in, get help.

Then it struck him.

They probably thought he was dead.

They knew where he'd gone. They must know that the fire had burned through here. They would expect him to have hauled his ass out of here by now. Though they knew his handheld radio couldn't reach them, the radio in his truck could. They would know from his silence that something had gone wrong.

Maybe they would send help.

*And maybe you'd better get out your first-aid kit and grab the emergency blanket.*

Okay, he could do that.

He lowered his pack to the ground and found it singed, small holes burned through the fabric by embers, some of the straps partially melted. He opened the front pocket and pulled out the folded square of reflective fabric. Cold must have dulled his brain because it took him a few minutes to figure out how to unfold the thing.

*It could be worse.*

He could be lying dead here.

He slipped on his pack again, wrapped the blanket around his shoulders, and set off toward the truck once more. With no forest to block his view, he could see part of his truck where it sat to the west and up on the road. It wasn't too much farther now—maybe three hundred yards.

He could make that—no problem.

One foot in front of the other.

His boots stepped on something that snapped. He stopped, looked down, saw bone and quill. The remains of a porcupine. It never had a chance. It had probably taken shelter in a tree. There's no way it could have outrun a conflagration like this on its stubby little legs.

*Damn it!*

Fire was a natural part of this ecosystem. Austin knew that. But he'd become a ranger because he loved the mountains, the forests, and all the creatures that lived here. This felt like standing over the corpse of a murdered friend.

God, he hoped the sheriff caught the bastard who'd started the blaze. All of this death and destruction because some asshole refused to follow the rules.

"I'm sorry, buddy," he said to the porcupine.

He moved on, stepping over charred branches, avoiding patches of brush that were still burning and trees that looked like they might topple. He climbed up the embankment toward the road. It would be easier and safer to follow it back to the truck than clambering around through the charred and smoldering remains of the forest.

He reached the road, and then he saw it clearly. "Son of a bitch!"

His truck was burned out, a smoking hulk.

He jogged toward it, hoping to find the radio still intact despite the damage. He reached the vehicle and glanced through a shattered window, holding his breath against the toxic fumes of methyl-ethyl-badstuff coming from burned wires, plastic, and upholstery.

*Fuck!*

The radio was slag.

He hoped Hawke or Sutherland had sent help. If not, it was going to be a long damned walk back to Scarlet Springs.

———

KENZIE HANDED the cage with the adorable little skunk kittens to Jack. The little creatures were curious, glancing around them, but they didn't seem afraid—thank goodness. No one wanted to get sprayed.

"Where's your mama?" Jack asked them.

"She was hit by a car." Winona walked up behind Kenzie, holding an aquarium with a snake inside. "Someone found them sitting near their mother's body up on the highway and brought them in."

"What happened to him?" Jack motioned toward the snake with a jerk of his head.

"A bicyclist ran over his tail—on purpose, they say."

"What the hell is wrong with people?" Jack disappeared inside his trailer with the baby skunks, Winona following him with the snake.

The trailer was almost full of animals of all kinds—mountain lion cubs, baby skunks, rabbits, raccoons, raptors, and now a snake, too. Kenzie didn't know what she and Winona would have done without Jack and Nate West or Marc, Julian and their friend Zach, for that matter. She and Winona wouldn't have been able to move all the animals on their own.

The plan was to transport the wildlife to the fairgrounds in the trailer, together with two dogs from Kenzie's vehicle, who would ride in Jack's cab, making room for Shota's crate in the back of Kenzie's truck. The wolf wasn't going to fit in Winona's old car. That much was certain.

Julian stepped out of the clinic carrying a large crate in which rested a wounded bald eaglet, a hood covering its eyes to keep it calm. "I think this is the last of the carriers. Hunter and McBride should be coming along in a moment with the moose calf."

He grinned, as if the thought of this amused him.

Then Harrison pulled up to the curb in his SUV.

*Thank goodness!*

She smiled, and waved to him, relieved to see that he was safely back from the rescue. But one look at his face told her something had gone terribly wrong.

He climbed out, walked over to her, the anguish in his eyes making her pulse skip.

"What is it? What happened?"

He looked behind her as if searching for someone, then lowered his voice. "We never made it. The fire burned through the camp, chased us out."

Kenzie's heart sank, her stomach knotting. "All those children."

"Most of the kids got out. One is missing. But Belcourt, his grandpa, Rossiter, and three camp counselors volunteered to stay behind because there wasn't room for everyone in the vehicles."

"Oh, God."

The Belcourts, Gabe Rossiter and Kat—they were friends, people she'd known for years.

"Kat and Naomi know. I told them."

Kenzie took her husband in her arms. "God, you're brave."

"If I had known there were still people at the camp… The fire had burned down to the road and got ahead of us. For a minute or two, I thought we were dead."

She held him closer, sickened by the thought. "Thank God you're safe."

"Yeah."

Kenzie knew some part of him would blame himself for this. He'd lost his best friend on Mt. Everest and had gone through hell in the aftermath, traumatized by the accident, wracked with survivor's guilt. The grief had almost destroyed him.

And now this…

A helicopter passed overhead, flying toward the reservoir to refill its water tank, hose dangling from its belly.

He drew back. "I need to tell Winona."

The knot in Kenzie's stomach tightened, her heart breaking for Win.

Kenzie turned toward the trailer, pointed. "She's in there. She's been so worried about them. God, I can't believe this. It doesn't seem real."

Winona walked down the ramp, saw Harrison—and stopped.

Kenzie's chest ached. She tucked her hand in Harrison's and followed him to where Winona stood, trepidation in every feature on her face.

"Did you get everyone out?" Win's voice was even, steady, calm.

Harrison shook his head, held Kenzie's hand tighter. "All but one of the kids and most of the counselors escaped. Chaska, your grandfather, Gabe Rossiter, and three counselors stayed behind because there wasn't room in the vehicles. We tried to get to them, but fire had already burned through the camp. We barely made it back ourselves."

The breath left Winona's lungs on a little cry, and her shoulders sagged, her eyes going wide. "So … they're all … *dead*?"

That last word was a whisper.

"We don't know that for sure. Maybe they found a way—"

"Did you say Gabe Rossiter?" Julian was there now, stunned surprise on his face. "He and Kat are good friends of ours."

Harrison repeated some of what he'd told Winona. "He, Chaska Belcourt, Grandpa Belcourt, and some camp counselors chose to stay so that others could escape. One of the kids is missing. The boy apparently hid when they evacuated the others. Hawke has asked a chopper to check for survivors."

A muscle clenched in Julian's jaw, his eyes hidden by sunglasses. "Fuck."

But at the word "survivors," Winona sank to the sidewalk.

Kenzie hurried to her side, knelt next to her, wrapped an arm around her trembling shoulders. "Chaska and Gabe are smart. If anyone can find a way out of this alive, they can."

Winona held tightly to her hand, her eyes squeezed shut.

"What about Kat? Does she know?" Julian asked.

Harrison nodded. "I told her. She's in a bus heading down the canyon with Chaska's wife, Naomi, and the counselors and kids from the camp."

Jack stepped out of the trailer, the lines on his face telling Kenzie he'd overheard. "What a damned awful thing."

A bawling sound brought everyone's heads around

Zach and Marc stood there with the moose calf on a makeshift halter, grim expressions on their faces.

"What happened to Rossiter?" Marc asked, an edge to his voice.

Kenzie hadn't realized all these people knew each other. She listened, still holding Winona's hand as Harrison repeated what he'd told the others.

Marc bent almost double at the waist as if someone had kicked him in the stomach, while Zach turned away from them, his head down.

"Winona's brother, Chaska Belcourt, and her grandfather stayed behind, too."

"What a damned awful thing," Jack said again.

The moose calf let out another cry.

Winona's head came up. With a single breath, she seemed to swallow both fear and grief. "He's scared. Let's get him inside."

She stood and, with tears still on her cheek, led the little moose into the trailer, speaking softly to it in Lakota and working with Jack to secure the little guy in one of the horse stalls. "Let's get the fawns. Then I need to tranq Shota."

———

ERIC LISTENED while Dispatch gave him the sitrep on rescue operations, struggling to hear over the engine of the SEAT as it flew overhead with a belly full of flame retardant.

"The rescue pilot says they're grounded. Engine trouble. He cannot get airborne."

*Damn it!*

If there were survivors at Mato Sapa, they needed urgent medical help. So would Taylor.

*If he's still alive.*

There wasn't time for engine repairs—or for another helicopter to fly in from Denver or Colorado Springs.

Eric clicked his mic. "Have Helicopter Ninety-Eight

Echo meet me on the hospital's helipad. I'll head to Camp Mato Sapa and Haley Preserve myself. I'm transferring Incident Command to Superintendent Tall Bull."

The helicopter wasn't big enough to carry lots of wounded, but he could at least start first aid and evacuate some survivors.

Tall Bull loaded his guys up for the drive to the top of Dead Man's Hill, which he and Eric had decided was the critical holding point. It was the last ridge overlooking Scarlet. Their combined crews would start another back-burn and work with the Skycrane and the two SEATs to stop the main head of the fire there. Tall Bull had called NIFC and the Rocky Mountain Control Center and asked for another Type 1 crew and the Supertanker—a 747 jet that could drop almost 20,000 gallons of flame retardant at a time.

Whether they would get it in time was anyone's guess.

If the blaze got around them this time, there would be nowhere for them to fall back to without surrendering the town.

Eric called for his best paramedic. "Silver!"

Silver stood not far away, refilling his water bottles. "Yeah, chief?"

"Load a couple advanced first-aid kits and a few burn kits into my truck, and let's roll. I've got a helicopter on its way to meet us on the hospital helipad."

Silver set off at a jog.

Eric walked over to Tall Bull, who'd overheard his exchange with Dispatch. "I'll be back on the line as soon as I can."

Tall Bull nodded. "Good luck."

Eric met Silver at the brush truck. "Did you find what we need?"

"Yeah."

Eric motioned to the photographer. "You coming?"

"Hell, yeah." Ramirez followed him and Silver to the truck, camera bag on his shoulder.

Eric didn't know any other way to say this, so he just came out with it. "If we find human remains, I won't let you take photos. These are our friends."

"One of them is my friend, too. If there are human remains, I wouldn't even try to take photos. I'm not an asshole."

Eric liked this guy. He, Ramirez, and Brandon climbed into the truck and started down the mountain toward town. The sheriff had closed the westbound lanes in Boulder Canyon, opening both to eastbound vehicles and resolving the traffic jam.

Ramirez called someone. "I'm fine. Don't worry. It's pretty bad up here. Gabe Rossiter and seven other people were entrapped at a camp. The fire burned through. I'm on a helicopter that's going to search for survivors. Yeah, I hope so, too. I love you, too."

He ended the call. "My wife Mia. She's nine months pregnant with our first."

Despite the heaviness in his chest, Eric found himself smiling. "Congratulations, man. That's great. You're going to love being a dad. My wife, Vicki, is expecting our second."

"No way!" Silver toasted them with his water bottle. "Congrats to both of you."

The helo was landing as they pulled into the hospital parking lot.

"Do you really think there's a chance they're alive?" Silver asked.

Eric didn't know how to answer that. "If they are, they need us."

They grabbed their gear out of the truck and ran to

the helipad, ducking down as they boarded. Eric sat in front where he could have the best view, Silver and Ramirez in back with their gear. He buckled in, put on his earphones, gave the pilot the GPS for Camp Mato Sapa. They would go there first.

"You know I can't carry more than six people at a time," the pilot said.

"We'll be very lucky if we end up facing that problem."

The pilot lifted off, nosed its way forward, gained altitude.

Eric typed out a quick text message to Vicki telling her he was on his way to look for survivors at Camp Mato Sapa and to find Taylor.

*That son of a bitch better be alive.*

Eric wouldn't be able to live with himself otherwise. He'd been the one who'd asked Taylor to head out to Haley Preserve.

"Holy fuck." Silver's voice came over the earphones.

Eric's stomach knotted at the sight. "Is that your professional opinion?"

"Pretty much."

The fire looked impossible to stop, a wall of smoke and flame stretching from the backside of Ski Scarlet, across the canyons, down the backside of the ridge they'd tried to hold, and off to the northwest to the highway. Soon, it would make a run through mountain homes to the top of Dead Man's Hill, where Tall Bull and his crew were already setting a backburn.

Silver nudged his arm, handed him a bottle of water. "I haven't seen you drink anything in a while."

"Right." Eric was always nagging his crew to stay hydrated. He needed to follow his own good advice. "Thanks."

He took a drink, capped the bottle, did his best not to

think beyond this moment, this rescue mission. If he let himself get caught up in grief, he'd be no good to anyone, and saving Scarlet Springs was still *his* responsibility, no matter who was Incident Command.

Wind blew the smoke plume eastward, compromising visibility, so the pilot radioed for permission to climb. Eric glanced at the radar, saw three blips that represented the two SEATs and the Skycrane, all of them on the way back to refill their tanks, the Skycrane at the reservoir just east of town and the SEATs at the airport.

"This is where it gets bumpy," the pilot said.

A big wildfire like this one made flying hazardous. Convective currents of hot air rose up from the blaze, causing turbulence. In Eric's experience, fixed-wing aircraft had a harder time managing it than helos, but he grabbed the handle near the door anyway.

*Thunk!*

Something hit the window next to Eric's head. At first, he thought it was a bird, but it flew into pieces.

The pilot cursed. "A fucking drone!"

Another thud. A mechanical whine.

The helo began to spin out of control, heading straight toward the flaming front.

*Holy hell.*

If they crashed in the fire, they would be dead in an instant.

"Fuck!" he heard Silver say.

"*Madre de Dios.*" That was Ramirez.

"We've lost our rear rotor. Fragments from the drone must have damaged it. We're going down!" He called it in. "Mayday. Mayday. Mayday. Helicopter Ninety-Eight Echo is going down. A drone hit the aircraft, and we've lost our tail rotor."

"Can you crash us away from the fire?" Not that Eric

wanted to tell the pilot how to do his job, but that seemed really important.

"I don't know, but I'm sure as hell going to try."

It was hard to tell which direction was which, the world spinning around them, the ground racing up at them as the helo lost altitude.

*I'm pregnant.*

Vicki's sweet face flashed through Eric's mind—her happy smile as she'd surprised him with the news, the sparkle in her eyes. He couldn't leave her.

Not now. Not like this.

The pilot fought with the machine. "Brace for impact!"

# Chapter 14

JESSE HOOKED the water hose to the last of the fan guns on Eagle Ridge, the highest point at Ski Scarlet. He walked back to the hydrant, cranked the handle, watched water surge through the hose. Then he walked back to the fan gun—and turned it on.

Water sprayed from the mouth of the machine, flying maybe thirty feet before falling to land on grass, shrubs, and trees.

It was the damnedest thing he'd ever seen—every fan gun the resort owned spraying water onto the upper reaches of the mountain in the middle of summer. In the winter, at the right temperatures, the fan guns made snow, enabling the resort to stay open when Mother Nature got stingy with the white stuff.

Today, it was all about rain—and a chance to stop the south head of the fire from burning through the slopes to threaten lives and mountain homes south of Scarlet.

The fire was almost here now, racing up the back of Eagle Ridge, embers carried high above him by the wind.

A crew of mostly volunteer firefighters stood by with UTVs, tools, and brush trucks to beat the shit out of any spot fires. But none of that stood a chance of working if the fan guns couldn't deliver enough water.

Two thousand gallons a minute.

That's how much water poured through the pipes when all of the fan guns were on full. The water was pumped at high pressure from the reservoir in the winter and returned to the reservoir as snowmelt in the spring. It was more moisture than any air tanker or helicopter could lay down.

Would it be enough?

Jesse had watched while the fire outflanked the back-burn. He'd watched it jump the narrow canyon and finger off, spreading through the forest on the flanks of the mountain. It had been his idea to try the snowmaking machines, and Matt and Hawke had given him the thumbs up. But it was no easy task to hook up the system—or to haul all twelve one-ton fan guns up dry slopes and into position.

Had they been fast enough? Would the trees and grass be wet enough?

If this failed, the fire would destroy the fan guns, setting the resort back millions. Worse, it would burn through the glades and advance on Scarlet from the south. There was little chance it would burn down the resort buildings, not with the pumper truck there to spray them down. But there were a lot of homes south of town.

At least Ellie and the kids were safe. She had texted to tell him she'd finally made it to her sister's house in Boulder.

He reached for his hand mic. "Forty-two to Dispatch. The last gun is running."

"I want everyone away from that ridge," Matt, his boss, replied.

He would get no argument from Jesse. The gases from the fire as it reached the top would be hot enough to kill in an instant.

"Copy that." Jesse motioned for his fellow patrollers to move away.

That's when he saw it—a helo spinning out of control.

It looked like it was heading into the fire.

"Son of a bitch." He wished he had his Team radio because he would know what the hell was going on and who was in that aircraft. Instead, he heard only radio traffic from the ski resort.

He called his boss. "Forty-two to Dispatch. I just saw a helicopter go down. It looked like it had lost its tail rotor. I think it crashed into the fire."

"A drone hit an observation helicopter. I heard the mayday. I think your buddy Eric Hawke was onboard."

The news hit Jesse like a blast wave, drove the air from his lungs.

*God, no!*

Hawke had been a mentor to him when he'd tried out for the Team. He'd helped him improve as a climber. He'd helped him land his ski patrol job.

He was one of the best men Jesse knew.

Matt's voice sounded in Jesse's earpiece again. "I'm sorry."

Jesse jogged to the top of the ridge again, looked toward the north, but smoke obscured his view. "Someone needs to get the hell out there with a rescue helo—now!"

"How long would it take a chopper to get airborne and reach them? If they landed in the fire, they're dead already."

Helplessness turned Jesse's dread and fear to rage. "For fuck's sake, we can't just stand here and do nothing while they burn alive!"

"If you've got a plan, tell me, and I'll call it in to Scarlet Command. If not, focus on keeping yourself and your fellow patrollers safe. Now, get the hell off that ridge!"

The fire was here.

The roar like a dozen fighter jets. Fist-sized embers. Black, choking smoke.

Son of a bitch!

*Hawke!*

Jesse ran down the slope, his fellow patrollers urging him on. He threw himself to the ground and glanced back as a hundred-foot wave of flame crested over the ridgetop, turning the world around him orange. Water from the fan guns became steam, and for a moment it seemed his plan wasn't going to work.

Then the length of the flames shrank. Fifty feet. Twenty. Ten.

The fire sputtered, hissed, went out.

Cheers.

"We've got a couple of spot fires in the glades," said a voice in Jesse's earpiece.

Crews scrambled to put those out, cutting down burning trees with chain saws, beating out the flames. But Jesse ran to his UTV and headed down the slope. He ditched the vehicle outside the ski patrol office and ran inside, where Matt sat listening to county's tactical frequency.

"… and we are deploying shelters!" Hawke shouted into his radio, his voice almost drowned out by the roar of the fire.

*Jesus!*

They had survived the crash, but they were entrapped.

*Son of a bitch.*

Sometimes the shelters saved lives, but they didn't guarantee survival by any means. Jesse had heard stories—some from survivors, some from people who'd had the terrible job of bagging and tagging the bodies of firefighters who'd died in their shelters of burns or asphyxiation from hot gases and smoke.

Now, every story came back to him as he waited, moments measured in heartbeats, seconds grinding by with unbearable slowness.

BRANDON DUG at the ground with the Pulaski, scraping away dried pine needles, twigs, and grass to expose the cool, mineral soil beneath. Hawke had given Ramirez a spare brush shirt and brush pants from his pack and was telling the pilot and Ramirez what they could expect.

"You're going to think you're burning alive, and you might get burned, but it's going to be a thousand times hotter outside the shelter than inside. Do not come out, no matter how afraid you are, no matter how hot or painful it gets. Do you understand?"

How could Hawke be so damned calm?

Brandon had trained for this, too. He'd done deployment drills over and over again. He'd watched videos, listened to survivor stories. But he didn't feel calm. He'd sworn to himself that he would never be careless enough to become entrapped. He hadn't imaged a helicopter would crash-land him in the path of a fire.

*Libby.*

Would he see her again? Would he die here in his shelter?

*Don't think. Dig.*

They'd run from the helicopter, searching for a good

place to deploy, somewhere with minimal fuels where burning trees wouldn't fall on them. The fire was moving much faster than they were, so they'd had just minutes to find a spot.

Hawke had chosen this place—a clearing that looked like it might have once been home to a miner's cabin. The cabin was long gone, but there was a sunken area in the shape of a rectangle toward the center of the clearing. It was as treeless as anything they could hope to find in the middle of a damned forest.

Hawke was doing his best to help the others. "You can do this. I'll be right here with you. We're going to check your shelters and make sure they weren't damaged in the crash."

The fire was close now, the heat already uncomfortable, the roar deafening, embers burning through Brandon's brush shirt and igniting spot fires all around them.

"That's good enough!" Hawke shouted to Brandon. "Toss your gear! Deploy shelters!"

*Shit. Fuck!*

This was it.

No drill this time. This was the real thing.

Brandon tossed the Pulaski, pulled his fire shelter from his pack, then doffed his pack and hurled it as far away from their deployment site as he could. It held flammable fusees and other things that might ignite.

"I'm taking my camera with me!" Ramirez shouted.

"Fine, but don't hold onto it! Hold onto the shelter!" Hawke shouted back. "The wind could tear it right off you! If you lose your shelter, you die!"

It was a good thing that Brandon had practiced this so many times, because adrenaline was kicking the shit out of his manual dexterity. He fumbled with the red tear ring on the outer bag, pulled on it, and removed the fragile shelter. Tab labeled *Left Hand* in his left hand. Tab labeled *Right Hand* in his right hand.

Clearly, they had tried to make the process both idiot- and adrenaline-proof.

He shook the shelter out, the wind catching it, hoisting it into the air like a sail. He wrestled with it, held onto it with clenched fists.

If he lost it, he would burn alive.

He managed to get one foot inside, then the other, catching sight of Hawke as he helped Ramirez and the pilot get inside their shelters. "Hawke, for fuck's sake, deploy!"

The fire was almost on top of them.

But Hawke didn't seem to hear him. He showed Ramirez and the pilot how to hold on, how to breathe cool air close to the ground. "Don't panic!"

"Damn it, Hawke! Deploy!"

Hawke heard Brandon that time.

He checked the others, pulled out his shelter, shook it out.

The heat was intense now, the fire rushing toward them like some vision of hell. Brandon dropped to the ground, feet toward the blaze, then slid gloved hands through the straps and pulled the shelter down around him.

A shiver ran through him.

It was like crawling into his own grave.

"Silver, are you good?" Hawke called to him.

"Yeah, chief!"

Hawke shouted encouragement to them. "Stay with me, all of you! We'll get through this! Burns heal! Fried lungs don't! Don't come out, no matter what!"

Something bumped against Brandon's shelter, and a

cottontail rabbit dug its way inside, hiding beneath his chin. The little thing was shaking like a leaf.

"Hey, buddy."

They would ride this out together.

Beyond his shelter, trees cracked, shrieked, moaned, the roar of the fire like the approach of a thousand freight trains. Wind from the blaze threatened to rip the shelter off his body. Radiant heat drove up the temperature inside the shelter, making it hotter and hotter until he was sure he couldn't take more. He lowered his face to the dirt where the air was a bit cooler and squeezed his eyes shut to protect them.

*Libby.*

He wrapped his mind around her, clung to the thought of her.

Libby bringing him her latest brew to taste. Libby making dinner at his house wearing nothing but tube socks. Libby curling up against him while they watched TV, her golden hair spilling across his chest, her skin like silk.

God, he loved her, loved everything about her. If she wasn't ready to commit, he could live with that—as long as he didn't have to pretend not to love her.

*Fuck!*

He cried out, something searing the back of his calves, the pain excruciating. The superheated shelter fabric—it had settled against him. He gritted his teeth and used an elbow to push it upward again—only to get burned on his elbow, too.

Someone cried out in pain.

Was it him? No.

Hawke? Ramirez? The pilot?

*Goddamn!*

For all he knew, the others were dying. All it took was a

gust of wind, a break in the fabric, a little exposure to direct flame…

It was hot, too hot, too damned hot. The air singed his nostrils and every bit of exposed skin, pain from his burns and adrenaline making him dizzy. Or maybe that was lack of oxygen.

He fought back a growing sense of panic.

"Stay with me!"

Had he imagined Hawke's voice?

Maybe. Maybe not.

*BLAM!*

The helo. Its fuel tank must have exploded.

He drew another breath, choked, smoke making his throat constrict until he started to drift away. He fought the darkness, fought to breathe, reaching for Libby with his mind.

*At least you told her you loved her.*

———

MARC STOOD with Darcangelo and McBride, watching as Jack eased his trailer onto the highway and headed down the canyon, Kenzie and Harrison Conrad following in two separate vehicles, one of which carried Winona and her wolf. Marc's relief at knowing that both people and animals would be safe didn't take away the ache in his chest.

If Gabe Rossiter was dead…

*Fuck.*

"Where did Jack say Kat was going?" he asked.

"On her way down the canyon toward the Boulder County Fairgrounds," McBride answered.

Darcangelo pulled out his cell phone. "We should let the others know."

"You're right." McBride gave Darcangelo a friendly slap on the back.

Darcangelo gasped, winced.

McBride stared at him. "I didn't hit you that hard."

"Burns from embers. I took off my shirt and wrapped Crank in it when I carried him outside." Darcangelo lifted the back of his shirt, exposing red, blistered burns the size of quarters scattered across his back and shoulders.

"Why didn't you say something?" McBride asked.

"He's stubborn," Marc offered.

"It's not that serious."

McBride wasn't convinced. "You should get checked out by medical."

"And what will they do? They'll tell me I have second-degree burns and do nothing. You two just keep your manly affection to yourselves."

"You're a pain in the ass, you know that?" Marc drew out his cell phone, typed a quick text message to Sophie.

Gabe and six others missing after fire burned through camp where he was staying. Kat knows. She evacuated to the BoCo Fairgrounds with the kids. Thought you'd want to know. We're safe. See you soon. Love you.

Sophie replied almost immediately.

OMG! How awful. Please stay safe!!!! I love you, too!

Deputy Marcs pulled up beside them in her vehicle.

"Thank God you're still here." For the first time all day, she looked shaken, her voice trembling. "Some fucking idiot was flying a drone over the fire. It hit the helicopter that Hawke was in and took out the tail rotor. The chopper crashed right in front of the fire. Four men were aboard—Hawke, Silver, a photojournalist, and the pilot. Help me find the son of a bitch responsible for that drone."

Marc stomach sank. "Photojournalist?"

Ramirez had been hanging with Hawke. It had to be him.

*Please don't let it be him!*

Deputy Marcs nodded. "I think they said he was from the Denver Independent."

"Fucking hell." Marc wanted to hit something.

*Not Joaquin, too.*

"*Mierda*." Darcangelo closed his eyes.

"Any idea who the little puke is or where we can look for him?" McBride asked.

"Witnesses said they saw two college-aged guys in the Food Mart parking lot holding what looked like a drone controller. They were wearing T-shirts and hiking shorts."

Marc didn't know what they could do with that kind of description. "That describes every young person in Colorado today."

"Sorry. That's all I've got. I'm setting up a roadblock to check the cars that leave town. If you could help..."

McBride nodded. "You got it."

Marc and Darcangelo got into Marc's vehicle, while McBride drove his. They started in the Food Mart parking lot.

"Where would I run if I were an idiot kid who knew I'd just fucked up bigtime?" McBride asked.

Julian pointed with a jerk of his head. "I'd run for the cover of that creek, and I'd ditch that controller as fast as I could."

They came up with a plan on the spot. McBride would drive around to the other side and follow the south bank of the creek to the reservoir, while Marc and Darcangelo walked along the north bank. If they found the little bastards, they would detain them and call Deputy Marcs.

Neither Marc nor Darcangelo spoke as they moved along, Marc sick at the thought of what might have happened to Joaquin. No, they didn't have proof he was gone, but if he was…

What a fucking awful way to die.

And with Mia about to have a baby…

Marc's chest constricted. He drew a breath, willed himself to focus on the search.

Sandbar willow grew along the bank, rising to almost six feet, creating natural cover for someone trying to hide. Trash littered the mud—used condoms, soda bottles, plastic vials from marijuana dispensaries.

Darcangelo pointed.

Two sets of fresh footprints.

They were heading east, toward the reservoir.

Marc fired off a text message to McBride and kept going.

A deer darted out from a thicket of willows, startled by their approach.

Marc's phone buzzed. He pulled it out of his pocket. "McBride says they're down at the reservoir. He says they just threw something into the water."

His phone buzzed again. "They saw McBride and rabbited. They're headed our way."

"That's convenient." Julian stepped into cover.

Marc did the same, the two of them crouching down in the willow.

Heavy footfalls. Splashing. Heavy breathing.

"Move! Hurry!" a young man whisper-shouted. "He knows it's us!"

"This is your fault!" another whispered back.

"You wanted to fly it, too!"

"*You* crashed it into the helicopter! You probably killed people!"

*Three. Two. One.*

Marc and Darcangelo moved as one, stepping in front of the kids. "Stop! Police!"

They froze, wide-eyed terror on their young faces.

Then one turned to run, only to find McBride walking up behind him.

"Going somewhere?"

Another started to bolt.

Marc stepped in front of him, touched a hand to the butt of his pistol. "*Don't* make me draw my weapon."

They handcuffed the kids and marched them to McBride's SUV, listening to their excuses and bickering the entire way.

"It was his drone. I was just there. I didn't actually fly it."

"He's lying. He flew it for a few minutes. He wanted me to fly it. You wanted to see the fire as much as I did."

"I didn't crash it into the helicopter. That was *you*."

The kids probably didn't realize they were confessing, and Marc didn't point that out to them. All of this would go into his report of the incident.

"You got cuffs?" Marc asked McBride.

"Always."

By the time McBride had them cuffed, Deputy Marcs had arrived, overheads flashing. She arrested them and put them in the backseat of her vehicle. "I'm taking you to the county sheriff's office for processing. You two might have caused the deaths of four good men, men with wives and kids and families. I hope you understand how serious this is."

One of the young men started to cry.

Marc started back toward the reservoir.

"Hey, Hunter, where are you going?" Darcangelo called after him.

"To find whatever they threw in the water."

He'd bet his ass it was the controller. If it was, it would clinch the case against them and give Mia and Joaquin and Hawke and all of them a little justice.

## Chapter 15

VICKI DROVE Lexi's car through nearly empty streets to The Cave, Libby following in her vehicle, Bob and Kendra still at the inn, shoving whatever they could into their Ford Bronco. It had felt strange to leave her own car behind, but then it was just a car.

Lexi needed her right now.

Lexi had insisted they stop at Team headquarters before leaving Scarlet so she could grab the hard drive that held all of the Team's old financial records. Lexi was a supporting Team member and had taken over as the organization's accountant after the previous one had been caught embezzling. How she could think of the Team when she was sick with worry over Austin, Vicki didn't know.

If Eric had been missing or presumed dead, Vicki would have been a wreck.

Eric had texted her not long ago to tell her he was going up in a chopper to rescue survivors at Mato Sapa and find Austin, but so far Vicki hadn't heard back from him. It didn't take long to travel by helicopter, so Vicki could only assume the news wasn't good. Otherwise, he'd have let her know right away.

Vicki pulled into the parking lot.

Lexi unbuckled her seatbelt. "It will only take a minute or two."

"I'll stay with Emily and Mack." Vicki kept the engine —and the AC—running.

Emily was asleep in her car seat, her pink blankie tucked beneath her chin, her red hair in tiny pigtails, blissfully unaware that the daddy she loved was missing and maybe or…

No, Austin couldn't be dead. The thought was just too terrible.

Lexi hurried inside, glancing over her shoulder toward the fire.

Vicki could see the wall of smoke in her rearview mirror—dark, ominous, menacing.

She'd sent a quick text message to let Eric know she was on her way down the canyon. With a raging fire threatening Scarlet, Austin missing, and people lying injured and maybe dead at Camp Mato Sapa, he needed to be able to focus on his job, not waste time worrying about her.

Libby rolled down her window, shouted to Vicki. "He called! Brandon called using someone else's phone. I guess he left his at the firehouse."

It was the first smile Vicki had seen on her face all day. "That's great!"

Poor Libby! She'd had a fight with Brandon, and then her house had burned down. If that didn't qualify as a shitty day, what did?

Lexi stepped out of The Cave with Megs, the stunned expressions on their faces and the way they looked at her making Vicki's pulse skip.

Something had happened.

She rolled down her window. "What is it?"

Megs motioned to her. "Come inside. You, too, Libby."

Vicki turned off the engine and followed Megs, leaving Lexi to get Emily and Mack. "What's going on? Tell me."

No one said anything.

Libby followed. "Did something happen to Brandon?"

They walked through the front door into the Ops Room, where Ahearn sat in front of the radio with a handful of other Team members—Nicole Turner, Bahir Acharya, Sasha Dillon, and Creed Herrera.

Vicki's mouth went dry, dread churning in her stomach. She looked from Megs to Ahearn. "Please just tell me —is my husband alive?"

Ahearn stood. "The helicopter he and Brandon Silver were flying in crashed in front of the flaming front. They survived the crash, but they had to deploy shelters. Dispatch has tried to raise them, but they're not answering."

Libby cried out, sank to the floor beside Vicki, covering her face with her hands.

But Vicki couldn't move, couldn't think, couldn't breathe, her heart thudding painfully, her pulse rushing in her ears.

A burst of static from the radio.

"Helicopter Ninety-Eight Echo, do you copy? Nineteen-oh-one, do you copy?"

*Nineteen-oh-one.*

That was Eric's fire department call number.

*Answer, Eric. Please answer! Say something!*

Silence.

This couldn't be happening. It couldn't be.

"No response from Helicopter Ninety-Eight Echo or its passengers."

Vicki took a step forward. "They can't give up. Why are they giving up? Why don't they keep calling?"

Megs knelt beside Libby, wrapped her arms around her. "They've been trying for the past five minutes."

Vicki's mind raced for explanations. "Maybe the fire hasn't burned through yet, or maybe their radios were damaged by the heat or…"

*Or maybe they're all dead.*

The world around Vicki blurred, pain seeming to shatter her breastbone. She sagged against the conference table, her throat going tight. "He can't be … *gone*. I'm pregnant. I just told him… I surprised him at breakfast."

Lexi came up beside her, smiling through tears. "A new baby. That's wonderful."

She wrapped her arms around Vicki and held her.

"To hell with this!" Creed surged to his feet. "I'm going after them. Who's with me?"

"You're not going anywhere." Megs stood. "Taylor, Belcourt, Rossiter, Hawke, and seven other people are missing! I don't want you to be next."

"I can't *sit* here and do nothing!"

"Sure, you can!" Megs' voice broke. "Do you think I'd be here right now if there were any chance at all that we could reach them?"

"Fuck!" Creed let out a frustrated shout, threw open the door to the vehicle bays, and stomped out.

Just then, Bob stepped through the front door.

"What's holding you up, Lexi? We're ready to…" He glanced around. "Hell. Did you get bad news about my son-in-law?"

Lexi stepped back, but held onto Vicki's hand. "Eric and Brandon Silver and two other men were in a helicopter that crashed right in front of the fire. They survived the crash and deployed fire shelters, but no one has been able to reach them since."

"Ah, shit."

At Lexi's words, Vicki's stomach revolted. She put a hand to her belly, drew a few breaths. "I think I'm going to be sick."

"Through there." Lexi pointed to the bathroom, following her inside, and closing the door behind them. "Morning sickness?"

"I don't know. I don't think so."

Lexi stayed while Vicki threw up, handing her a wet paper towel when it was over. "I can't believe this. It's worse than my worst nightmare."

But Vicki had lived with the fear of Eric being hurt or killed in a fire since she'd watched him put out that blaze at Hank's place.

"I need to call Eric's mother."

———

AUSTIN OPENED HIS EYES, found himself staring up at a familiar face, hair from a long beard tickling his fore-head. "Bear?"

"Austin Taylor." Bear looked down at him, concern in his eyes.

Austin tried to remember. He'd left the lake, hiked back to his truck, and started for Scarlet. "What am I doing on the ground?"

"Sleeping."

*Hypothermia.*

Shit.

"I came to warn you about the fire, to get you out."

"You came … for me?"

The surprise in Bear's voice put an ache in Austin's chest. "I needed to make sure you were safe."

"Mama said when fires come, run to the mine."

So, Bear had been safe in an old mine all this time.

Didn't it just figure?

Austin fought to sit up, got an assist from Bear, and saw that he'd collapsed only a hundred or so yards from his truck. Not good. "I'm sorry about your cabin."

"The things of this world will pass away."

"I took these to keep them safe." Austin reached into his backpack, which Bear had apparently removed from his shoulders, and drew out the diary and the photograph.

Bear stared. "You took Mama's book and picture."

"I'm sorry. I just wanted to save them."

Bear crushed him in a big hug, gave a little sob.

"It's okay, buddy. It's okay." But then Austin couldn't resist. "Do you know which of these little boys in the photograph is you?"

Bear pointed to the oldest child.

The journal entry had been written in 1959. The two younger children hadn't been born yet, and the middle daughter had been a nursing baby. Bear must have been six when the entry had been written. He looked like he was around ten years old in the photo. That meant he must be almost sixty-five years old now.

*Holy shit.*

Austin tried to remember what he'd read. "Your name is Matthew, right?"

Bear stared open-mouthed at him, tears in his eyes.

"No one has called you that in a long time, have they, buddy?"

Bear pointed at the image. "Mama. Papa. Luke. Paul. Mary. John. Elizabeth."

"That's your family—your parents, your brothers and sisters."

Bear nodded. "They're waiting for me in heaven."

What an awful thing it must have been for Bear to lose them all.

"Can I put these in my pack to keep them safe while we walk to town? You can have them back any time you want."

Bear nodded again, yielding the precious items to Austin's care.

Austin did his best to explain the situation—how he'd run from the fire, how he'd taken refuge in the lake, how the cold water had left him dangerously hypothermic. "I need to get to the hospital."

Bear stood. "Old Bear will take you to Winona."

Bear sometimes took sick and injured wildlife to Winona.

Austin chuckled. "Okay. Thanks."

In the next instant, he found himself hauled to his feet, Bear half-carrying him down the dirt road. The man was a lot stronger than Austin realized. Then again, he'd lived his entire life in the wilderness, fending for himself, and was taller than Austin, who was six-three, by a good four inches.

"Have you seen any helicopters?"

"No."

*Damn.*

They plodded down the road, passing through a smoky wasteland, charred snags and smoldering logs all that remained of a once-thriving forest, green replaced by black and gray. Austin stumbled more than once. He'd have fallen to the ground again if Bear hadn't been there to hold him up. Neither of them said much, Austin because he was struggling to remain conscious and Bear because, well, he was Bear.

Austin was exhausted. Just being awake was painful. "Don't let me fall asleep, Bear. If I do, I might never wake up."

Bear started singing, old hymns, whether to pass the time or to keep him awake, Austin couldn't say. Austin didn't know the lyrics, but delivered in Bear's rich baritone, the words were comforting.

Austin found himself wanting to ask Bear what had killed the rest of his family, how old he'd been when he'd been left alone, and how he had managed to survive. But he didn't want to hurt Bear with careless questions. Besides, he could scarcely think.

What he wouldn't give to see a rescue chopper head their way. A heated blanket, some warm IV fluids, some warm oxygen, and he'd be good. But there was no chopper, not even the beating of the rotors in the distance.

Why wouldn't they send someone? Hawke knew where he'd gone. He'd surely send someone to make sure Austin was okay. Unless…

Maybe the situation was too dire and they couldn't, or maybe …

*Maybe they truly believe you're dead.*

Well, hell.

*If only you'd thought to take your phone out of your pocket before jumping in the water...*

Right. Next time he was entrapped in a wildfire and took shelter in a freaking lake, he'd remember that.

On and on they walked. They couldn't be far from Camp Mato Sapa. Then again, the landscape looked so different without the forest that Austin couldn't be sure precisely where they were. He fought to stay on his feet, fought to keep going. Lexi was probably worried sick. He needed to get back to her, needed to let her know he was okay.

*I'm still here, Lexi. I'm still here.*

Then he heard it.

*Thwop-thwop-thwop-thwop*

The sound brought his gaze skyward. It sounded like…

"It's about time." Austin waved to the chopper, but it wasn't as if the pilot could miss seeing them—the only two moving, breathing beings in sight.

Bear stopped in his tracks, went rigid.

Austin sank to the dirt, his strength long gone. "It's okay, Bear. Don't be afraid. There are men inside. They're here to help me and take us to Scarlet. Do you want to fly with me?"

Bear stood beside him, watching the helicopter.

The bird set down fifty yards away, rotor wash sending up a cloud of dust and ash. Two people jumped out and ran toward them carrying first aid kits.

One of them called out to him. "Austin Taylor?"

Austin raised a hand. "That's me. This is Bear."

"Hey, Bear. I'm glad we found you, Mr. Taylor." The paramedic knelt. "You've had a lot of people worried."

"Sorry about that. I sheltered in a lake when the place burned over and became hypothermic. My truck was destroyed. Bear has been helping me. He doesn't talk much, and I think the chopper scares him."

"We're going to take good care of Austin, Bear." The paramedic reached for his hand mic. "Dispatch, Rescue Ten. We've located Austin Taylor and someone named Bear. Both are alive. Taylor is hypothermic but otherwise appears to be uninjured."

"Thank God for at least one happy ending," said the other paramedic.

That caught Austin's attention. "Has something happened?"

"A helicopter carrying the fire chief, another firefighter, and a journalist was hit by a drone and crashed into the fire. No one has heard from them since. Another chopper is on the way to check that out. Some other folks were trapped at a kids' camp in the box canyon when the fire came through. We were just there, looking for survivors, but saw no one—no survivors, no bodies, nada. You're the first living people we've seen."

*Oh, fuck. No. No. No.*

———

THE OPS ROOM exploded into cheers.

Lexi stared in shock and amazement toward the radio, her body boneless with relief, her eyes blurring with happy tears.

Austin was alive. He was alive and safe—and Bear, too.

*Oh, thank God! Thank you, God!*

"Where are they taking him?" Lexi had to see him.

"Boulder Valley Hospital," Ahearn answered.

Vicki hugged her tight. "I'm so happy for you, Lex. That's the best news."

Creed punched the air with his fist, laughing. "Leave it to Taylor. Who the fuck becomes hypothermic in a wildfire?"

"Oh, I think I know this one—a guy who jumps into a lake to avoid burning to death, maybe?" Megs rolled her eyes.

Lexi wanted to jump for joy, but she couldn't. The rescue helicopter hadn't found bodies at Camp Mato Sapa, but it hadn't found survivors either. Chaska, Grandpa

Belcourt, Gabe, those poor camp counselors, and that little boy were still missing.

And no one had heard from Eric or Brandon or the photojournalist, either.

Vicki, Naomi, Winona—they were still trapped in the hell of not knowing. How could she celebrate when so many people were still missing … or dead?

The door opened and a deputy Lexi didn't know stepped inside. "I'm here on behalf of Sheriff Pella to make sure everyone who isn't on duty as a Team member evacuates to safety now. That fire is burning up the back of Dead Man's Hill. It's going to be in town before you know it. I don't see how they're going to stop it now."

His words sucked the light out of the room like someone blowing out a candle.

Lexi's father stood, Kendra beside him. "That's it. Come on, Lexi-girl. You, too, Vicki and Libby. Time to go."

Libby got to her feet, shook her head. "I'm staying. Brandon is out there, and I want to be where I can get the news."

Vicki wiped the tears from her cheeks and handed the keys to Lexi. "I'm staying, too."

The deputy stood a little taller. "I'm afraid I can't let you—"

Megs cut him off. "I'm in charge here, and I'll handle it. Thanks."

Muttering something to himself, the deputy turned and left the building.

"Promise me you'll let me know as soon as you hear anything," Lexi said. "Waiting like this … not knowing … I know how hard it is."

Vicki hugged her. "Thanks. Now, go be with Austin."

CHASKA STOOD WITH ROSSITER, hoping the helicopter would come back. The two of them had waved and shouted, but the pilot hadn't seen them. It would have helped if they'd thought to bring the rope into the cave with them. They'd have been down on the ground by now. As it was, they'd forgotten about the rope, and fire had torched it.

"Why didn't they see us?" Dean asked.

Chaska turned to him, tousled his hair. "They were looking at the ground. They didn't think to look for us up here."

Rossiter looked down at the wall of rock below them. "I should have downclimbed."

Chaska shook his head. "Not worth the risk, man."

Chaska knew that Rossiter was thinking of Kat and what she must be going through, believing him injured or dead. Chaska knew Naomi must be suffering, too. But it was one thing to risk a crazy-ass free solo when your other option was burning to death. It was another thing altogether when the only consequence of *not* climbing was hanging out in a cave for a while.

Rossiter looked over at Chaska. "They'll send a rescue party to do a ground search."

Both men knew it, but they didn't say it. Next time, rescuers would come prepared to search for bodies amid the debris.

Old Man picked up the drum again from its place on the singed remains of the blanket. "Our ancestors sometimes took shelter in caves in the Black Hills. When they had to wait, they would pass the time by sharing stories."

Chaska pretended to be annoyed for Dean's sake, rolling his eyes. "Here we go."

Dean laughed.

But in truth Chaska never tired of Old Man's stories or the sound of his voice or the beat of the drum. He knew he didn't have much time left with his grandfather. Sooner rather than later, Old Man would be making the journey, and the stories would be Chaska's to tell.

But for today, they were still alive, still together. Today was a good day.

Chaska sat down beside Dean to listen.

## Chapter 16

NAOMI SWALLOWED her fear and dread, willed herself to seem calm. "Here we are, kids. Remember to hold hands with your travel buddy. No one is to go wandering anywhere by themselves or leave the group with any other adult."

She waited till the bus came to a stop, then walked down the center aisle. She'd spent most of the drive talking to counselors, trying to calm them down and focus them on the job at hand. They had thirty-nine confused and frightened children who needed them. They had no time for their own personal fear or pain.

That's what she'd told them. But inside, some part of her wanted to cry, to curse, to scream. The man she loved was missing, maybe dead. He'd sent her away to save her and the baby. He'd been willing to sacrifice his life for theirs, and now she didn't know if she would see him again.

*Chaska.*

"Let me just find out where they want us to go." She

stepped out of the bus, her big belly making her motions awkward, and glanced around at what seemed like chaos.

Soldiers from the Colorado National Guard directed traffic as cars, trucks, and horse trailers from Scarlet Springs poured into the fairgrounds. In the shade of a pavilion, two of the guys from Timberline Mudbugs played guitar while a few people danced.

A young woman in uniform spoke with a man hauling a small horse trailer. "Horse trailers that way."

Naomi approached her. "I'm from Camp Mato Sapa. I've got forty children and a dozen or so adults who have nowhere to stay for the next few days. They're thirsty and hungry, and I have nothing to give them."

"Can their parents pick them up?" the soldier asked.

"No, they can't. They're all from South Dakota. The fire burned through the camp. We left everything—clothes, food, first aid supplies. We almost didn't make it." She couldn't keep the quaver out of her voice, tears threatening to break through. "I have nowhere to take them between now and when they head home in four days."

The soldier called someone on her radio, explained their situation. "The captain says to send you to the Exhibit Building. That's the squarish building just over there. That's where we're putting people who've lost their homes. You let the kids off and then park the bus over here."

"Thanks." Naomi got back on the bus and told the driver where to go.

It was a short drive, but it gave Naomi's fear for Chaska and the others time to rush back, despair rising like bile in the back of her throat. She drew in a few deep breaths, fought back her emotions.

These kids needed her. There would be time to fall apart later.

The bus pulled to a stop in front of the Exhibit Building, its front and back doors opening with a hiss.

"Hold hands, kids, and follow your counselors." Naomi thanked the bus driver, then gathered the children and counselors together and walked inside.

The Exhibit Building was essentially a big box with a high ceiling and—*thank God!*—air conditioning. Uniformed Guard soldiers were busy carrying in cases of bottled water and other supplies, folded cots sitting in neat rows.

A man in olive drab walked up to her. "You're the woman from the kids' camp."

"Yes." Naomi held out a hand. "Naomi Belcourt."

"Captain Peter Langeland." He gestured around the room. "I thought you might be able to set up here. You'd have your own space, with a kitchen, bathrooms, a shower, and better security. If I had forty kids in a situation like this, I'd want a door I could lock."

Naomi hadn't even thought about that. "Thanks. This is perfect."

"We'll have cots or sleeping bags for them by tonight. In the meantime, there's bottled water out in the main room. Do any of you need medical attention?"

"No. Thank you." Naomi had to ask. "Do you know what's going on up there? My husband, his grandfather, and several others stayed behind at the camp so that we could escape. There wasn't room in the vehicles. The fire burned through, and I don't know if they found a way out or whether..."

Captain Langeland's eyes filled with sympathy. "I'm sorry, ma'am. I don't have any contact with the Incident Command in Scarlet Springs."

Naomi's gaze fell to the concrete floor, her heart with it. "I understand."

A hand came to rest on her arm. "If you'd like, I can

pass this up the chain of command and see whether our Incident Command here can get in touch with the IC up at Scarlet Springs."

Naomi's head snapped up. "You could do that?"

"I can try." He stepped back, glanced at his watch. "You just rest now and take care of yourself and these kids, and let us worry about the rest of it."

His kindness broke through the wall she'd tried to build around her emotions, tears blurring her vision. "Thank you."

"That's what I'm here for. If I hear anything, I'll let you know." He reached for his hand mic, turned and walked away. "No, I said no llamas in the horse barns. They spook the horses. Zero llamas in the horse barns. Zero is that number that comes before one. There shouldn't be a single llama in the horse barns."

Naomi took a bathroom break—she seemed to need to pee all the time now, especially when the baby decided to dance on her bladder—then washed her hands and splashed cold water on her face. When there was no sign of tears, she walked back out to where the children and counselors stood together. "They've set this space apart just for us, kids. Isn't that wonderful? There's water over there. Let's make a line. Everyone get a bottle of water, and then we're going to have some circle time."

They would talk through what had just happened, let the kids share their experiences, see how they were coping, and then—

"Naomi?"

Naomi turned to see Winona and Kat standing just inside the door, Kat's kids around her, all of them looking shaken.

Winona hurried over to Naomi, hugged her. "I'm so glad you and the baby are okay."

Words spilled out of Naomi. "One of the boys hid. I didn't know. I thought we had them all. I did a headcount, but it must have been wrong. Or maybe he hid afterward, and I didn't see him go. Chaska and Grandpa stayed behind with—"

"I heard." Winona stepped back. "We need to pray and stay strong."

Winona was right. Fear and tears wouldn't change anything.

"I had to evacuate all of the animals," Winona said.

"Shota, too?"

Win nodded.

"How did you manage that?"

"I had lots of help. I need to go check on him now, but I wanted to let you know that I'm here." She took Naomi's hand, gave it a squeeze, and turned to go.

Kat stepped forward. "I thought we'd stay with you for now—if you don't mind."

Naomi saw the same fear in Kat's eyes that she was feeling.

"I'm so glad you're here."

———

JOAQUIN RAISED HIS HEAD, opened his eyes, coughed. As his panic subsided, the pieces came together—the quiet, dissipating heat, pain.

The fire. It had passed.

He was still alive—burned but alive.

*Madre de Dios.*

That was as close to hell as Joaquin had ever been or ever hoped to be. He didn't know if he'd been in this shelter for a minute or an hour, but never in his life had he been more uncomfortable, more terrified—or more certain that he was going to die.

From beyond the walls of his shelter came a crinkling sound.

Someone coughed. "Ramir—"

More coughing.

"Ramirez!" It was Silver.

He and Hawke had saved Joaquin's life. If not for their quick action and encouragement, Joaquin would never have made it through this.

Someone peeled back the edge of his shelter.

"You still with me?" Silver looked down at him, blisters on his face, his skin red. "You're a bit toasted. How's your breathing?"

Joaquin coughed, nodded.

Silver moved on to the pilot. "Come on out, buddy. We're safe now."

"Jesus!" The pilot's voice held raw terror. "Jesus!"

Joaquin willed himself to let go of the straps that had enabled him to hold onto the shelter despite the terrible wind created by the fire. That's when he noticed the blisters on his hands and wrists. He looked as bad as Silver.

*Shit.*

No wonder he hurt so much—his face, his lips, the backs of his legs, his neck, his ass. Every bit of exposed skin and every part of him that had touched the foil of the shelter, even through the clothes Hawke had given him, was burned.

He pushed the shelter away and sat up, gasping at the pain caused by even the slightest movement. His skin felt like it was still burning. "Fuck."

"Chief, you still with us?"

Joaquin glanced over, saw that some of the silver foil had come loose from one side of Hawke's shelter.

"Hawke?" Silver hurried over to him, peeled back the shelter. "Fuck."

Hawke lay there face down, unconscious and unmoving.

Silver rolled him onto his side, checked his pulse.

Joaquin fought to stand, his body starting to shake. "Is he breathing?"

Silver bent low over Hawke, listened for breath. "Yes. He's in shock, I think. His shelter had partial failure. He's got some third-degree burns on his right leg."

Hawke rolled onto his back, moaned, his face contorted with pain. He opened his eyes, looked up at Silver, frowned. "I hope to fuck you didn't just give me mouth-to-mouth."

Silver grinned. "No, chief."

"Thank God." Hawke coughed, fought to sit up. "Is everyone okay?"

Silver answered for them all. "We're all a bit toasted, but we're all alive."

Hawke reached into the front pocket of his brush shirt. "I took these … out of the med kit. I hope to fuck they still work."

He held out his hand to reveal seven little black tubes with yellow tips, the word *Morphine Sulfate* written in all caps on the side.

Silver took them. "You first, chief. You're hurt worse than the rest of us."

"I won't … argue."

Silver opened one, hit Hawke in the thigh.

Almost immediately, the lines of pain on Hawke's face eased. He sank back to the ground. "Got a radio?"

Silver shook his head. "Sorry. I threw mine with my pack."

Hawke grinned. "You, too?"

Silver clearly didn't think this was funny. "Fuck."

"I've got my cell phone." Joaquin reached into his camera bag, the nylon straps of which had melted in places, and pulled it out. "It's not working."

"It probably got a little cooked. They'll send a helicopter to search for survivors." Silver met Joaquin's gaze and then the pilot's. He glanced down at the morphine pens and up again. "I'm not sure how long that will be."

Joaquin understood.

Once they used the morphine, there wouldn't be more until help arrived. Silver wanted to save it all for Hawke.

*Mierda.*

Joaquin had been looking forward to some relief, but if Silver could stand it, then so could Joaquin. Hawke needed it more than they did. The man's lower right leg was badly burned. Without him, Joaquin might not be alive right now.

The pilot looked miserable. "I'm sorry I couldn't keep us in the air."

"You did … one hell of a job … landing that wounded bird." Hawke's voice sounded a million miles away. "We'd all be dead … if not for you. What's your name?"

"John Wright."

"Thanks, John."

A cottontail rabbit hopped by, seemingly unhurt.

Silver pointed to it. "That little guy hid in the shelter with me."

"Good." Joaquin watched the rabbit. "For a moment, I thought I was seeing shit."

He glanced around at a changed landscape, forest replaced by blackened tree trunks and smoking ash, the blue sky hidden. The clothes he'd put on this morning lay against the ash, charred black, synthetic fibers melted. The fire had moved eastward, toward Scarlet.

All at once it hit him—how close they'd come to dying. He trembled uncontrollably now, whether from shock or stress he didn't know.

*Mia.*

Had she heard? He hoped to God no one had called her. If she heard his helicopter had gone down in front of the fire…

*Hell.*

He needed to call her. He tried his phone again.

Nada.

Silver glanced over at Joaquin's camera bag. "Did your camera make it?"

Joaquin took it out, turned it on, looked at the lifeless screen. "Nah."

"Bummer." Hawke said. "Sorry."

"Don't worry about it." Joaquin set the camera down, reached inside the front of his underwear, and pulled out the memory card. "My photos are safe at least."

The other men stared at him.

Joaquin held up the memory card. "I figured if my dick melted, photos wouldn't matter much anyway."

The others burst into laughter, interspersed with coughing fits, Joaquin laughing—and coughing —with them.

Holy Mother of God, they were alive. They were alive.

*What about Rossiter?*

The thought ripped away Joaquin's momentary euphoria.

Rossiter and the others with him hadn't had fire shelters.

Silver pulled shelter fabric over Hawke, who had begun to shiver. "We're probably all going to get a little shocky. Keep warm. If you've got water, drink it."

No one had water.

Joaquin needed to get to Mia. "Maybe I should hike out, get help."

Silver shook his head. "They had our position when we went down. They'll find us as soon as they can get a rescue chopper in the air."

Minutes dragged by as they waited, pain grinding Joaquin down. John asked for an injection of morphine, but Joaquin held out, wanting to do all he could for Hawke, who was now drifting in and out of consciousness.

Silver was worried—Joaquin could see it on his face. He gave Hawke another injection, took his pulse, stayed beside him.

Soon, a desperate thirst joined Joaquin's list of miseries, his body needing fluids to replace what had been lost from his burns.

And still there was nothing to do but wait.

———

MARC NUDGED the drone's controller out of the water with his boot and held it in place while Deputy Marcs slipped her hands into a pair of nitrile gloves. It had taken all of two minutes of wading in the reservoir to find the damned thing.

She picked it up, bagged it. "Thanks for your help with this. You three sure come in handy in a crisis."

"We're just doing our jobs," McBride answered.

They all looked to the west toward the dark wall of smoke. Every time it seemed to have moved more than Marc would have imagined it could. It wouldn't be long now till it reached the backburn. If it got past the fire crews there, nothing short of a miracle would save Scarlet.

Deputy Marcs put the evidence in her trunk. "Where are you off to now?"

Marc met Darcangelo's gaze and then McBride's. "I think we'd like to stay here. If there's anything we can do to help bring in survivors…"

Darcangelo came right out with it. "We can't leave with our friends still missing."

Deputy Marcs seemed to understand. "I'll take you over to The Cave—Rocky Mountain Search and Rescue Team's headquarters. Rossiter is a tenured member, so you'll be among friends. If there are survivors to bring in, the Team will be involved in that effort."

McBride gave her a nod. "We'd be grateful."

They climbed into their vehicles and followed her through thickening smoke to a big, square building with two enormous vehicle bays—probably an old firehouse. They parked and followed Deputy Marcs in through an open bay door.

"The Cave," Darcangelo looked around at the cavernous space, its walls hung with climbing and rescue gear. "I see where they got the nickname."

They passed through another door and found a handful of people gathered around the radio. Heads turned as they entered.

"Julia." An older woman with shoulder-length gray hair stood, lines of worry etched into her face. "Any news?"

"We caught the kids who were flying the drone. These guys helped with that. They helped with the evacuations earlier, too." She quickly introduced Marc, Darcangelo, and McBride to the others, a flurry of names passing by in a rush.

"This is Megs Hill, the Team's founder, and her spouse, Mitch Ahearn, also a founder. Nicole Turner, Sasha Dillon, Bahir Acharya, Creed Herrera—all Team members and friends of Gabe Rossiter's."

"He's a good buddy of ours, too." Marc shook their hands.

Herrera eyed him and Darcangelo, his lips quirking in a half smile. "He's told us about the two of you. He calls you 'Marcangelo.'"

McBride chuckled. "Marcangelo. I like it."

Marc and Darcangelo shot him a withering look.

One of the women—Sasha?—smiled, tear stains on her cheeks. "I feel like I know you."

Marc wasn't sure how to take that. "We're here to help bring Rossiter and the others in. Joaquin Ramirez was in the chopper that went down. He's a good friend of ours, too."

Megs nodded, the anguish in her eyes at odds with the hard set of her jaw. She was suffering as much as they were —maybe more. "Thanks for your help today."

She sat, went back to listening to radio traffic.

"Can I get you three some water?" Nicole asked.

Now that she mentioned it …

"That would be great. Thanks."

Marc followed her to a small kitchen, Darcangelo and McBride beside him.

Nicole opened the fridge, took out three bottles of water. "This has got to be the worst day ever. Gabe, Chaska Belcourt, and Chaska's grandpa are missing. Eric Hawke and Brandon Silver are missing. They're our friends. They're like family. They're the heart of the Team."

Darcangelo twisted off the top to his bottle. "We can't give up hope—not yet."

"At least they found Austin Taylor alive—and Bear, too."

Marc wasn't sure who Austin Taylor or Bear were, but

a life saved was always a reason to be grateful. "That's good news."

"Megs and Ahearn—they never had kids. I think we're like their kids, you know? She never says it, but I know she loves us. If Eric, Chaska, and Gabe are all dead …" Tears welled up in Nicole's eyes. "I don't know how any of us will deal with that, but I think it will kill Megs."

"We know their wives and kids." Marc couldn't bring himself to say more.

Nicole rested a hand on Marc's arm, a moment of shared distress between strangers. "The woman with the dark hair sitting next to Megs—that's Eric Hawke's wife. She just told him today that she's pregnant. The woman with the strawberry-blond braids—she's Brandon's girl-friend. They refused to evacuate. They're waiting for news."

Marc couldn't blame them.

He and Julian followed Nicole out of the kitchen in time to see Megs slam her cell phone down on the desk. "They say the governor is aware of the situation and is leaving the deployment of resources to the appropriate agencies. What a load of bullshit!"

"Doesn't he care about our town?" Sasha asked.

"Not enough to send the Supertanker. Bastard!" Megs looked over at Marc and the others and filled them in. "Hawke called for it before he went up in that chopper. The super of the hotshot crew requested it, too. As far as I know, no one has gotten back to them."

"Sheridan." Marc looked from Darcangelo to McBride.

McBride's cell phone was already in his hand. He tapped in a number, lifted the phone to his ear. "Yeah, Sheridan. It's McBride."

Marc met Darcangelo's gaze, listened while McBride

brought Lt. Governor Reece Sheridan up to date on the situation, giving him the bad news about Rossiter and Ramirez. Sheridan was a good buddy of theirs. His wife, Kara, had worked with Sophie and Tessa at the *Denver Independent*, and the three women were best friends.

If anyone could help, Sheridan could.

"They've got a handful of local crews and one hotshot crew battling this monster, with two small air tankers and a single helicopter making bucket drops. They've asked for the supertanker but are getting bullshit and red tape instead. Can you kick the governor in the ass and get some help sent our way?"

At this, every head in the room turned, people staring at McBride with astonishment.

"Hurry," McBride said. "There isn't much time. If help doesn't arrive soon, Scarlet will burn to the ground, and more lives may be lost."

He ended the call.

Megs stood. "What did he say?"

McBride slid his phone back into his pocket. "He says he'll do everything he can."

"When Reece Sheridan says he'll do everything he can, he means it," Darcangelo reassured her.

Marc thought they should know. "He's a good friend of Rossiter's, too."

Megs exhaled. "Thank you."

Marc hoped to God that Sheridan would be able to pull the right strings in time. The survival of Scarlet Springs might well depend on it.

## Chapter 17

CONRAD LIFTED the kennel out of the living area of Nate West's enormous horse trailer and carried the dog to the section of the barns that had been set aside for them. He didn't know their names the way Kenzie did. "Here's the last one."

Kenzie looked into the kennel. "Hey, Buster."

She checked the pooch off her list. "They're all here."

"Do you want me to start taking them for walks?" asked Quinn, Kenzie's manager.

Kenzie had set up a schedule for her staff so they could work despite the evacuation. Conrad was just glad she would have help caring for twenty dogs in a new, unsecured environment. It was going to be a big job.

"That would be great, Quinn. Thanks." Kenzie pointed. "I managed to grab a few leashes on the way out."

Quinn held one up. "I found them."

"I wish we didn't have to leave the dogs kenneled." Kenzie set the clipboard aside. "I want to check on Winona and see if she needs help."

"I'll come with you."

The Boulder County Fairgrounds had become Scarlet Springs in microcosm. Rose sat in the shade of a tree giving free tarot readings to evacuees, while Joe and Rain, who had brought food from the restaurant, made sandwiches for folks who were hungry. A few members of the Mudbugs were taking a break but had promised the full band would get together for a free evening show. Familiar faces were everywhere, everyone doing their best to get through this.

"You didn't even bring beer?" Hank asked Joe.

"No beer, Hank. Want some water?" Joe held out a bottle.

Hank took it. "Life is cruel."

Wasn't that the truth?

Megs had sent a text to all Team members telling them about the chopper crash that had landed Hawke, Silver, and two other men in the fire's path. They had survived the crash and deployed fire shelters, but no one had heard from them since. She'd also told them that a rescue chopper had found Taylor and Bear but that neither bodies nor survivors had been found at Camp Mato Sapa.

Nothing would be the same after today. Homes had been lost and probably lives, too. The homes could be rebuilt, but Scarlet would be changed by loss and grief. Vicki and Hawke were so in love—Naomi and Belcourt, too. Naomi was expecting a baby.

*Fuck!*

Life was so damned unfair.

They found Winona in a small outbuilding sitting beside Shota's crate, slipping him ice cubes. They kept their distance, not wanting to alarm the wolf.

Winona glanced up, and for a moment there was hope on her face.

Conrad hated to take that from her. "They found Austin and Bear, but we haven't heard anything new from the camp."

"Sorry," Kenzie said.

"I'm glad Austin is okay." Winona turned back to Shota, slipped another ice cube through the bars on his crate. "I'm trying to keep him cool and hydrated."

Kenzie glanced around. "Where are the other animals?"

"The baby moose and fawns are in the barn with the llamas, but the rest are gone," Winona said. "Jack and Captain Langeland got in touch with other wildlife shelters —the ones in Lyons and Golden and the raptor sanctuary in Fort Collins. They drove down and took as many animals as they could handle. It's better for the animals this way. Being here with all the noise and strange smells—it would have been too stressful for some of them."

Every once in a while, something happened to restore Conrad's faith in humanity. "I'm glad it worked out that way."

Kenzie crouched down, looked toward the wolf's crate. "How's Shota?"

"He's still dopey, but he won't be for much longer. He can't stay here. It isn't safe for him or anyone else. That wolf sanctuary near Conifer has a truck on the way. They'll be taking him in—at least for a while."

What did she mean by that?

Winona loved that wolf. Everyone knew that.

Before either he or Kenzie could ask, Winona changed the subject.

"Are the dogs settled?"

Kenzie nodded. "Quinn is taking care of them for now. Chip and Charles went to get food and water bowls. I'm going to try to find ice."

"Ask Captain Langeland," Winona suggested.

"Let us know if you need anything, okay?" Kenzie said. "Thanks."

Conrad and Kenzie left her alone and walked back, hand in hand, to find Inez watching the dogs and Nate West waiting for them.

"I'm about to head out," he said. "I thought I'd check to see if you needed anything else."

Kenzie gave him a hug. "I don't know how to thank you. What would we have done if you hadn't come along?"

"You'd have found a way. I'm just glad I could help." Nate pulled off his cowboy hat, ran his fingers through sweaty hair. "What are you going to do now?"

"We'll stay here until we get the all-clear to go home again. Most of the dogs' owners are out of town. If the kennel burns…"

"If the kennel burns, we'll set you up at the ranch until you can rebuild." Nate took his wallet out of his pocket, drew out a card, and handed it to Kenzie. "Call me if you need anything. I'm leaving the trailer here. We'll come back and help you transport the dogs back up the canyon when it's time."

Conrad shook his hand. "Thanks, man. We're grateful."

"What are neighbors for?" Nate tilted his hat at them and set off toward his trailer.

That was the thing about the Wests. They were filthy rich—and modest as hell.

For the first time since the evacuation began, Conrad was alone with Kenzie.

He drew her into his arms, wanting to comfort her, needing the comfort of her. He knew she must be hurting as much as he was.

"Oh, Harrison, it's just awful. I feel sick thinking about

what Eric, Chaska, Gabe and the others must have suffered."

He kissed the top of her head, held her close. "We don't know anything for sure yet."

Kenzie looked up at him through blue eyes filled with tears. "If they're gone … What will Vicki and Naomi do? Naomi's about to have a baby. Winona will be crushed. She and Chaska are so close."

"We'll do all we can to support them." There wasn't anything else they *could* do.

"At least Austin is safe."

"Yeah." That had been much-needed good news.

"If they didn't find bodies at the camp, does that mean they got away?"

"Maybe." It might also mean that the bodies were so charred or buried in debris they hadn't been visible from the air, but Conrad couldn't bring himself to explain this to her. "As soon as it's safe, the Team will head up to the camp to search."

"They'll need an HRD dog."

Gizmo and Gabby were both certified in HRD—human remains detection—but Conrad didn't want Kenzie up there.

"It doesn't have to be you, babe."

"Yes, it does." The determined look on her face told Conrad her mind was made up. "My staff can handle caring for the dogs. We should head back up to Scarlet with Gizmo and Gabby. Our Team stickers will get us through the roadblock, won't they?"

"Yes, but it could be rough up there." He knew she'd seen corpses before, but this would be different.

"I know, but they're our friends." A tear spilled down her cheek. "It's our job to bring them home. I don't want it to be anyone else."

"Yeah." Conrad drew her close again, kissed her.

"Sorry to interrupt…" Rain stood there, worry on her face, Angel in a carrier on her back. "Have they found Austin? We haven't heard any updates since we left."

Conrad looked into Kenzie's eyes, nodded. "They found him, and he's going to be okay. He's hypothermic from riding out the fire in a lake. Bear is okay, too."

"Oh, thank God!" Relief blossomed on Rain's face.

"I'm afraid there's bad news, too," Kenzie said.

Rain's smile vanished. "What is it? Tell me."

---

ERIC'S BODY ached for water, not even the morphine taking the edge off his thirst. It followed him into unconsciousness, gnawed at him, shredded him, his mind churning up images of lakes, creeks, rivers, glasses and bottles full of cool, clear water.

As a paramedic, he knew it was his body's response to his burns, but that didn't make it easier to bear.

He drifted off again until his own moans woke him. "Water."

"Sorry, chief." Silver took the cap off another autoinjector, jammed it into Eric's right quadriceps. "We don't have any."

Then it hit Eric.

They'd only had seven morphine syringes, and he'd gotten four of them.

"You haven't given yourself a shot, have you?"

"The pilot got one, but Ramirez and I are okay. We're doing alright."

"Yeah, man, we're good." The lines of pain on Ramirez's face told a different story.

"Liars. Second-degree burns hurt more than third-degree burns. You should give yourselves a shot—now."

"No, chief. You've got deep second- and third-degree burns. You're in a lot worse shape than we are. There are two left. We're saving them for you."

Stubborn son of a bitch.

"You're fired."

Silver grinned with blistered lips. "Okay."

Eric drifted again.

When he next woke, his face was turned toward the east where there was nothing but charred forest heading toward town. The sharp edge of regret cut at him. "Scarlet … It was my job to protect the town. I was supposed to—"

"Hey, you did your best. If that bastard Robertson had listened to you and handled initial attack the way you wanted, I doubt we'd be here right now."

"I should have evacuated Mato Sapa myself."

"Not even you can be everywhere at once, chief."

But Eric barely heard Silver's words, the pain trapped inside his chest beyond the reach of morphine. "I sent Taylor to Haley Preserve, and now … *God.*"

And then he was drifting again.

*Vicki.*

She held out a glass of water, smiled at him, touched a hand to her belly.

A baby.

"Chief! A chopper. Look."

Eric jerked open his eyes, saw a helicopter circling high in the sky above them. "It's about damned time."

*Thank God.*

Silver got to his feet and reached toward the sky, holding up four fingers.

Four survivors.

The pilot gave them a thumbs up.

Eric must have drifted off again because the next thing he knew, Silver was pouring water over his lips.

"Drink. Just a little."

It felt so good, like life itself. "More."

"Sorry. No more than a sip. We'll get you hydrated." A paramedic Eric didn't know, a woman with auburn hair, finished putting an IV in his arm. "I'm opening your fluids wide. It should help with the thirst."

Eric had said that very thing to people before, people with burns and blood loss. "What took you … so long?"

"They had to call us out of Denver. We had to assemble the crew, run a safety check, get airborne, and then fly here."

A stab to the thigh.

More morphine.

Even with a full load of narcotics, getting him onto the litter was no picnic.

He gritted his teeth. "The others. They're hurt, too."

"We're on top of it."

"My wife. Call her. Tell her … I'm not dead."

The paramedic put an oxygen canula beneath his nose. "We've radioed in already. She'll get the word."

Eric floated as they carried him to the helicopter and slid him into the bird, its rotors still running. The paramedic climbed in behind him, Silver, Ramirez, and Wright buckling into seats beside him, each carrying their own IV bag.

"I hope we don't run into any drones this time," Ramirez said.

The doors closed, and the bird lifted off, swinging in a wide arc around the forest and heading eastward.

Eric tilted his head back, caught sight of a wall of flame surging toward the new backburn, and beyond that, Scarlet Springs.

His home. The town he loved.

"It was my job to keep everyone safe. It was my job."

Then his eyes drifted shut, and he was aware of nothing.

———

HEART THUDDING, Vicki looked to Megs to make sure she'd heard right. "*Four* survivors?"

Libby repeated her words. "Did they say four?"

"They surely did."

"Oh, thank God!" Vicki turned to Libby, hugged her. "They're alive."

As far as Vicki was concerned, it was a miracle.

"Hawke knows what he's doing, man," Creed said. "He's not going to take risks."

Megs held up a hand for silence.

A voice came over the radio once more.

Vicki couldn't understand everything they were saying, their words garbled by static and made up of slang she didn't know.

Megs translated for her. "All four are responsive. Silver, the pilot, and the photojournalist have second-degree burns, while Hawke has second-degree with third-degree burns on his right leg. He suffered partial shelter failure. All need medical treatment. They're being flown to the burn center in Denver."

Vicki's stomach sank. *Third-degree burns. Shelter failure.* "Oh, God."

Megs took her hand, gave it a squeeze. "He's alive and responsive, so that's a good sign."

Vicki shot to her feet. "I've got to get to the burn center."

Libby stood, too. "I'm coming with you."

"My car is at the Forest Creek Inn." Vicki started toward the door.

Megs stood, blocking her. "You're not driving."

"I'll take you." The tall man who'd called the lieutenant governor stepped forward, Gabe's friend. "I met your husband today. He's a good man."

"Thank you."

"He helped me evacuate," Libby said as if to vouch for the man.

Vicki headed toward the door, then turned back. "Text me when you get news about Chaska, Gabe, and the others, okay? And, Megs, thank you."

Megs acknowledged this with a nod. "You go be with your man."

Vicki followed the man outside to his vehicle, Libby beside her, both of them holding a hand over their mouths to shield themselves from the smoke. It was so thick she could barely see twenty feet ahead.

The man opened the two passenger-side doors for them, then hurried to the driver's side and climbed in.

"I'm sorry, but I don't remember your name." Vicki was ashamed to admit this. She was usually good with names.

"Chief Deputy US Marshal Zach McBride." He backed out of his parking space. "How would the two of you feel about me switching on my overheads and running hot?"

"Oh, hell, yes!" Libby blurted.

They drove through empty, smoke-filled streets, passing a single sheriff's vehicle but seeing no one else as they made their way to the canyon.

Vicki called her mother-in-law to share the news, knowing that Robin was suffering every bit as much as she. "Yes, he's alive, but he's got third-degree burns on his right leg. I'm on the way to the burn center now. I'll call as soon as I have more news."

Vicki ended the call, lapsing into silence. She didn't have the heart for conversation, her thoughts wrapped around Eric and what he must have endured, questions chasing through her mind. Why had his shelter failed? Were they taking care of his pain? Was his life in danger? Was he at risk of losing his leg? Would he be able to walk again?

The canyon passed by outside her windows unseen. When they reached Boulder, Zach flipped on his sirens. Traffic pulled over, enabling them to move quickly through the city and onto Highway 36 toward Denver.

It was only when they passed the hospital that Vicki remembered her promise to text Lexi when she got word. She typed out a quick message and sent it.

"Do you think they'll let me see Brandon?" Libby asked out of the blue. "I'm not his wife. I'm not sure he'll even want to see me."

Vicki turned to look back at Libby. "Are you kidding? He's going to be so happy that you're there. Just tell them you're his significant other."

But Libby looked unconvinced.

Forty minutes later—it felt like much longer than that —they pulled up in front of the Denver Burn Center, stopping just outside the emergency entrance. "You two head in. I'll park and then come in to check on my buddy Ramirez."

"Thanks so much."

"I'm happy to help."

Vicki climbed out and followed Libby through the sliding glass doors.

## Chapter 18

LEXI FOLLOWED the RN in blue scrubs back to the emergency department.

"He was seriously hypothermic when they brought him in, but he's doing much better now," the nurse said. "We're going to keep him under heated blankets and continue giving him warmed IV fluids and oxygen until his core temperature has normalized completely. He should be ready to go home this evening."

"Thanks so much."

The nurse motioned to one of the bays, a blue-and-gray striped curtain drawn across it for privacy. "He's in there."

"Thanks." Lexi nudged the curtain aside. "Austin?"

The head of the bed was raised so that he was sitting up, but he was sound asleep, blankets covering him up to his chin, an oxygen mask on his face, an IV tube disappearing beneath the blankets.

She pressed a kiss to his cheek, tears filling her eyes.

She'd come so close to losing him, so close to never seeing him again.

Needing to feel his touch, she took his right hand from beneath the blankets, held it against her cheek, her gaze moving over his face, studying every dear and precious feature. Those long, dark lashes. His high cheekbones. The line of his nose. The stubble on his jaw. The lips that drove her crazy.

He was safe and alive.

*Thank you, God.*

His eyes fluttered open, and he smiled, squeezed her hand. "Lexi."

"Hey, sleepyhead." She smiled through a new rush of tears. "How do you feel?"

"Like I've been hit by a bus." He took his hand from hers, wiped a tear from her cheek. "Hey, it's okay."

She'd told herself that she would keep it together, but she was failing. "I was so afraid, Austin. When they said the fire had burned through your last known location and that no one could reach you, a million terrible things went through my mind. I thought…"

His gaze went soft. "I'm so sorry."

"It's not your fault." She sniffed, smiled. "You were trying to rescue Bear."

"Bear didn't need rescuing. He was safe all along."

Lexi listened while Austin told her about reaching the cabin to find that Bear wasn't there. He told her how the fire had moved faster than he'd imagined, his description of running for the truck and realizing he wouldn't make it sending chills down her spine.

"I ran for Azure Lake instead. I knew that if I didn't make it, I would burn alive. I would never see you or Emily again. Emily would lose her father like you'd lost your mother."

His words struck a sore spot inside her, the place in her

heart that had never healed. "But you made it. You made it."

"The fire was right behind me. By the time I reached the lake, it was close enough to melt the straps on my backpack. If I had tripped, if the lake had been another ten feet farther away… The heat was unbearable, and the way the trees seemed to shriek…"

Lexi felt almost sick, his descriptions bringing vivid images to her mind. "That's awful."

"I've always had a lot of respect for firefighters, but after today…" Austin's body tensed as if he'd just remembered something. "Hawke. Have they found him?"

"Yes. He's alive, but he's hurt. He, Brandon Silver, and the others are being flown to the Denver Burn Center."

"What the hell happened?"

Lexi shared the little she knew. "Eric and the others were heading to search for survivors at Camp Mato Sapa and to find you when they were struck by a drone. It took out the helicopter's rear rotor. The chopper crashed right in front of the fire. Vicki said they deployed fire shelters, but Eric's shelter failed. He has second-degree burns all over and third-degree burns on his right leg."

Austin squeezed his eyes shut. "Christ. I can't imagine."

"Vicki's pregnant." Lexi wasn't sure why this was relevant, but it was.

So much had been at stake today.

Austin let out a breath. "Thank God he's alive. I'd have had to kick his ass otherwise."

Lexi squeezed Austin's hand. "That's big talk for a guy who can't stay awake."

"What about Camp Mato Sapa?"

"Nothing new there."

"Shit."

Lexi didn't want Austin to worry about things he couldn't change, not when he was still recovering. She changed the subject. "You said Bear was safe. Where did you find him?"

"He found me. My truck was burned out, the radio melted. I started to walk back to town, but I lost consciousness. The next thing I knew, Bear was there, looking down at me. He helped me up and told me he'd take me to Winona."

Lexi smiled. "Like all the injured animals he finds?"

"Exactly like that." Austin told her how Bear had half carried and half dragged him down the road until the helicopter arrived. "He was scared of the helicopter, but I talked him into get onboard with me. I've never seen a bigger smile on anyone's face than when he looked down at the ground."

"Where is he?"

"I'm not sure. When I opened my eyes again, I was here."

They talked for a while, Lexi telling Austin how hard it had been to evacuate and leave their home and everything in it behind.

"Where's Emily? Where's Mack?"

"They're with my dad and Kendra. They took them both to a park. I didn't want Emily in the ER with sick people, and they wouldn't let Mack in anyway."

Austin's gaze met hers. "Let's have another baby—a brother or sister for Emily."

His words surprised Lexi, made her laugh. "Where did that come from?"

They had talked about having another child, but life had kept them busy. It had never seemed like the right time.

"There was a moment in the lake when I thought I was

going to die. There was so much smoke. I thought of you and Emily and how I'd always believed we'd have more children."

Tears blurred her vision again.

She cupped his cheek with her palm. "Oh, Austin. If I had lost you …"

But she hadn't lost him. He was going to be okay.

She smiled. "I would love to make another baby with you."

They kissed, his lips cool against hers.

He drew back. "I almost forgot. I've got something to show you. Can you grab my pack? I think it's in a plastic bag under the bed."

She bent down, saw a large plastic bag with his name on it, and tugged it off the shelf under his bed. "This is heavy."

Inside were his boots and his backpack, both reeking of smoke. The sight of both made her stomach knot. His boots were covered with ash and soaking wet. The fabric of his backpack had been burned through in places, and some of the nylon straps had begun to melt.

Good God.

It had been *that* close.

He took the backpack, opened it, drew out what looked like a framed photo and a book. "This is a photo of Bear's family and his mother's journal. His whole family is buried out there not far from where the cabin stood. The place burned to the ground, but I managed to save these. I promised him I'd keep them safe."

"Oh, Austin." Lexi stared, amazed. "Do you realize what you have here? No one knows anything about Bear's past."

He grinned, pointed to a boy in the photo. "That's him there. His real name is Matthew."

And Lexi knew. "You risked your life for these, didn't you?"

His brow furrowed. "I couldn't leave them."

Lexi caught his face between her palms and kissed him again. "I could not possibly love you more."

———

KENZIE SAT on a wooden bench in the shade, watching while Harrison walked to stand beside Joe at the microphone. Rain had asked Harrison to come and share what he knew with folks in a kind of impromptu town meeting.

"There are so many rumors flying," she'd said.

"Remember to check the list of missing persons." Joe pointed to a piece of paper pinned to a nearby kiosk. "Right now, I think we're down to about twenty-eight people. If you're on the list, check in with Captain Langeland so we can get you crossed off. If you believe someone is missing, let him know."

Joe paused for a moment. "I've asked Harrison Conrad to come share the news with us. He's on the Team, as you all know, so he's getting updates."

Harrison stepped up to the mic. "As you might have heard, Austin Taylor was sent to find Bear and bring him to safety. The fire burned through that area while Taylor was there, but he found shelter in a lake. So, he's hypothermic but okay. As it turns out, Bear found him."

Quiet laughter.

"The fire also burned through Camp Mato Sapa— Naomi and Chaska Belcourt's camp. Although most of the kids and staff got away, Gabe Rossiter, Chaska Belcourt, Grandpa Belcourt, and three counselors stayed behind so that the others could get away. One of the kids apparently hid during the evacuation and is missing, too."

A flurry of gasps.

"Oh, God!"

"That's awful!"

"Some Team members and I tried to reach the camp to evacuate them, but we couldn't get through."

Kenzie's heart constricted at his humbleness. He didn't say a word about nearly being trapped and having to drive through flames, probably because he still believed he had failed.

"A helicopter went to search for survivors but found nothing—no bodies, no survivors."

Harrison went on. "Our fire chief, Eric Hawke, went up in a helicopter to try to find Taylor and to check for survivors at Camp Mato Sapa, but a couple of college kids were flying a drone to film the fire. The drone struck the chopper and took out the tail rotor. The helicopter crashed in the path of the blaze."

"Oh, heavens!"

A sob.

"No!"

"Captain Brandon Silver and a photojournalist were onboard, too, as well as the pilot. I just heard that they were all found alive—"

Cheers.

"Thank God!"

Harrison held up a hand. "They're alive but injured. They've been flown to the Denver Burn Center. Hawke has third-degree burns. That's about all I know."

The crowd fell into whispers of dismay.

"Is my house still standing?" Rose asked.

"Can't you look into your crystal ball and see for yourself?" Hank blurted.

Snickers.

Harrison could see that Rose was truly worried. "I

don't know. I don't have any information on the extent of damage to property. I know Hawke's crew is fighting hard to save our town and they've got help. Whether it will be enough, I can't say. Kenzie and I are on our way back up to join the rest of the Team to search Camp Mato Sapa as soon as it's safe."

"God bless you!" someone called.

"Stay safe!"

"Thank God for the Team!"

Harrison acknowledged their good wishes with a nod and rejoined Kenzie.

Joe stepped up to the mic once more. "The Timberline Mudbugs will be playing a special free show tonight, performing their new single, 'My House Burned Down, But I Still Got You, Babe.' As I'm sure you've heard, two of the band's members have lost their homes, but they're going to play for us anyway. How's that for keeping Scarlet strong?"

Whistles and applause.

"Some local charities are joining with Knockers to provide meals tonight. A church group is offering to house families with small children and to provide toiletries to those who need them, so we're grateful for that. Esri Tsering is offering free counseling for people who are feeling shaken up. And now Father Penberthy has asked to say a few words."

The priest stepped forward. "We stand here today as children of Scarlet Springs, united in a time of trouble, as our ancestors were when fire threatened them. Now, as then, we turn to each other and to God for strength."

He paused a moment, bowed his head. "Let us pray."

Kenzie wasn't Catholic, but she bowed her head, too, her fingers twining with Harrison's.

"God, our Father, give us the strength to think not of

ourselves during this trial, but of our neighbors who are suffering. Keep the men and women fighting this fire safe from harm, and guide them in their noble work. We pray especially for those who've been injured in the line of duty and ask for swift healing for Austin Taylor, Eric Hawke, Brandon Silver, and the others who crashed in the helicopter whose names are unknown to us."

When Father Penberthy had finished—he went on for some time—Kenzie and Harrison whispered "Amen" in unison.

Harrison gave her hand a squeeze. "Ready?"

"Yeah."

They turned to go.

"Bear!"

He stood not far behind Kenzie, looking like a child on Christmas morning, a broad grin beneath his beard. "I flew in the air."

Kenzie hugged him, joined almost immediately by Rain.

"I'm so happy to see you." Rain slipped her arm through his. "Are you hungry?"

Bear nodded.

Rain led him away.

The question came suddenly to Kenzie. "How do you think he managed to survive? Austin had to take shelter in a lake."

"Bear knows that country better than anyone. He must have a few tricks up his sleeve to have survived all these years."

They walked to Harrison's SUV, Gizmo following at their heels. When the dog was in his crate, they drove in silence back toward the canyon to do a job both of them were dreading—searching for the bodies of missing friends.

LIBBY PACED around the periphery of the waiting room, stopping to make herself a cup of tea that she didn't drink.

What if they wouldn't let her see Brandon? What if Brandon didn't want to see her? What if she had finally succeeded in pushing him away just like she'd done with every other boyfriend she'd ever had?

No, she couldn't let that happen.

Brandon was different. He wasn't like the others.

*You told him to leave.*

He'd told her he loved her, and she had kicked him out.

"Libby and I work together at Knockers," Vicki was telling a very pregnant woman with red hair named Mia. "Her boyfriend is one of my husband's shift captains."

Mia's husband had been on that helicopter, too. Two friends sat with Mia doing their best to reassure her, one named Sophie and the other named Tessa. The pilot's wife was there, too. The women were all making conversation, but Libby didn't have the patience for that.

The double doors opened, and a man in blue scrubs and a white medical coat walked in. "Who's here for Joaquin Ramirez, John Wright, and Brandon Silver?"

Mia stood. "I'm Joaquin's wife."

"John is my husband."

Libby tossed the tea in the trash. "I'm here for Brandon. Is he okay?"

"We've treated their burns and gotten their pain under control. They were both badly dehydrated, so we're giving them intravenous fluids. I'll take you back."

Vicki stood. "Any word about my husband, Eric Hawke?"

The doctor nodded. "He just went into surgery. Doctors

are cleaning and debriding his burns. I'm not sure how long it will take them—perhaps an hour, maybe longer. I'll have one of the nurses come out and give you updates."

"Thank you." Vicki sank back into her chair.

Libby followed the doctor through the double doors—and there he was. "Brandon!"

He stood at the nurse's station, wearing only a pair of scrub pants, bandages on his wrists and hands, surprise on his handsome face. "Libby?"

She ran to him, wrapped her arms around him. "I thought you were dead."

He held her close. "For a while there, so did I."

It was only then that Libby noticed the IV in his wrist and the IV pole beside him and the blisters on his face and lips. Was she hurting him?

She drew back. "You should be resting."

"I was trying to borrow a phone so that I could call you."

"Really?"

"Really."

Libby walked with him back to his hospital room and kept his IV line from getting tangled as he got back into bed. There were blisters on his hands, elbows, shoulders, the backs of his legs, and his neck, too.

She wanted to hold his hand, but was afraid to hurt him. She rested a hand on the curve of his bicep instead. "Are you in pain?"

"Not anymore. They gave me morphine on the way here and then some pills." He looked into her eyes. "I'm so glad you're here. I was afraid—"

"I'm sorry. I was an idiot." She steeled herself to say words she'd never said before.

"I shouldn't have pushed—"

"I love you, Brandon." There. She'd said it. She'd gotten it out.

"You… what?" Brandon stared at her.

"Don't act surprised. *You* said I loved you before I said I loved you."

His lips quirked in a lopsided grin. "I guess I did."

"You were right." Libby closed her eyes, tried to fight the tears. "I felt sick after you left this morning. I was afraid I'd ruined everything. When I heard you'd been in a helicopter crash, that you'd crashed into the fire…"

Her voice failed, her throat too tight to speak.

He slid a hand behind her head, drew her against his bare chest. "It's okay."

She'd sworn that she wouldn't cry but she couldn't stop herself, sobbing out the anguish of the past few hours in his arms.

He held her, kissed her hair, let her cry herself out.

*Get it together, chick! He's the one in the hospital bed, not you.*

She raised her head, saw that he was smiling. "What?"

"I'm just so happy that you're here. A couple of hours ago, I was pretty sure it was game over. Now, I'm sitting here with you, buzzed on pain meds."

She reached for a tissue, dried her eyes, sniffed. "It must have been terrible."

The smile left his face. "It was like something straight out of hell."

Libby listened while he told her about the drone hitting the helicopter and how he'd realized they were headed directly toward the fire.

"I prayed I would die in the crash so that I wouldn't burn to death, but somehow the pilot managed to land us far enough from the flaming front to give us a fighting chance."

He told her how they'd run, looking for a good

deployment spot, and how he'd prepared the site while Hawke had gotten the other two ready. "When he shouted for us to deploy, some part of me couldn't believe it was really happening. My hands were so clumsy. Somehow, I got my shelter out. When I got inside, I had the feeling that I was crawling into my own grave."

"Oh, Brandon."

"The fire was rushing straight at us. The roar was unreal, and the heat... Hawke was still helping the others. I shouted at him to deploy, and then it was too hot. I pulled my shelter down around me."

Brandon closed his eyes as if the memories were too much. "God, Libby, it was the worst five minutes of my life."

"I'm so sorry."

"It got so hot that I was sure I was going to die. The fabric of the shelter kept blowing against me, burning me wherever it touched my clothing—my ass, my shoulders, the backs of my legs. I kept pushing it off me with my elbows, but they burned, too. Do you know what kept me together?"

She shook her head. "Courage?"

"No." He gave a little laugh. "*You* did."

"I did?" She gaped at him.

"I wrapped my mind around you and didn't let go."

If Libby hadn't already been in love with him, that *right there* would have done it. "Did you really?"

He nodded. "Just before the fire passed, I started to lose consciousness. I thought I was dead. My last thought was, 'At least you told Libby you loved her.'"

Libby was stunned by this, a strange ache in her chest. "No one has ever loved me like that. Guys say they love you, but when they get what they want, they always disappear. Not even my dad bothered to stick around. He used to beat me and my mom. I never told you that, did I?"

"I guessed it was something like that." He ran a thumb over the curve of her cheek. "Forget him, Libby. Forget all of them, and give me a chance. I won't let you down."

Then he kissed her, his blistered lips rough.

She left it to him to shape the kiss, afraid she would cause him pain.

When he drew away, the tenderness in his blue eyes made her heart skip. "I love you, Libby. I would walk through fire for you."

"God, please don't do that." She ran a hand up his chest, smiled. "But, hey, my house burned down. Can I move in with you?"

## Chapter 19

JOAQUIN OPENED his eyes to find Mia there, looking beautiful and worried at the same time. "*Mi amor.*"

He could see she'd been crying.

She smiled down at him, rested a hand against his arm. "How do you feel?"

"Sleepy. The pain pills are kicking my ass, but I'm not complaining." He reached out, tucked a strand of red hair behind her ear. "How are you?"

"Me? I'm fine now." She reached for his water pitcher, held the straw to his lips. "They said you were dehydrated. Drink."

He took a few deep swallows, found her studying him.

Yeah, he looked like hell, and he knew it.

"Your poor face."

"The doctor said I might have scars where the burns are deepest."

"You'll still be as handsome to me as you ever were."

What had he done to deserve her?

"How long have you been here?"

"About an hour. Sophie and Tessa drove down from the

Cimarron when they got the news. They stayed with me and then drove me here."

"I'm glad you weren't alone." He'd never doubted that his friends would be there for Mia if anything happened to him, but it was nice to know he'd been right.

"Alone?" She laughed. "Are you kidding? I called your parents, and ten minutes later most of your family and the entire cousin mafia was at our place, cooking, praying, lighting candles. I had to sneak upstairs to get away from it all."

He could believe that. "I'm sorry. I didn't mean to worry you."

"Yeah? Well, think about that next time you selfishly decide to be in a helicopter crash in the middle of a damned wildfire."

He chuckled. "I love that smart mouth."

Her chin wobbled, her composure fading. "They told me you'd survived the crash but said they hadn't heard from anyone since. I was certain I'd lost you. I couldn't understand how life could be so cruel to take you from me now."

"Eric Hawke—he saved my life. Without him…." Joaquin would never be able to repay the man. "He gave me a spare set of firefighter clothes. He said mine would melt and cause bad burns. He showed us how to use our shelters. When that fire was running straight at us, he kept me focused on survival. He was the last to deploy his shelter because he was helping us. The man has balls of steel. How is he?"

"Last I heard, they were cleaning his burns."

Joaquin hoped they'd knocked him out.

Mia went on. "I met his wife, Vicki. She's in the waiting room. She was very kind to me. She's pregnant, too—their second."

Then Joaquin told Mia the story from the beginning, hesitating when he got to the worst of it. "I was sure I was going to suffocate in there—or burn to death. I kept remembering what Hawke said about it being a hundred times hotter outside of the shelter. The noise was deafening. Then I heard him cry out, and I knew something must have gone wrong. I just closed my eyes, tried to breathe close to the ground the way he'd showed me, and prayed—for him, for myself, for all of us."

"I can't imagine."

"Brandon Silver, he's a good guy, too. He got me out when it was over. He took care of Hawke, gave him morphine. He and I refused any for ourselves because we didn't want to run out before help arrived. God, Mia, it was a long wait. The thirst, the pain—it was tough. I just kept telling myself that I was alive and I was going to see you soon."

"Oh, Joaquin." She reached for his hand, stopped herself. "I want to touch you but I'm afraid to hurt you."

He closed his hand over hers—then remembered. "Any word about Rossiter?"

Mia shook her head. "Nothing."

Joaquin's stomach sank. "*Mierda.*"

"Sophie says that Marc and Julian are still up there. They're planning to help that rescue team search for remains as soon as they can get through."

"Good." Rossiter deserved that.

Mia stood, rubbed her lower back.

Joaquin sat up. "Can I get you a better chair?"

Mia shook her head. "Sophie, Tessa, Zach McBride, your parents, your grandma, a few of your cousins—they're all waiting for a chance to see you. No matter how much I want to, I can't keep you to myself. Besides, I need a bathroom break."

Oh, right. All that baby on her bladder left her needing to pee all the time.

"I'll be back."

Sophie and Tessa were the first to enter his room.

"You look like hell," Tessa said, her curly blond hair held back in a ponytail.

Joaquin laughed. "Thanks."

"Are they keeping you comfortable?" Sophie asked.

"I've had morphine, Percocet, some kind of numbing gel, a tetanus shot. I'm good."

"Thank God for painkillers." Sophie sat beside him. "What happened up there? How did you all survive?"

He gave them the short version of the story until the two were staring at him wide-eyed.

"God almighty, Joaquin." Tessa shook her head. "A helicopter crash *and* a raging wildfire. It just wasn't your time, was it?"

Sophie gave his hand a careful squeeze. "I can't decide if you were incredibly unlucky today or whether you're the luckiest guy I know."

"I'll go with lucky." Then he remembered his photos. "Can you get into my stuff beneath my bed?"

"Sure." Sophie grabbed the bag, set it on the bedside table, took out his camera. "This looks bad."

"It's ruined. My phone, too." He reached for the bag, felt around inside for the smaller plastic bag the nurses had given him. "But this is fine."

He opened the bag and took out the memory card.

"How did that survive?" Sophie asked.

He handed it to her. "I tucked it inside my underwear."

"This was in your crotch?" She held the memory card at eye level. "This is a new and unexpected level of intimacy between us, Joaquin."

Joaquin chuckled. "Can you get it to Tom?"

Sophie nodded. "Of course. Anything to help."

Tessa took the memory card. "I'll do it. You stay in the car, Sophie. Tom might ask you to clock in otherwise."

Sophie's eyes went wide. "Oh, right. Good call."

"I saw Hunter and Darcangelo up there." Joaquin figured they'd like to hear about their husbands. "They were helping with the evacuations."

Tessa smiled sweetly, a note of sarcasm in her voice. "Yes, I'm sure they're staying out of danger like they always do. They're such wallflowers."

Sophie's brow furrowed at this. "They scare the hell out of me."

Mia stepped inside the room again. "Your mother and grandmother are getting impatient to see you."

"Zach is out there, too." Sophie pulled out her phone. "We should go and give them a turn. But first a quick selfie so we can show everyone you're alive."

She and Tessa arranged themselves with Joaquin and Mia between them.

*Click.*

Sophie glanced at the photo. "Perfect."

"We'll get these to the paper," Tessa said.

Sophie found a safe place to plant a kiss. "Feel better, okay?"

Tessa did the same. "I'm so glad you're safe. Mia, let us know if you need anything."

Mia hugged them both. "Thanks for being there. It meant so much to me."

The two turned and walked away as Joaquin's mother and grandmother walked in, his dear, old *abuelita* holding her rosary.

"¡*Pobrecito!*" His mother hugged him. "You scared your mother to death."

JESSE CLIMBED into the brush truck, breathing hard. He'd been working a small backburn in the canyon on the fire's southern flank, trying to keep the blaze from fingering off again. He was slick with sweat, covered with soot, and thirsty as hell.

Jenny Miller handed him a cold bottle of water. "Here."

"Thanks." He twisted off the top, drank.

He and some of the other volunteers had been pulled off the line to work with Jenny and Hawke's A-shift in a last defense of Scarlet Springs. They would start on the western edge of Scarlet proper, spraying down houses and businesses so that embers carried off the ridge by high winds wouldn't start new fires.

"We need to protect the town so it will be here when the head of the fire comes to burn it down," Ryan, Hawke's A-shift captain, had joked.

Chuckles.

But everyone was wondering the same thing: Did they stand a chance against this beast?

Thanks to the fan guns, the blaze was twenty-percent contained, but it was the other eighty percent that worried Jesse.

Jenny wet a pink bandana and wiped her face. "Any news about Hawke and Silver?"

Jesse shook his head. "Nothing since they found them."

They drove through smoke from the backburn above Scarlet down into town, turning left to reach the western-most edge of the town proper. The houses on the thickly forested slopes above them were too dangerous to protect, but this space in the valley was defensible.

They parked in the hospital parking lot, where Ryan gathered everyone together.

"Listen up!" Ryan looked up at the smoke above them. "We don't have much time. We're going to roll through town starting with Quarry Street, and we're going to water down the rooftops and the trees. Before the flaming front reaches the backburn on Dead Man's Hill above town, the wind is going to start showering this place with embers. We're going to put those out. But if the fire breaks past the backburn and backs down the mountainside, we will evacuate to the reservoir. Quarry Street is our get-the-fuck-out trigger. I don't want anyone else to end up at the burn center. Is that clear?"

Heads nodded.

"Any news about the chief and Silver?" someone called from the back.

"Not since they were evacuated."

Ryan divided them up, assigning crews to different trucks, and set them loose. "Let's do this for Hawke!"

"For Hawke!"

Jesse moved off with Jenny and a couple of other guys in the brush truck. They took out the hoses that had already seen so much action today, hooked one end to a fire hydrant, and aimed the other at a row of homes that included his own.

It felt surreal to stand there dousing the place—the roof, the walls, the wooden fence, the wood pile, the trees. He couldn't help but think of the time he and Ellie had spent inside those four walls. She'd lived here the night he'd met her. He'd carried the twins through that front door when they'd been sick with strep, and, yeah, he'd gotten sick himself. They'd lived there when he'd proposed, when they'd gotten married, when Dylan had been conceived and born.

If the fire took it all, they would rebuild—but it would hurt.

They moved to the next house and the next until they'd soaked that entire block.

Jesse wished they could get the fan guns down here and hook them up to hydrants, but he knew that wouldn't work.

Their connections weren't compatible with fire hydrants, and the machines only functioned with water kept under intense pressure.

But that was okay. That was all right.

They'd beat this fucker one way or another.

The big Skycrane flew overhead, hose dangling from its belly. The helicopter was working on spot fires, while the SEATs were protecting homes and bombarding the canyons that led into Scarlet, trying to bottle up the blaze.

If they could funnel the flaming front into the backburn…

The first ember landed in the grass not far from Jesse's feet.

Still holding the big hose, he stepped to the side and stomped it out. He reached for his hand mic and called it in. "Wind is carrying embers our way."

But Ryan had already seen and called it into Scarlet Command.

At first it was just an ember here or there, small ones carried aloft by the wind. Then spot fires started on the mountainside above them.

"Fuck!" Jenny shouted.

But Jesse had known this would happen. He heard through his earpiece when Ryan called this in, too. Scarlet Command responded by diverting one of the SEATs and the Skycrane to the spot fires above town.

Jesse looked to Jenny. "We are *not* giving up!"

"Giving up?" Jenny grinned. "Hell, we're just getting started."

They kept at it, drenching houses and trees in their little corner of Scarlet while the mountainside above them ignited, one spot fire at a time.

The Skycrane didn't have far to go to refill its tank and seemed to pass overhead every few minutes, while the SEATs took much longer. Where was that fucking Supertanker?

"Three o'clock!" Jenny shouted.

Jesse looked to his right, saw that embers had ignited the leaf litter in someone's gutter. They turned the hose on it, put it out.

But as the fires on the mountainside above them grew in size and number, it seemed to Jesse that they were fighting a losing battle.

———

MARC STOOD NEAR THE DOOR, glancing outside every so often, the inaction wearing on him. He wanted to do something besides stand here. He wanted to get out there, to go after Rossiter and the others. Instead, he was standing here, waiting.

He glanced at his phone, smiled at the photo of Sophie and Tessa with Mia and Joaquin.

"He looks pretty good for a guy who almost died twice today." Darcangelo leaned back against the wall, winced, stood upright again, a scowl on his face.

The man was hurting, but he was too damned stubborn to do anything about it.

Across the room, Megs sat at her desk listening to radio traffic, the others double-checking gear they would take with them when they finally had the green light to head up to Camp Mato Sapa. There were ropes, litters that broke down into two pieces, medical kits—all kinds of shit—spread out around the room. People were just passing the time, keeping their hands busy.

It gave Marc an idea.

"Hey, is anyone here an EMT?" he asked.

Heads came up, and almost everyone raised a hand.

"Is something wrong?" Megs asked.

Marc pointed to Darcangelo with a jerk of his thumb. "This guy got second-degree burns on his back when we evacuated some pets earlier today. He's being stoic about it. I think he needs treatment."

Darcangelo shot him a look that could kill. "I'm fine."

Megs stood, hands on her hips. "I'll be the judge of that. Show me."

Darcangelo took off his shirt, turned so Megs could see his back, and lowered his voice to a whisper. "You're dead, Hunter."

Marc grinned.

Megs pointed to a chair. "Sit. He's right. You need medical attention."

Darcangelo glared at Marc but did as Megs asked.

"Nicole, bring me a burn kit." Megs looked over the wounds. "Some of these are fairly deep. Many of the blisters have popped, leaving open burns."

Nicole returned and handed Megs the medical kit.

Megs pulled on a pair of gloves, then took out a tube of gel that she opened and quickly blotted onto the burns, a look of concentration on her face.

The scowl on Darcangelo's face faded, replaced by relief. "Thanks."

"You still planning to kill me?" Marc asked.

"Hang around and find out," Darcangelo muttered.

Creed chuckled. "Yeah, Rossiter says you two bicker all the time."

Marc pretended to be offended. "Rossiter said that?"

Megs worked on Darcangelo for about ten minutes, covering the burns with sterile gauze. "Unless you've had one recently, you should get a tetanus shot."

"Really?"

"That's standard these days." She stripped off her gloves. "You're done for now, but you'll still need to see a doctor."

"Thanks. That feels a lot better." Darcangelo stood to put on his shirt.

"You're welcome." Megs tossed her gloves in the trash.

It was then Marc noticed that Sasha and Nicole were staring at Darcangelo's chest. They liked what they were seeing, too. When they realized Marc had caught them, they looked at each other and shared a guilty laugh.

Yeah, they didn't fool him. Women were every bit as horny as men.

It was the sound of voices outside that drew Marc back to the front door.

"Fire crews," he told the others. "It looks like they're hosing down the rooftops or something."

Megs hurried over, peered outside. "That's exactly what they're doing. God, someone give them respirators or face masks. It can't be good for them to be working in such poor air quality."

Smoke rolled through the streets like fog. The sharp scent of it permeated The Cave and clung to Marc's clothes, but at least he and the others were indoors. The firefighter crews were out there, doing hard, physical work in the thick of it.

"Some of these guys are volunteers from nearby departments," Megs said. "I don't recognize them."

The volunteers were working in this smoke, trying to save a town that wasn't their own—and they weren't getting paid for it. Marc had to admire their spirit of service, even if he thought they were a little crazy.

*And what exactly are* you *doing here, Hunter?*

That was different. He was here for Rossiter.

That's when he saw it—a glowing ember. It drifted to the ground like a snowflake from hell, landed on the sidewalk, and went black.

Darcangelo walked over, looked outside, too. "Embers."

Herrera joined them at the door. "The fire's got to be close now."

A burst of static.

Megs hurried over to the radio, listened to a rush of radio traffic. "This is it."

They walked outside all together and stood looking up at the wall of black smoke rising over Dead Man's Hill above town.

If the backburn worked, it would halt the flaming front in its tracks. If it didn't, the fire would start backing down the hillside, and Scarlet would be doomed.

Megs pointed to the small fires on the mountainside beneath the ridge. "The fire is already spotting."

"That's it then." Nicole looked like she might cry. "Even with the backburn, they can't stop it now."

Megs slipped an arm around her shoulders. "Don't say that yet."

A Sikorsky S-64 Skycrane rose off the reservoir and moved in on the spot fires, dousing one as another flared up. Then it turned its nose westward and disappeared.

"Where the hell is he going?" Creed pointed to their left. "The reservoir is that way."

Then a roar shocked the air. It wasn't coming from the fire.

"Look!" Sasha pointed to the east, eyes wide.

Marc stared. "Holy fucking shit. How…?"

A 747 Supertanker tore up the canyon, flying so close to the rooftops of Scarlet Springs that it looked like it was going to slam into the mountainside.

Well, that explained why the Skycrane had disappeared.

The supertanker banked, hugging the contour of the slope, a seemingly unending stream of orange slurry leaving its hold, blanketing the spot fires on the mountainside and the top of Dead Man's Hill. Then it gained altitude and disappeared to the south.

Marc found himself shouting and cheering with Darcangelo and everyone else.

"Way to go, Sheridan," Darcangelo said.

"I'm going to buy that man a drink." Marc shot Sheridan a quick text to thank him.

But the fire wasn't out.

On the mountainside, a few spot fires still burned, and on the ridge above town…

Cheers faded to silence, everyone looking to the west, embers falling like a rain of fire, thick, dark smoke churning skyward.

Marc found himself holding his breath, time measured in heartbeats.

A wall of flame at least a hundred feet high flared up—and disappeared.

Again, Marc stared. "They did it."

The backburn had worked.

For a second time, Scarlet's smoky streets echoed with cheers.

## Chapter 20

THE SWEET SOUND of Vicki's voice drifted over Eric, a hand stroking his hair. "I'm right here, Eric. Can you hear me?"

Was she crying?

He wanted to answer, wanted to open his eyes, but couldn't.

"He's still a little out of it from the anesthesia," said a voice he didn't recognize. "He'll come around soon."

"I don't want him to suffer. He's been through enough."

"We'll do all we can to keep him comfortable."

Then he was off again, drifting in and out of awareness.

When at last he opened his eyes, he found Vicki still beside him.

She smiled, stroked his hair. "Welcome back."

"Vicki." He reached for her with a bandaged hand.

She took her palm in his. "I don't think we'll be able to hold hands for a while."

"Is oral sex out?"

She smiled, laughed. "As soon as you're home again, you will get *all* the head."

He liked that idea.

Sadly, he wouldn't be leaving any time soon. "Did you talk to the doctor?"

She nodded. "He explained all of it—the temporary skin grafts, how they'll eventually take some of your own skin for permanent skin grafts on the two worst areas. He says you're probably going to be here for a month with physical therapy and possible follow-up surgery after that. He also said he expects you to recover and to walk normally once you're healed."

They had stitched sheets of lab-cultivated pig skin onto his leg to cover the deep second-degree burn area—the biggest part of it. Those would protect him from infection and help his skin heal faster and scar less. They'd done the same with the worst areas of full-thickness burns, but those would have to be replaced with sheets of his own skin from donor sites. The doctor had warned him that it was going to be painful, and he was going to spent a lot of time in this bed.

But, hey, he was alive.

He raised his hand to Vicki's face, the weight of his own failure weighing on him. "I let everyone down, Vicki."

She smiled, shook her head. "No, you didn't. Your plan worked. You saved Scarlet. The fire isn't out, but it is contained."

Maybe it was the morphine, but Eric could hardly believe what he was hearing. "Contained?"

She held up her phone so that he could see the photo she'd gotten from Megs of the 747 Supertanker dropping retardant on spot fires above town. "Check this out."

It was the most beautiful thing he'd ever seen.

He closed his eyes, relief sweeter than morphine.

The town was safe. Scarlet was safe.

Then he remembered. "What about Taylor?"

"Austin is fine. He sheltered in a lake and became hypothermic. Bear found him. He's at a hospital in Boulder, but Lexi says he's going home soon."

Austin was safe. Bear was safe, too.

Eric exhaled. He wasn't sure he could have lived with knowing he'd sent his best friend to his death. "Camp Mato Sapa?"

The smile left Vicki's face, giving Eric his answer. "No news yet. The Team is heading out to search for them soon."

"Jesus." Eric knew what they were going to find—charred bodies twisted in positions of agony, the last writhings of friends. Hours had gone by since the fire burned through Mato Sapa. The fact that no one had seen them and no one had heard from them could only mean one thing.

"It's not your fault. You did everything you could."

He squeezed his eyes shut, fighting not to imagine how much his friends had suffered. "Tell that to Naomi and Kat."

"Oh, my poor, sweet man." Vicki stroked his hair again. "Please don't do this to yourself. You've been through hell already."

Slowly, the story came out of him. The argument with Robertson. The first backburn. The news about Taylor and Camp Mato Sapa. The chopper crash.

"I thought we were dead. We were spinning, heading straight for the fire, but John, the pilot, held on. The man is a hero in my book."

"I can't wait to meet him."

"When I realized we were alive, the job became survival. The fire was headed straight for us. Silver knew what to do, but John and Ramirez, the photojournalist, didn't. We grabbed our gear from the chopper and ran. I chose a deployment site. Silver cleared it, while I told the other two what to do."

"You must have been terrified."

"I didn't have a lot of time to be afraid."

He told her how he'd been the last to deploy and how he'd noticed too late that the plastic package that held his shelter had been slashed in the crash. "I knew that meant the shelter might be compromised, but I didn't have time to run back to the helicopter and search for another one. The fire was on top of us."

Understanding dawned on Vicki's face. "That's why your shelter failed."

"I crawled in and hoped for the best, but ..." The memory of unbearable heat and excruciating pain made his skin shrink, goosebumps prickling his arms. "I knew the moment the shelter failed. I thought I was dead."

Vicki cleared her throat as if fighting not to cry. "It must have been so painful."

"Worse than anything I could have imagined. I screamed and fought not to thrash around. I knew if I moved, I'd let in more hot gas and maybe lose my grip on the shelter."

Tears spilled down Vicki's cheeks now, distress on her sweet face. "You just had to lie there and burn? Oh, God, Eric."

He told her how the shelter's failure let in hotter air, how he'd clawed at the earth with his fingers while still keeping his hands in the straps just to reach soil that was cool enough to enable him to breathe.

"The last thing I remember was taking a breath with my face in the dirt and feeling the darkness close in." Eric's throat went tight. "I asked God to watch over you and Caden and the new baby."

Vicki smiled through her tears. "He took care of you, too."

"The next thing I knew, Silver was staring down at me." He told her about the terrible thirst and how Silver and Ramirez had given their morphine to him. "How are they doing? Have you heard?"

"They're on another floor. They're going to be okay, too—thanks to you. I met the photojournalist's wife. She's a nice person. She's about to have their first baby." Then Vicki's face crumpled. "I thought I'd never see you again, that our kids would have to grow up without you. It was bad enough believing that I'd lost you, but knowing you'd died such a horrible death… I just couldn't bear that."

"Come here." He reached for her, drew her head against his chest, let her cry it out, her tears seeming to wash away his anguish, too.

━

KENZIE SAT in the passenger seat as Harrison followed Rescue 1 and Rescue 2 and the Pine Ridge Hotshots up the road to Camp Mato Sapa, Marc and Julian and the rest of the Team following behind. The hotshots had asked to be a part of the rescue when they'd heard Lakota people from Pine Ridge were involved.

"They're our people," Tall Bull, the superintendent, had told Megs. "Chaska Belcourt and I went to high school together."

Megs had agreed.

Kenzie had done more than a few searches for human remains in her career as a search dog trainer, but she'd never done a search like this.

Seven people. Three of them her friends. One a child.

The destructive power of this fire was apparent every-where Kenzie looked. Where there had once been dense mixed-conifer forest and stands of aspen there was now only ash and charred tree trunks, wisps of smoke twisting in the wind.

"We were right here when we turned around. The entire road was engulfed."

"You did the right thing." Kenzie reached over, put her hand on his thigh. "If you hadn't turned around, I'd be out here searching for you, too."

Survivor guilt had come close to breaking Harrison after the Everest disaster. She wasn't going to give it a second chance at him.

He looked over at her, doubt in his eyes. "If I had seen any way to reach them…"

"You would have gone after them, like you came after me in that blizzard. Trust that you did the right thing."

The crease between his brows deepened. "Yeah."

The sun was close to setting, the air still heavy with the scent of smoke. Not knowing where Gabe, Chaska, and the others might have run in their desperation to escape, they parked their vehicles at the entrance to the campground and stood together, surveying the destruction.

There were no buildings, no structures of any kind, no sign that a thriving kids' camp had stood here just a handful of hours ago.

"God in heaven." Megs stared at the desolation. "No one could have escaped this. There's nowhere to run."

"I was here a few weeks ago to help Chaska set up the ropes course for the kids." Sasha wiped tears from her face. "It's all gone—all of it."

Her steps leaden, Kenzie went around to the back of

the vehicle and opened the liftgate. "Are you ready to go to work, Gizmo?"

She tried to act like this was any other search, but her voice quavered.

Gizmo whined, sensing her despair.

She opened his crate, leashed him, and lifted him to the ground. He wasn't a young dog any longer, and she didn't want him to hurt himself.

She put protective booties on his paws to keep him from getting burned in case there were any hot spots out there. The people all wore fire boots for exactly that reason, and Kenzie never risked her dogs' safety.

She led Gizmo to the edge of the camp, tried to still the thrumming of her heart. Then she knelt, petted him. "These are our friends, buddy. Help us bring them home."

She removed the leash, stood. "Okay, Gizmo, search!"

Gizmo was off, walking back and forth, his nose guiding him.

Kenzie followed, letting him find his own way through hazardous terrain, while the others held back, not wanting to distract him.

He'd gone maybe twenty feet when he stopped, raised his head, and barked. Then he took off, running as fast as his covered paws could carry him toward the far side of the camp.

Stunned, Kenzie shouted for him, tried to get him to come back. "Gizmo!"

When that failed, she ran after him. "Gizmo! Stop!"

He ignored her, veered to the left, crossed a little creek, and sat, staring upward.

Breathing hard, Kenzie splashed her way across the creek to Gizmo's side.

"Hey, Kenzie!"

Kenzie looked up, stared open-mouthed, blood rushing to her head. "G-Gabe?"

He was bent down, peering at her from the mouth of what looked like a little cave a hundred feet above her. "You look like you've seen a ghost."

"You're alive!" Happiness washed through her, a golden wave of joy.

"Hell, yes, we're alive—all seven of us—and we're hungry."

Kenzie turned back toward the Team, pointed at the cave, and found herself shrieking and jumping up and down like a kid on Christmas morning. "They're here! They're up here!"

The rest of the Team ran toward her.

Chaska peered out from behind Gabe. "Hey, Kenzie."

Harrison was the first to reach her. He stared up at the cliff wall, stunned. "What the hell? How did you get up there?"

"We climbed."

Creed, Jesse, Marc, Julian, Bahir, and the hotshots were there now, too. Creed and Jesse whooped. The Hotshots stood together in a group, laughing.

"*Hau, kola!*" Tall Bull called up the Chaska, who looked astonished.

*Hello, friend.*

"Tall Bull?"

Marc glared up at Gabe. "You son of a bitch! I'm going to kick your ass!"

Gabe apparently thought all of this was funny. "Hey, Hunter, you're here, too? Darcangelo, hey, man. Good to see you!"

Julian stared. "You have more lives than a fucking cat!"

Naomi, Kat and the kids—are they safe?" Gabe asked.

"Yes!" Kenzie shouted back. "They all made it out."

Creed walked up to the rock, studied it, clearly trying to figure out how Gabe and the others had done it. "How did you pull this off, man? There's not much here."

"We had a lot of incentive."

Jesse looked back at the burned forest. "I bet they did."

Gabe grinned, waved. "Hey, Sasha, Nicole, Megs."

Sasha and Nicole did what Kenzie had done, jumping up and down, hugging each other, and shrieking. But it was the relief on Megs' face that brought tears to Kenzie's eyes.

She bent double as if to catch her breath, then stood upright, and called up to Gabe. "I see you did what you do best!"

"Old habits die hard!" he called back.

Then Megs reached for her hand mic. "Scarlet Command, sixteen-oh-one, we have seven survivors."

Her voice quavered. She released the mic.

Was Megs crying?

"Damned smoke." She blinked, wiped her eyes, cleared her throat, and then took hold of the mic again. "Yes, seven survivors. They sheltered in a freaking cave about a hundred feet off the forest floor. Make sure someone notifies their families."

Chaska stuck his head out again. "So, I've got a plan for getting us out of here. Anyone want to hear it?"

"Sure," Jesse answered. "Hit me."

Kenzie's work as part of the Team was done. While the others talked through the rescue, she knelt next to Gizmo and gave him a whole handful of treats. She'd sent him to find bodies, and he'd found living people instead.

She rubbed his silky chest, ash and soot on his fur. "Good job, Gizmo. Good job."

CHASKA WAS the last to set foot on the ground. He was greeted with cheers, slaps on the back, hugs, and a kiss on the cheek from Sasha. Then someone shoved a cold bottle of water in his hands. "Thanks."

He tore off the top and drank the entire thing.

Rossiter swept Megs up in a hug. "Sorry to worry you. I love you, Megs."

"If the next words out of your mouth are, 'like a mother,' you're dead."

They made their way back to the vehicles in the twilight, Dean sticking close to Old Man. The two of them had bonded in that cave.

Tall Bull waited for Chaska. "Good to see you alive."

He and Chaska had gone to high school together. That seemed a lifetime ago.

"Thanks. Good to see you, too, man."

"I hear you got a pretty Lakota wife and a baby on the way."

God, Chaska couldn't wait to hold Naomi in his arms. "How about you?"

"On my second wife. Three kids. There aren't a lot of women who can handle being married to a man who's away from home for almost half the year."

Chaska could see how that might be hard. "See that boy with Old Man? He hid when we evacuated the camp because he thought he was going home. From what he's told us, life there is pretty rough. We're going to get in touch with tribal authorities, but do you think you can look in on him once in a while when you're around?"

"I can do better than that." Tall Bull left Chaska and joined Old Man. "Hey, Grandfather, who is this boy who survived the fire with you in the cave?"

"This is Dean."

"Is he a brave boy?"

Old Man rested a hand on Dean's shoulder. "What he did today—waiting out the fire in that cave—was very brave."

Tall Bull tousled Dean's hair. "Dean, since you're such a brave boy, would you like to ride back to town with me, Old Man, and the other hotshots?"

Chaska couldn't help but smile.

Dean looked up at Tall Bull, clearly star-struck, and nodded.

Tall Bull looked over his shoulder at Chaska, their gazes meeting.

"We're going to get you all cleared by medical, and then you can go home," Megs said.

"Scarlet is still there?" Rossiter asked.

"It's still standing, though a lot of homes in the mountain to the west burned. They're still mopping up spot fires." Megs opened the door to Rescue 1. "We'll catch you up on the way into town. But first, I need to hear how you got up there."

Rossiter rode down with his buddies, while Chaska rode with Megs. He told her how they'd spotted the cave and how Rossiter had free soloed his way up and set up a make-shift pulley system.

"Rossiter is a bad ass." Creed grinned.

Chaska had to agree with Creed. "I free soloed part of the route while they were pulling Old Man up. Those holds were thin. I'm not sure I could have done it. Rossiter tossed me the rope and pulled me up just as the fire reached us. Without him, I probably wouldn't have made it. None of us would have made it."

"We need to give him a raise," Megs joked.

Team members were volunteers. No one, not even Megs, earned a wage.

"What happened in Scarlet?"

"Hawke did one hell of a job," Megs said. "I wish he'd seen that Supertanker fly over town. Oh, you two don't know about Hawke, do you? Or Taylor?"

Chaska listened as Megs told them what had happened —the fire overtaking Taylor, his mad dash to a nearby lake, Bear finding him hypothermic afterward. "Talk about a close call."

"He'll be coming home, soon." Then Megs told him about Hawke.

Chaska felt sick for the man. "Third-degree burns?"

"He's out of surgery and stable. Vicki is with him. The doctors told her he's going to be there for at least a month and that he'll need skin grafts. Silver and the others have second-degree burns. They're keeping them overnight."

"Please tell me they caught the bastards who flew the drone."

Megs nodded. "Rossiter's friends caught them—a couple of college kids."

Chaska knew this had to have been hell on Megs. "How are you holding up?"

Megs drew a breath. "Now that I won't be going to your funerals, I'm dandy."

Sasha turned around, looked back at them from the front passenger seat. "You scared the hell out of us. I've been crying all day."

For sunny Sasha, that was something.

They pulled into the parking lot at Mountain Memorial, where a skeleton crew had stayed on to offer triage to firefighters. Chaska walked over to the hotshot buggy, watched as Old Man climbed out, drum under his arm, Tall Bull and Dean behind him.

Dean wore a look of awe on his face. "Can I be a hotshot, too?"

"If you stay healthy and strong and work hard, yes."

Tall Bull bent down to Dean's level. "How about I come check on you when I get back to the rez?"

Dean smiled again, nodded.

Tall Bull stood, looked over at Chaska. "See you around, brother."

Then he climbed back in the buggy.

Dean stared after him, watched the buggy drive away.

Old Man stood beside the boy, put a hand on his shoulder. "Now you know what a true warrior is."

Megs came up to Chaska, handed him her phone. "Someone really wants to talk to you."

The sound of Naomi's voice put a hitch in Chaska's chest. "Yes, we're all fine. We're on our way down to you now. We just need to get cleared and find some wheels. See you soon. I love you, too."

In the ER, the seven of them were given a quick exam and some crackers and then released. Chaska and Old Man stayed close to Dean, who probably wasn't used to the technology, let alone being around so many white folks.

Back outside, Chaska found Conrad waiting for him.

"Rossiter is heading down with Hunter and Darcangelo. You, your grandfather, and the others can ride with Kenzie and me."

Wendy from the newspaper rushed up to them, a woman Chaska didn't recognize beside her. Both held up digital recorders. "God, I'm glad you're okay. Everyone thought … Can you tell us what happened up there?"

But all Chaska wanted in the world right now was to hold Naomi. "Ask Megs. She can tell you all about it. I want to see my wife."

## Chapter 21

NAOMI HAD NEVER BEEN MORE relieved or more exhausted in her life. They were all safe and whole and alive—Chaska, little Dean, Grandpa Belcourt, the three camp counselors. But somehow the good news had left her feeling limp as a ragdoll.

When she'd gotten the call from Megs, Naomi had expected the worst. She'd thought she'd get confirmation that Chaska and Grandpa Belcourt had been killed, along with three camp counselors and another woman's child—a child whose life had been hers to protect. Instead, she'd gotten the best news possible.

Megs had explained to her how the eight of them had survived, taking shelter in a cave a hundred feet up the side of a cliff. Then she'd handed the phone to Chaska.

Naomi had heard his voice—and burst into tears of sheer relief. Afterward, she'd gone in search of Kat, but Kat was already speaking with Gabe and getting the story from him. That left Winona, who had come running from the pavilion when she'd gotten Naomi's text message.

That had been a half hour ago.

They would be here soon.

Naomi willed herself to stay focused. The children had had a rough day, too, fleeing a wildfire, seeing the adults around them driven to near-panic. She divided the kids into four groups, settling each with a camp counselor. They were playing games suggested by Esri, who was a trauma therapist, to help the kids process their experience today—games about feelings and games like Simon Says to help kids focus on the here and now by using their bodies.

Everyone was being so kind. One of the local churches had brought hot meals for the kids—spaghetti with meatballs and salad. A daycare center had donated some storybooks and toys. A local grocery chain had brought breakfast cereals, cookies, and milk.

Kat's two older kids sat in a circle with the younger children, participating in one of the games, while Kat helped a soldier set up cots for the kids, little Noelle playing with toys Kat had brought inside from her vehicle.

Naomi walked over to Kat, spoke quietly. "I'm going to go splash water on my face."

Kat fluffed a pillow. "You've done a great job, Naomi. Go take a break."

Naomi stepped inside the bathroom, leaned back against the door, and exhaled, rubbing a hand over her belly, the baby kicking restlessly.

Had she been crazy to think she could run a camp like this?

Someone with more experience and training might have thought to keep a vehicle on hand that was capable of transporting everyone. Maybe they would have thought to have a satellite phone rather than relying on a landline. Maybe they would have noticed one of the children running away and hiding.

If Chaska and Grandpa Belcourt and the others had died…

She would have had to go on without Chaska for the sake of the baby, but she would never have been able to forgive herself for their deaths.

*That's not how it turned out. Don't dwell on things that didn't happen.*

Naomi splashed cold water on her face, dried off with paper towels, and stepped back out into the main room.

One of the groups was playing the Gratitude Game.

"What are you grateful for, Mona?"

Mona smiled shyly. "Pusketti."

"You like spaghetti, don't you?"

"How about you, Alissa?"

"My daddy is going to come home."

And then Chaska was there, standing just inside the doorway, his dark hair tousled, soot on his face. Dean stood beside him. Behind them came Grandpa Belcourt with his drum, Gabe Rossiter, and the three camp counselors.

All conversation in the room came to a stop, kids craning their necks to see.

Naomi bit back a sob as Chaska came to her and lifted her off the floor. She wrapped her arms around him, held on tight. There was so much she wanted to tell him, so many things she wanted to say, but now wasn't the time. "Chaska."

He set her on her feet again, touched a hand to her belly. "Are you okay?"

She blinked back tears, nodded. "I am now."

"There's a party going on out there. Have you seen? The Mudbugs are playing, and people are dancing. It's crazy out there."

"I've been busy here."

Little Alissa squealed, jumped up. "Daddy!"

Kat dashed out of the back room, hurried straight over to Gabe, who scooped up his daughter and drew his wife into his arms, neither of them speaking.

Naomi reluctantly let Chaska go, knelt, and hugged Dean. "I'm so glad you're safe! You gave me such a scare. I want to hear about your adventure today."

Dean grinned. "I rode with the hotshots. Tall Bull said I can be a hotshot, too."

Naomi had no idea who Tall Bull was. "Is that what you want to be—a firefighter?"

Dean nodded, still smiling. He seemed like a different child than the angry, frightened boy who'd been throwing punches this morning.

Then Naomi hugged Grandpa Belcourt, her throat going tight. "I'm so glad you're safe. I was so worried."

God, how she loved the old man.

He chuckled. "It was an interesting day."

Winona burst through the door. "Grandpa!"

Grandpa Belcourt held his granddaughter, speaking softly to her in Lakota.

Then Winona made her way over to Chaska—and hugged him hard.

"Hey, little sister." Chaska chuckled, then drew back. "What's wrong?"

Winona shook her head. "I'm being silly. That's all. Shota went to the wolf refuge. It's better for him than staying here."

Understanding dawned on Chaska's face. He hugged his sister again.

Naomi told the counselors to continue with the games, while she took the three who stayed behind to the back-room. It was clear to her that the three of them were exhausted and a little shaken up. They all smelled strongly of smoke.

"What you did today goes so far beyond your job description. You were willing to sacrifice your lives for the children and other counselors. I don't know how to thank you."

"Food?"

Naomi laughed. "There's leftover spaghetti in the kitchen area and a bathroom with a single shower. I'll see if we can get towels for you. After the kids are asleep, we're meeting to talk about what happens next."

They disappeared as a group into the kitchen.

Kat walked up to Naomi. "All the cots are up. Unless you need anything else, Gabe and the kids and I are heading home."

"Thank you—for everything. I couldn't have gotten through this without you."

Kat hugged her. "I was going to say the same thing. Thank you for letting me stay with you. Being here made it easier for me to cope."

Out in the main room, Chaska and Gabe hugged.

Chaska slapped Gabe on the back. "You saved our lives."

"I couldn't have done it without you, brother."

Kat and Gabe collected their kids, said their goodbyes, and were gone.

Chaska gathered the children into a big circle. "Old Man wants to tell us a story."

Grandpa sat, drum in hand, and began to beat on it. "Who can tell me about the beating of this drum?"

Dean's hand shot in the air, and he blurted, "It's the heartbeat of our ancestors."

Grandpa nodded. "It's the heartbeat of our ancestors, of the Lakota, Dakota, and Nakota people. Our people have been through many hard times, but we survived them all because we are strong. As long as the drum beats, our ancestors and our people live on. Today was a hard day for us, but we survived. Now, let me tell you the story of Mato Sapa, the Great Black Bear, and the angry Fire Spirit."

Chaska came to stand beside Naomi, slipped his fingers through hers, whispered in her ear. "He's making this up."

---

JESSE DROVE down the canyon into Boulder, the tail end of a day-long adrenaline rush like too much caffeine, exhaustion creeping in around the edges. He called Ellie to let her know he was coming—and to tell her their home was undamaged.

"I can't wait to see you," she said. "I heard about Eric and Brandon. The news reports say Eric has third-degree burns. How awful."

"Yeah. The man is lucky to be alive."

"I'm so glad Gabe, Chaska, and the others are okay."

"Me, too."

"Cedar is grilling Portobello mushrooms, but I told him you'd need something more substantial after a day of fire-fighting. He got you a T-bone."

Jesse was *not* a vegetarian. "You're the best. See you soon."

Images from the day kept running through his mind as he drove. That ominous wall of dark smoke. A tsunami of fire meeting the spray of the fan guns. Hawke's chopper spinning, going down. The destruction at Camp Mato Sapa. Belcourt, Rossiter, and the others laughing down at them from that cave.

Yeah, it had been one hell of a day.

Not that it was over yet. The fire was contained, yes, but there were still spot fires and lots of smoldering timber. Mopping up this blaze was going to take a while.

He threaded his way through Boulder traffic to Martin Acres—called Martian Acres by locals—to Claire and Cedar's bungalow on 32$^{nd}$ Street and parked at the curb.

The door flew open, and Ellie ran out.

He stopped her from hugging him. "I'm hot and sooty and sweaty. I'll get your clothes dirty. Let me take a shower, and we'll pick up right here."

Daisy squealed as Jesse stepped through the door. "Daddy!"

Daniel was right behind her. "Daddy's home!"

Ellie caught them. "Your daddy needs a shower. He'll give you big hugs as soon as he gets out of his dirty fire-fighter clothes."

"Hey, man." Cedar stepped out of the kitchen, a microbrew in his hand. "I've got beer chilling in the fridge when you're ready."

"God, that sounds good."

"Hey, Jesse." Claire, his sister-in-law, appeared, carrying a fussy Dylan. "Good grief! You look like a chimney sweep."

She handed the baby to his mother and led Jesse to the guest bathroom, where Ellie had already put their toiletries. "There are towels and washcloths under the sink. I think Ellie brought clothes for all of you."

"Thanks."

The shower felt like redemption, soap, shampoo, and warm water washing away salt, soot, and stress. He willed himself to relax, to focus on the relief of water massaging his tired muscles and sluicing over his skin. When he stepped out of the shower, he felt less tense, more awake, and clean.

He opened the bathroom door wearing only a towel and found a pair of jeans, a T-shirt, and some boxers sitting just outside the door, with a note from Ellie that said, "I love you."

She was always doing things like that, always finding ways to show him that she cared about him.

He dressed and joined the others, who were outside on the deck now, his T-bone on the grill next to three Portobello mushrooms.

Vegetable steaks.

As far as Jesse was concerned, that was an oxymoron.

Ellie sat at the glass patio table nursing the baby. "Better?"

"God, yes." He bent down, kissed her cheek, lifted Dylan's little fist from her breast with his pinkie, felt a hitch in his chest when the baby grasped his fingertip. "Hey, little guy. Daddy missed you. Where are the twins?"

"I think they're downstairs drawing pictures for you."

Another hitch in the heart.

Damn, he loved being a father.

"Have a seat." Cedar rose, walked to a cooler, grabbed a beer. "Tell us all about it. We watched the coverage on TV, but half the time they're clueless."

Jesse took a swig of his brew and told them about his day, from the alarm he'd felt when he'd spotted that first wisp of smoke to his astonishment at seeing Rossiter, Belcourt, and the others alive.

"They could have died of smoke inhalation in there." Ellie had worked her share of hours in the hospital emergency room and wouldn't miss a detail like that.

"Belcourt says they covered the opening of the cave with a big woolen blanket his grandpa had on hand. He and Rossiter held it in place until the fire passed."

Cedar grabbed him another beer. "So, it was your idea to use the snowmaking machines? That's genius."

"I'm just glad no one was killed. Are Eric and the others going to be okay?"

"It will be a long haul," Ellie said. "But, yes, they'll recover."

Daisy and Daniel stepped outside, whispering to each other.

"I'll give him my picture first," Daisy said.

"We can give him the pictures at the same time," Daniel was saying.

It was good to see him stand up for himself against his more talkative, outgoing sister.

"Yes, give them to Daddy at the same time." Ellie lifted a sleeping Dylan from her breast and buttoned her blouse.

Jesse set his beer aside, ready to give the twins his full attention. He hauled them, drawings and all, onto his lap. "First, I want hugs. Here's my Daisy. Here's my big boy, Daniel."

He held them tight, one child in each arm, grateful beyond words that they were safe. "Okay, let's see what you drew."

They each held up a sheet of paper with stick-figure drawings that appeared to be him with lots of orange and yellow flames.

"Wow. Look at these! Did the two of you see news about the fire on TV?"

They nodded.

Daniel's drawing showed stickman Daddy holding what was meant to be a firehose spraying blue water toward a burning tree, a smile on his face.

Jesse studied it, saw a child's worry. "There were lots of trees that burned down today, but not the ones in our yard. Thank you, Daniel. Good work."

Daisy's drawing showed even more fear. This time,

Stickman Daddy stood in the center, surrounded by a ring of fire.

"Great job, Daisy. Look, I'm surrounded by fire." He looked into his little girl's eyes. "The fire never got close to me. I was very careful. Do you know why I was careful?"

She got a shy little smile, shook her head.

"I had to keep myself safe so that I could come home to you, Daniel, and Dylan."

Daisy and Daniel looked at each other, doing their twin thing, and smiled.

Cedar stood, got the steaks off the grill. "Who wants steak sauce?"

After supper, Jesse helped Ellie give the kids baths and put them to bed. Dylan was already sleeping in his portable playpen.

Out in the hallway, Jesse caught Ellie around the waist, nuzzled her neck. "How about you and I get in bed—and not sleep."

Ellie tilted her head to the side, gave him room to play. "We'll have to be quiet."

Jesse chuckled. "I hate to break it to you, honey, but I'm not the noisy one."

―――

KAT PUSHED Gabe back on their bed, straddled him, ran her hands over the hard muscles of his chest, the lamp on the nightstand casting a glow over his skin. Her gaze locked with his as she reached down, took his cock in hand, and guided him inside her.

He inhaled, a quick shuddering breath, a crease appearing between his brows as she slowly took all of him.

It felt so good, his cock stretching her, filling her, stroking that deep ache. She began to move, grinding herself against him, the sensation almost too sweet to bear, pleasure making her forget, chasing away the lingering shadows of a terrifying day.

He knew just how to drive her crazy, teasing her nipples, cupping her breasts, sending jolts of arousal straight to her womb.

Somehow, their sex life kept getting better, the bond between them deeper. He was her half-side—her perfect, matching half—and she was his.

She kept up the rhythm, her nails digging into the skin of his chest, pleasure drawing tight inside her. He reached down with one hand to stroke her clit with his thumb, his blue eyes dark. Her gaze still locked with his, she came, bliss washing through her, a blaze of golden light that left her breathless.

The moment her peak had passed, he flipped her onto her back and caught her legs with his shoulders, forcing her knees back and opening her fully to him. He thrust into her, driving hard, carrying her toward a second shattering climax. This time he came too, spilling himself inside her.

They lay together afterward, her head on his chest, his fingertips tracing her spine.

"What you did today—it's the same thing you did the night you lost your leg." She'd thought a lot about this on the drive home.

His voice was deep, soft. "How?"

"You took a situation where death was imminent and turned it into a chance for life."

"I was where I needed to be today."

Kat smiled to hear him say that. "Yes, I guess you were."

When she'd met him, Gabe hadn't believed in anything —no higher power, no religious tradition, not even himself.

Her mind flashed to the last moments together before she'd driven away with the kids.

*"I'll stay here and wait for the next sheriff's vehicle. Deputy Marcs got a call off to Dispatch. They know we're here."*

*"Are you sure they're coming?"*

*"I'll be fine."*

"You stayed behind knowing that no one could get through, didn't you?"

"I didn't have a choice—at least not one I could live with afterward. I couldn't drive off and leave others behind to die."

Gabe told the whole story, filling in the details. "When we reached the cave and everyone was up and out of harm's way, I was hit by the reality of what had just happened. I was so afraid the fire would overtake you and the kids on the road."

Kat had worried about that, too. "When I saw Megs and the others on their way up, I felt so relieved. She said they were going to get you. We got caught in a traffic jam in Scarlet, and then Conrad walked up to the car. I knew then that they hadn't made it. He told me that the fire had already burned through the camp. I jumped out and threw up beside the road. The thought of you all burning to death…"

He kissed her hair, spoke in a soothing voice. "That didn't happen."

"Conrad went to Naomi next and gave her the news. Somehow, seeing how devastated she was helped me pull myself together. I tried to focus on helping her."

"You think I'm brave, but of the two of us, you're the truly strong one."

Kat propped herself on her elbow, looked down at the man who had turned her life upside down. "That's crazy talk."

"Is it? You've had three babies without drugs, and you—"

"I'm hardly the first woman to do that." Her grandmother had given birth in *hogaans* squatting on dirt floors and beneath trees, sometimes alone.

But Gabe wasn't done. "I get trapped by a wildfire and climb to safety. Okay, cool. High fives. But you believe you've lost your husband and still find the strength to go on with the day and help someone else who's suffering. That took a lot more courage than on-sighting a hundred feet of rock."

"I think we'll have to agree to disagree on that. Besides, what choice did I have?'

He tucked a strand of hair behind her ear. "We sure have been through some shit together, haven't we?"

That was the truth.

She pressed her palm against his heartbeat, the feel of it precious. "I've known from the beginning that I might have to finish this journey without you."

He started to speak, but she pressed a finger to his lips to stop him.

"I know you would never risk your life for kicks the way you used to do, but I live with the tension of being proud of the man you are and what you can do, and, at the same time, feeling afraid that your courage and abilities are going to get you killed."

His gaze went soft. "I know that scares you, but try not to worry. You and I are going to grow old as the hills together. You'll look like your Grandma Alice, with no teeth and wrinkly like an old apple."

Kat laughed at that image—and came up with one of her own. "You'll look like that old white-haired guy who used to live next door—stooped over with trousers that go all the way up to your chest."

The two of them laughed together, the feel of it sweet after so much worry.

Gabe kissed her, stroked her hair. "One day, many years from now, when we're gone, our kids will stand together and say, 'Our parents loved each other well.'"

Kat rested her cheek against his chest. "I like that."

She closed her eyes, snuggling against him as he drew up the sheet around them. Soon, they were both asleep.

## Chapter 22

MARC SAT at a long table on the Wests' deck at the Cimarron, trading stories about his day with the others while the children played on the lawn below, Sophie holding Marc's hand, the breeze cool, the sky full of stars.

Marc took a swig of his beer. "Then we look up, and there they are, just hanging out, having a good time in a cave."

Julian, who'd been treated in the ER before leaving Scarlet Springs, picked up the story. "Rossiter had free soloed a hundred feet up the cliff wall, fixed a pulley in the rock with a piton, and pulled the others to safety."

Heads shook, and people laughed.

Zach shifted his sleeping boy from one arm to the other. "Why am I not surprised?"

Nate looked amazed. "You have to be in complete control of your body's adrenaline response to do what he did with a hundred-foot wall of flame coming at you."

Jack picked up his whiskey. "That man has an unnatural relationship with gravity."

"Bless his heart," said Natalie, Zach's wife, glass of wine in her hand. "Are we sure he's actually human?"

Janet didn't seem to find anything funny in this. "Think what would have happened if he had fallen or hadn't been there. All of those people…"

Jack took his wife's hand. "Life is hard enough without dwelling on the 'what ifs.'"

The conversation drifted after that.

Jack's and Nate's experience rescuing stranded horses and being a Noah's Ark for everything from Australian cattle dogs to fawns and eagles. Zach calling Reece, who'd won the day for Scarlet Springs with the 747 Supertanker. Natalie watching all of this unfold on the television and through text messages from Zach.

"I felt so helpless."

Then Sophie and Tessa shared their visit with Joaquin and Mia.

"I looked at his photos when Tom went through them," Tessa said. "They were incredible. There was one shot of the fire chief, covered in sweat and soot, standing in front of the fire as if he were daring it to come and get his town. It gave me chills."

Nate shared what he'd heard about Hawke's condition. "He has a long road ahead of him, but he'll get through it."

Megan put her hand over his. "You know better than anyone what that's like."

Nate twined his fingers with Megan's. "I've already told Vicki that if she needs anything, she can count on us."

Jack tossed back the last of his whiskey. "A lot of people are going to need help getting back on their feet. I'll call Joe, and we'll put something together."

Sophie knew that Jack and Nate would reach into their

own pockets to help. They were among the most generous people she knew.

"Hawke is a hero," Marc said. "He fought like hell for his town."

Sophie shared a conspiratorial smile with Tessa and Megan. "What did the two of you do today? You were up there for most of the day."

She didn't miss the quick glance Marc shot Julian.

Julian avoided eye contact the way a person does when they're about to lie. "We helped with the early evacuations and then hung out with the members of the Rocky Mountain Search and Rescue Team, waiting for the green light to go search for Rossiter and the others."

Marc nodded. "We also caught the idiots who were flying the drone that made the helicopter crash."

"So, you were never in any danger up there?" Tessa asked sweetly.

They shook their heads.

"Nah, man," Julian said.

"It was pretty chill day for us." Marc took a drink of his beer.

Megan shook her head, poked a finger at her brother. "You are *such* a liar."

Sophie turned to Marc. "Sheriff Pella called and talked to Megan this evening before you got here. He told a different story. He said the two of you are heroes. He said you evacuated a street that was already in flames to save a cat and a dog and how someone in town told him that Julian had gotten second-degree burns in the process."

"Crank is a cool dog," Julian protested.

"Hey, I got scratched by the cat." Marc held up his hands. "Don't forget that. I rescued the guys' wedding photo, too. They were very grateful."

Megan took it from there. "Pella says he's amazed the two of you made it out alive. But, yeah, it was a chill day."

Tessa looked Julian square in the face. "You and I are going to have a conversation when we get home."

Julian gave Tessa a slow, sexy smile. "Aren't you going to take care of me? I *am* wounded."

Tessa narrowed her eyes at him. "Oh, I'll take care of you all right."

Sophie noticed Marc watching her, as if trying to gauge how she was feeling about it all. "To tell you the truth, hon, I wasn't even surprised."

Marc frowned. "You weren't?"

When the laughter died down, Jack got to his feet. "Who wants coffee and a slice of my cherry pie?"

"Is that even a question?" Natalie asked.

It was close to midnight when Sophie and Marc loaded sleeping kids into the car and headed back to Denver.

Sophie looked over at the man she loved. "You can't help it, can you?"

He glanced over at her. "What do you mean?"

"You just can't sit on the sidelines. When there's trouble, when someone needs help, when lives are on the line, you have to be in the thick of it."

His brow furrowed. "I *can't* do nothing."

Sophie laughed. "No, you really can't, can you?"

He took his right hand off the wheel, threaded his fingers through hers. "I didn't tell you all of it because I didn't want to upset or worry you."

"I know." Sophie raised his hand to her lips, kissed it. "It's one of the reasons I fell in love with you, but it scares the hell out of me sometimes.

"Remember the graduation party? You saw those meth heads bullying me, and you stopped them. You didn't even know me—not really—but you risked your safety for my sake."

Marc grinned. "Remember what happened *after* the graduation party?"

"How about we reenact that when we get home? I'll be the shy virgin—"

Marc snorted. "Shy? You were a virgin, but I don't remember you being shy."

Sophie let that go. "You can be the hunky guy who rescues and deflowers me."

"I like where you're going with this."

"You're my hero, Hunt. You always will be. Just don't get yourself killed, okay?"

He gave her hand a squeeze, serious now. "You got it."

⸻

AS QUIET FELL over the fairgrounds and evacuees took to their cots, the wind died down, and the temperatures dropped, giving firefighters a chance to rest.

As the sun rose the next morning, the latest edition of the Denver Independent hit the streets with its stunning front-page photo of a firefighter facing down a wall of flame—and the story of how he and the man who'd taken the photo had almost been killed.

In the early morning cool, fire crews put out the last of the big spot fires and started the long work of mopping up —finding hot spots, cutting down dangerous snags, clearing roads of ash and fallen timber. By mid-afternoon, the wind picked up again, but this time it brought rain, and the fire was finally out. The evacuation order was lifted, and the residents of Scarlet Springs began the hard work of returning home.

In all, forty-six homes had burned to the ground,

together with their barns, sheds, and everything inside them. Three public campgrounds and Camp Mato Sapa had been destroyed as well. But, not a single human life had been lost.

To everyone who'd seen the fire, that seemed like a miracle.

Lt. Governor Reece Sheridan came to visit Scarlet Springs that afternoon. He wore jeans and a T-shirt with the Colorado flag on it, shaking hands with firefighters and people who'd lost their homes, promising to do all he could to support the town's recovery. The media followed him, of course, one intrepid photographer getting a photo of climbing legend Megs Hill kissing him square on the cheek. Then, without the media horde, Sheridan paid a quiet visit to the Denver Burn Center, spending time with good friend Joaquin Ramirez and visiting the others wounded in the blaze as well.

Moved by the media coverage, communities around Colorado and the nation joined together to help Scarlet Springs, donating money, clothes, and food to those who had lost everything. The director of the YMCA children's camp in Estes Park heard of the plight of Camp Mato Sapa and took the children and camp counselors in, giving them a safe and fun place to spend that last three days of the session.

Almost immediately, signs began to go up at the end of people's driveways, on corners, and in storefronts. Some were hand-written on poster board, while others were spray-painted on scraps of plywood. They all carried the same message.

"Thank you, firefighters!"

"God bless our fire chief."

"Scarlet Strong."

Joe and Rain sent photos of the signs to Vicki, who

showed them to Eric, who was in and out of it on morphine.

"See? People love you," she told him.

As the investigation into the fire was set in motion, Terry Robertson announced his immediate retirement, leaving the top county firefighting post open. More than a few people thought Eric Hawke should have that job.

———

AUSTIN DROVE Lexi's car up the canyon in heavy traffic, listening while she told him what she'd learned from Bear's mother's journal, which she had read last night.

"They all got sick with something—high fever, nausea, seizures. His father refused to come into town for a doctor. He thought God would heal them."

"How did that work out for him?" Austin hated shit like that.

It was one thing for an adult to risk their own life on faith-healing. It was another to use religious beliefs as an excuse to deprive a child of life-saving care.

"Elizabeth, the youngest child, died first. Then Abel, his father, who'd had pneumonia that previous winter, died. Matthew—Bear—got sick next and was in bed with a fever for a long time. One by one, the other children got sick and died."

"Why didn't their mother go to Scarlet for help?"

"By the time her husband died, she was sick, too. She wrote this heartbreaking entry about trying to find the strength to dig graves for Mary and Paul. In the end, it was just the two of them, Bear and his mother."

"How old was Bear then?"

"He would have been about thirteen."

"Hell of an age to watch your whole family die."

"Bear slowly got better, but when he was upright again, he wasn't the same boy he'd been. His mother said the fever had damaged his mind somehow. She also wrote that fever had left her all but blind. She lingered on, doing her best to teach him how to care for himself, knowing she was dying. She wrote that he remembered every Bible verse she read to him but that he seemed to have the mind of a small child."

What disease could cause brain damage and make a person go blind? Scarlet fever maybe? Meningitis? Viral meningoencephalitis?

Hell, entire families had been wiped out by fevers in Scarlet Springs back in the day.

"In her last entry, Rebecca wrote that she warned Bear against going to town or trusting people from Scarlet Springs because they would lead him astray."

"I guess Bear got lonely enough or hungry enough to ignore that—or at least part of it. He's never been open to talking about where he lives or where he's from."

"It breaks my heart to think of him up there alone." Lexi held something up. "I found this old document tucked in the back of the journal. I'm not sure what it is. It's pretty faded."

Traffic had brought the canyon to a standstill, so Austin reached over, took the document, unfolded it. At first, he couldn't make sense of it. Then he saw a familiar stamp at the bottom.

*Forest County Clerk & Recorder*

He stared. "This is the deed to the land."

"It's … what?"

"It's the deed to the property where the cabin stood. The land belongs to Bear."

Since the day Austin had discovered the cabin, he had worried the county administration would find out Bear was there and force him off the land. Now, they would have to concede that the land belonged to Bear outright.

"Does that mean he'll be able to stay up there?"

"The county might choose to contest it or try to condemn the land, but they'll have everyone from Scarlet on their back if they do. Of course, we need to talk to Bear first, see how much he understands and what he wants us to do. These things belong to him, not to us. We're just keeping them safe."

Traffic nudged forward again, winding toward home.

"It's going to be burned to the ground," Lexi said.

"Yeah."

They had both resigned themselves to finding an ash heap. They'd heard on the news that most of the homes beyond Quarry Street had burned. Their home sat high above Quarry Street, midway up Dead Man's Hill overlooking town.

They rounded the last corner, and Scarlet Springs came into view.

Austin stared. "Holy shit."

"God, look at that."

From the top of the mountain stretching westward to the high peaks, south to Ski Scarlet, and northward toward Estes Park, the conifer and aspens were gone, replaced by a landscape of gray. No trees. No houses. Nothing but ash.

Austin refused to let his spirits sink. He'd gotten a second chance at life. Nothing was more important than that. "We have a lot to be grateful for."

Lexi reached over, rested a hand on his thigh.

They found Julia Marcs directing traffic where the highway entered town, a big smile on her face. "Welcome home!"

Bear stood in his roundabout, preaching encouragement to those who drove by. "It is the Lord who goes before you. He will be with you. He will not leave you or forsake you. Do not fear or be dismayed!"

"Seeing him, knowing what he's been through—it breaks my heart," Lexi said.

Austin waved. "Hey, Bear!"

"Austin Taylor!"

They drove on through town and up the highway toward home.

"God, look at this." Austin glanced around at charred tree trunks and stone chimneys that marked the homes of friends and neighbors.

"Oh, Austin. It's terrible."

"It's going to be okay." He turned the corner onto their street. "A year from now…"

"Oh, my God!" Lexi squealed, pointing. "It's there! It's still there!"

Their house stood by itself in the middle of the block, the orange-red tint on the exterior and the surrounding vegetation telling the story. The fire had burned to within ten feet of the house before it had been stopped.

"It looks like we took a direct hit from one of the slurry bombers."

"Thank God! Thank you, slurry bomber pilot!"

Austin turned into the driveway. "Honey, we're home."

━━

PAIN WOKE ERIC. He heard himself moan, opened his eyes.

Nate West was standing beside his hospital bed.

"Hey."

"Hey, brother." Nate pushed the call button. "He needs a bolus of morphine."

"I'll be in to check on him in a—"

"Now."

"Thanks, man."

Eric closed his eyes, breathed. It did no more to relieve his pain than it had Vicki's when she'd been in labor.

Nate rested a hand against his shoulder. "Hang on. She's coming."

The nurse entered the room. "So, you're having some pain?"

Eric couldn't respond without shouting, so Nate answered for him.

"He needs morphine."

A few minutes later, Eric was floating. "Thanks. I appreciate it."

"Happy to help." Nate grinned. "You're looking good, man."

"Good to see you, too."

He and Nate had gone to high school together. Eric had gone off to fight wildfires, while Nate had joined the Marines. Eric had always respected the man.

"How are you feeling?"

"Better than I was a few minutes ago."

"I bet." The burn scars on the right side of Nate's face were proof that he knew more about what Eric was going through than Eric did. "Joaquin Ramirez told me what happened. He says you saved his life and the pilot's."

"How is he?"

"He's going home today—Silver and the pilot, too." Nate held up a newspaper. "He wanted me to bring you this."

It was today's *Denver Independent*.

"Wow." Eric remembered the exact moment when this shot had been taken. He'd heard the click of the camera and ordered Ramirez to get out. "Ramirez is good."

"He's kind of a big deal. He won a Pulitzer some years back."

"Rossiter told me about that. Can I keep the newspaper?"

"It's yours." Nate took it from him, set it on his bedside table.

"Thanks for helping with the evacuations. We would have lost a lot of horses if not for you and your old man."

"Not just horses." Nate told Eric that his father had helped Winona evacuate the wildlife clinic. "It made his entire year to have a baby moose and fawns in his trailer."

"A baby moose?" Eric hadn't known that.

"Yep. So, tell me about your situation."

Eric told Nate what the doctors had said. "I'd show you my leg, but it's all wrapped up now. They've got temporary skin grafts on it. I guess they take skin from a donor site at some point and use that."

Nate listened, nodding. "They want the burn site to stabilize first. They won't want to risk losing an autograft to a hematoma or some other problem."

"I just got to say, it doesn't sound like fun."

Nate looked Eric straight in the eyes. "I won't sugar-coat it. It's going to be tough. For a time, every day is going to be a bitch, but it will get better. I promise. A year from now, you'll be looking at this in your rearview mirror."

Eric wondered what it was like for Nate to be here. Did it stir up bad memories for him? Eric couldn't see how it wouldn't. Nate had spent the better part of a year in a burn center in San Antonio and had gone through dozens of surgeries to reconstruct his face and enable him to use his right hand. And still, he was here.

"How did you get through it?"

"One day at a time. One hour at a time. Sometimes, it was minute by minute." Nate pulled over a chair, sat. "I don't have many memories of the first weeks. I was unconscious a lot of the time. The first time my fiancée saw me with my face unbandaged, she decided she couldn't handle it and broke things off. It felt like my life was over."

"Bitch."

Nate chuckled. "I appreciate that, but she did me a favor. She got out of the way and made room in my life for Megan. You've got Vicki, so you're set. And, hey, congrats. I hear you're expecting another baby. That's great."

"Yeah." Eric fought to stay awake. "Vicki is trying to find a rental nearby, somewhere furnished where she and my mom can stay with Caden until I'm discharged. It's too much to drive in from Boulder or Scarlet Springs every day."

"I've got a friend here in Denver who's a realtor. She can help Vicki narrow her search and handle the rental agreement for her."

"Can you text Victoria … the realtor's number?" The morphine was really kicking in now. "She's got so much on her mind."

"You got it. If you or Vicki need anything else—help with medical bills, meals, someone to drive, watch Caden, go to the grocery store—please let me know. I've got your six. You're a hero to the people of Scarlet and to me."

"Thanks." Eric's throat grew tight. "Coming from you, that really means something."

Eric didn't realize his eyes were closed until Nate spoke again.

"You rest, buddy. You did your part. Just heal and let us take it from here."

## Chapter 23

BRANDON FOLLOWED Libby through his front door, glad to be home. "Smoky with subtle undertones of smoke."

He'd left the windows open, and smoke from the fire had gotten in. It hadn't done any lasting damage and would clear eventually. Then again, the entire area around Scarlet Springs still smelled of smoke.

Libby set his bag of junk down inside the door. "Let's get you comfortable."

Wearing overall shorts and a yellow tube top, her hair in three ridiculous braids, she buzzed into his bedroom—their bedroom—and turned down the bed. "I washed the sheets last night. I wanted everything to be clean so you don't get an infection."

"That was sweet of you. Thanks." He didn't want to spend the day resting, but his body said otherwise.

He pulled off his T-shirt and crawled carefully into bed, wearing only the shorts she'd brought him and his underwear. His lower legs were heavily bandaged. Doctors had stitched sheets of lab-grown pig skin onto the deepest

burns to help them heal—which made wearing pants difficult. His hands and elbows were bandaged, too, but
without the temporary skin grafts.

And his face…

His doctor said those burns would heal, but the scars
would take time to fade. Brandon didn't really care. What
mattered to him was dashing around the house right now,
wearing three silly braids, and fussing over him.

He wouldn't lie. He liked that.

"I'll bring you your pain pills and some water."

"I can get them myself."

"No, you rest." She left the room.

He grinned, laid back onto his pillow. He would need
to find room for her stuff, clear out space from his closet,
on his bookshelves, in the bathroom cabinet.

She reappeared with a glass of ice water in one hand
and a bottle of Percocet in the other. "You're supposed to
take your next dose in two hours. I'm going to set the oven
timer so you don't miss it."

He caught her wrist. "Hey, come here."

She hesitated. "I don't want to hurt you."

He patted his bare chest. "See any burns here?"

She shook her head, smiled, stretched out carefully
beside him, resting her cheek on his chest. "I've spent so
much time here it already feels like home."

"That's good." Brandon kissed her forehead. "I'll clear
out space for you soon. Where is the stuff you managed to
rescue from your house?"

She pointed.

He lifted his head, saw a small suitcase, her TV, and a
few plastic garbage bags sitting in the corner of his room.
"That's it?"

*Damn.*

She nodded. "I only took the important stuff—my

record collection, my beer bottles, my nail polish, my TV and computer, my sex toys, some clothes."

"Vinyl, beer bottles, electronics, nail polish, and sex toys." He couldn't help but chuckle. "You've got your priorities straight."

"Some." She raised herself onto her elbow, looked down at him. "I took that stupid music box—the one my dad gave me before he disappeared. I don't know why."

"It must mean something to you."

He'd thought a lot about what she'd told him—the violence and abandonment she'd experienced as a kid. That kind of pain cut deep. It was bound to affect their relationship again and again. But he would rather spend his life on a rollercoaster with Libby than walk a smooth, straight path with anyone else.

He loved her. It was as simple as that.

Her lips curved in a little smile. "The plastic bag holding my sex toys broke on the way out to my car. The Deputy US Marshal who helped me evacuate was standing right there when it happened. He saw *everything*. I had to run inside and get the suitcase. Then these other two guys walked up—"

Brandon couldn't help it. He burst out laughing, the mental image of Libby scrambling to pick up vibrators, dildos, and cock rings under the supervision of a deputy US marshal more than he could handle.

"You think that's funny?"

Brandon was laughing too hard to answer.

Libby stood, peeled off her overalls, pulled the tube top over her head, freeing her breasts. "I think I need to test them to see whether any were broken."

Brandon got a hold of himself. "You should wash them before you do that."

She grabbed a handful of things out of the suitcase,

disappeared into the bathroom, and returned a few minutes later.

Brandon settled in, ready for a show.

She picked the pink one first—a run-of-the-mill cylindrical vibe—and turned it on, the buzzing sound proof that it worked. Then she reached over, those beautiful breasts swaying, and rubbed the damned thing over the bulge in his shorts.

Sure, it was arousing, but it wasn't going to get him off.

"Libby, I'm all doped up. I doubt—"

She jerked his shorts down far enough to free his half-hard cock and gave him a lick, teasing the head with her tongue.

And just like that, he was hard as a rock.

She looked at him from beneath her lashes. "You were saying?"

"Huh?" He couldn't remember saying anything.

She drew him into her mouth, worked the head of his cock with her tongue, teased the shaft with the vibrator.

Okay, it felt good—and strange.

He reached out to fondle her breasts, but she turned away, set that vibrator aside, and picked up the vibrating cock ring.

"Let's see if this one still works." She turned it on, touched the vibrating part to the underside of his cock where he was most sensitive, her tongue flicking the tip.

He jerked, gasped. "Shit."

He liked her mouth more than the vibrators and her vagina more than her mouth, but there was something about this, something irritatingly arousing.

"How does that feel?"

"Libby!"

She stopped, smiled at him, stroking his length.

"No more vibrators. I just want you."

She straddled him backward. "I don't want to bump your legs."

"Okay." Brandon didn't give a shit at this moment.

She moved the crotch of her panties aside and guided him inside her.

Brandon groaned, grasped her hips, guiding her as she rode him, her ass cheeks bouncing in a way that drove him crazy. He could tell from the motion of her right arm that she was stroking her clit, and that drove him crazy, too.

He took hold of one of her braids, gave a tug, pulled her head back, his hips driving into her from below. "God, *yes*."

She came with a cry, the sound of her pleasure driving him over the edge, orgasm drenching him with bliss.

She snuggled against his chest afterward, careful of his burns. "I love you, Brandon. It scares the hell out of me, but I love you."

"We'll take it one day at a time." He tried to stay awake, to stay with her.

She got up, bent down, kissed him. "Sleep."

An orgasm and Percocet.

Did he have any choice?

---

CHASKA DROVE down a winding country road, Naomi in the seat beside him, Old Man and Winona in the back. Ahead on his right, he saw it—a large wooden sign that read Wind River Wolf Sanctuary. "Here we are."

He and Naomi exchanged a quick glance.

The day had finally come.

Chaska parked near a red-brick ranch-style house and climbed out, Naomi and the others joining him.

"This way." Winona led them toward the house.

A blond woman in jeans, cowboy boots, and a white T-shirt stepped outside. "Hey, Winona. It's great to see you again."

Winona introduced the woman to the rest of them. "This is Heather. She runs the sanctuary. Heather, this is my Grandfather, my brother, Chaska, and my sister-in-law Naomi."

Heather shook hands with each of them. "Great to meet you."

"Heather and I met online years ago. She runs the sanctuary. They offer a home to wolves and wolf hybrids."

Heather gave them a quick overview. "We've got about seven hundred acres and, at the moment, twenty-two wolves and wolf-dog hybrids. They have lots of room to run, some natural game to eat, and full-time monitoring and care."

"I brought Shota's crate."

Heather smiled. "Great. Let's go see him."

Winona nodded, a forced smile on her face. "Yes. Thanks."

Heather loaded them onto a muddy UTV, talking as they drove through the property. "A lot of people don't know what they're getting themselves into when they adopt a wolf. Maybe they've always had big dogs, but wolves aren't like big dogs. There's a part of them that stays wild. I've seen them tear through drywall and rip crates apart in minutes. We take in wolf hybrids at risk of being euthanized and wolves that can't live in the wild."

Like Shota.

Chaska wasn't sure how his sister was holding it together. She loved Shota like a mother loved a child. She'd hand-reared him, cared for him around the clock, saved his furry life. For her to give him up was both incredibly brave and utterly selfless.

She had agonized about it these past few days after Heather called to tell her that Shota had bonded with a female named Aput. Wolves were pack animals, and though Shota was attached to Winona, she wasn't a wolf.

"I can't be there with him all day every day like pack-mates would," she'd said. "If I ever find a boyfriend or have children, I'll have to worry about Shota's reaction. He'll have so much more room there than he does here. He'll be with other wolves. I'll be able to move out of the house, get my own place, get out of your hair."

Naomi had taken her hand. "You're welcome to stay here. It's your home, too."

But Winona was determined to do the right thing for Shota—and for herself.

As Old Man had said, "Sometimes, doing the right thing means doing the hard thing."

That's why they'd all come.

They were here to support Winona while she said goodbye to a dear friend.

"I'm going to stop on this rise." Heather pulled a pair of battered binoculars out from under her seat. "They're over there."

Winona took the binoculars, looked in the direction Heather had pointed, her lips curving in a tremulous smile. "Oh, she's pretty! She's pure white. They're playing."

"They bonded through the fence almost immediately. Aput—that's an Inuit word for snow—has been by herself for a while. She's an alpha female to her core. She took to Shota right away. I put them in together to see how it would go, and they just clicked."

Winona turned, handed the binoculars to Chaska, tears on her cheeks.

He held them up, looked in the same direction Winona had.

There they were—romping, chasing each other. Then Aput dropped to the ground, lying on her side in a gesture of submission. Shota wagged his tail, nipped her, licked her muzzle.

Heather drove on, Chaska handing the binoculars first to Old Man, who chuckled, and then to Naomi, who looked like she might cry, too. Shota had saved her life, after all, and brought her and Chaska together.

They stopped fifty yards from the fence that marked the boundary of the enclosure.

Heather gestured toward the fence. "Go say hello, but be careful where Aput is concerned. I can't say how she'll react if you stick your hand inside."

Winona walked forward, Chaska following with Naomi and Old Man.

Shota saw her immediately. He trotted to the fence, gave a welcoming yap.

Winona reached inside to pet Shota, speaking to him softly in Lakota.

Aput didn't look like she liked this and moved closer, head down, teeth bared.

Shota snapped at Aput, stopping her in her tracks.

Winona scratched Shota behind his ears. "You look happy here, Shota. You have a new friend. That's good. A wolf needs a pack. I love you, and I will miss you so much. But this is your home now. I want you to be happy. I'll come to visit you sometimes. I promise."

*Shit.*

Chaska's throat grew tight.

"You have been a good friend. I'm so happy to have known you. Walk well, Shota. I will see you again."

There was no word in Lakota for goodbye.

At that, Winona took a step backward, anguish on her face as Shota bounded off with the other wolf. As they drove away in the UTV, Shota turned to face them once more—and howled.

Winona smiled through her tears. "He's saying thank you."

Heather nodded. "He sure is."

———

*Five weeks later*

ERIC SAT in the passenger seat while Vicki drove into Scarlet Springs. Tonight was the big fundraiser at Knockers. Joe and Jack West had put it together, and they'd wanted to wait until Eric was out of the hospital and able to attend.

They'd left Caden with Eric's mom. This was Eric's first evening out since before the fire, and Vicki wanted the two of them to be able to relax.

Eric wasn't altogether sure he wanted to be there, but he couldn't say that. He didn't like being called a hero. He hadn't done anything special.

"I know a secret," Vicki said. "Joe seeds the pot."

"What do you mean 'Joe seeds the pot'?"

"He throws money into the donation jar when people aren't looking. He knows he has more to give than anyone else in town, but he wants people to invest in their own community and have a sense of ownership in the outcome of these events."

"So, he makes it look like donations are coming thick and fast from everywhere." Eric was impressed. "I always wondered how a community as small as Scarlet could raise a hundred grand. Who told you?"

"Rain."

Of course.

"She figured it out a long time ago but never said anything to him about it."

Eric chuckled. "Yeah, Old Caribou Joe—he's a clever one."

The parking lot at Knockers was packed, but someone had reserved a spot for them near the front door, a hand-painted wooden sign that read "Eric & Vicki Hawke" sitting at the curb.

"They don't want you to have to walk far."

"I can walk just fine." Okay, so it wasn't always comfortable, especially with the compression sleeve on his calf. But he *could* walk.

He climbed out, made it to the door before Vicki did, and opened it for her. "I told you I can walk just fine."

"Show off."

They walked inside, heads turning their way.

"He's here!"

"Hawke is here."

"He looks good."

"Eric Hawke!" Bear sat at a table near the door, dinner and a tall glass of milk on the table in front of him.

"Hey, Bear." Eric was happy to see him whole and alive.

Part of the proceeds from tonight would go toward rebuilding Bear's cabin. Joe had hired an attorney to fight for Bear's ownership of the land. The proceedings hadn't gotten far before a former county employee had admitted to burying the deed so the county could claim the land.

Rain met Eric and Vicki, gave them each a hug. "God, it's good to see you again, Eric. The Team saved places for you at the usual table."

They made their way to the back corner near the climbing wall, but it was slow going. Everyone seemed to be here tonight. Chip and Charles. Herb, the pharmacist.

Zach McBride, Marc Hunter, Julian Darcangelo, and their wives. They were hanging with Julia Marcs, Joaquin Ramirez and his wife Mia, who was holding their two-week-old baby boy.

"He's so cute! Can I hold him?" Vicki asked. "What did you name him?"

"Érik—after your husband." Mia laid the bundle in Vicki's arms. "Érik Matías Ramirez."

"I'm touched, really." Eric gave Ramirez a hug. The two had stayed in touch, and Eric considered him a true friend. "Congratulations, man. How do you like being a father?"

Ramirez's face lit up. "It's the best."

Lt. Gov. Reece Sheridan was with them, too. "This is my wife, Kara."

Kara shook Eric's and Vicki's hands. "I've heard so much about you."

Brandon was there with Libby, the two of them sitting with John Wright and his wife, Susan. "Chief."

Eric hugged Silver and shook John's hand. "You two look like shit."

Where they'd had blisters on his face, they now had red patches just like Eric.

Silver grinned. "You, too, man."

The Wests had a table to themselves—Jack, Janet, Nate, and Megan. They stood as he and Vicki drew near, shook his hand. They had done so much this past month to help Vicki and make the burden of Eric's recovery easier on her.

Vicki kissed Jack and Nate on the cheek. "I don't know how to thank you all."

"You just did," Jack said. "You're welcome. We were happy to help."

"You're looking better," Nate said.

"You were right. It gets easier."

Rose kissed Eric on the cheek.

Bob Jewel socked him on the shoulder. "The Inn has survived *two* fires now, thanks to you. I've got a bottle of scotch for you."

"If he doesn't drink it first," Kendra joked.

Finally, they reached the Team table.

"Look who's here." Sasha jumped up, came around the table to hug them both. "It's so good to have you back."

"It's good to be back." That was the understatement of the century.

Nicole was next, followed by Lexi.

"We missed you."

Taylor grinned. "We saved seats for you."

"Thanks." Eric greeted the others. God, it was nice to see them all. "Hey, Belcourt. How you doing, Naomi? Winona, how's it going?"

"I'm doing fine. How about you?"

"Better." Eric had heard about Shota and Winona's decision to leave him at the wolf sanctuary. He could only imagine how hard that had been for her. "Keeping out of trouble, Herrera? Hey, Acharya. O'Brien. Where's Megs?"

Ahearn pointed. "She's up at the bar with Joe."

Eric sat beside Taylor, a little overwhelmed by the crowd and the noise after so many weeks in the quiet of a hospital.

Rain walked up, Angel on her back, and set down a dozen menus. "Joe says to tell you all to keep your filthy money to yourself. All emergency responders eat free tonight. And that goes double for you, Eric and Vicki."

Eric knew the menu by heart, but he picked it up anyway. He was trying to decide between a cheeseburger and going all out with a ribeye when Joe stepped up onstage.

"I want to welcome everyone to tonight's fundraiser. We've got friends new and old with us tonight. It's a real pleasure to have you all here. All sales of Libby's new Limited Edition Smoke and Fire IPA go toward the recovery effort. Here she is to tell us about it."

Libby bounced onto the stage. "Hey, everyone! Smoke and Fire IPA is a hoppy brew with overtones of citrus to capture that sense of summer and smoked shishito peppers to give it a smoky burn. I hope you'll enjoy it as much as I do."

"Smoked shishito peppers?" Eric would have to buy some and save it for when he could drink again. It wasn't safe to mix alcohol with pain meds.

"I've got to try it," Taylor said.

Joe took the mic again. "The Timberline Mudbugs have a special show for us tonight, but before they take the stage, there are some folks here who deserve our thanks."

"Uh-oh." Eric met Vicki's gaze. "He's not going to…"

Vicki smiled. "Of course, he is. You know Joe."

"I'd like to turn the microphone over to Councilwoman Megs Hill."

Cheers and applause.

"There are a lot of unsung heroes in this crowd tonight, so I've come to name names."

She described each person's actions, asking those who'd made special contributions to stand. Hunter, Darcangelo, and McBride for helping with evacuations and catching the guys who'd flown the drone. Julia Marcs for going above and beyond the call of duty in trying to evacuate Camp Mato Sapa. The West family for saving horses and critters of all kinds. Moretti for getting creative and using the fan guns to save Ski Scarlet. Lt. Gov. Reece Sheridan for moving heaven and earth to get the Supertanker. The IHC Pine

Ridge Hotshots, who weren't there but were named nonetheless. Rossiter and Belcourt, who'd been willing to sacrifice their lives for others—and then lived to laugh about it.

Then Megs thanked Scarlct's fire crews, singling out Silver, Jenny, and Ryan.

Hell, they deserved it—and more.

"One man fought harder than anyone that day to save this town. He put everything on the line for us, and he almost lost his life. He doesn't like attention, but he's getting it anyway." Megs' gaze met Eric's from across the crowded pub. "Eric Hawke, I'm talking about you."

Embarrassed, Eric got to his feet and waved.

The pub exploded with cheers and applause, people rising to their feet, even his fellow Team members.

Eric turned to Taylor. "What the hell is wrong with all of you?"

When people had resumed their seats again, Megs went on. "In honor of your courage that day and your unfailing devotion to this town, the Scarlet Town Council has voted unanimously to change the name of Dead Man's Hill to Hawke Hill and to place a marker on the spot where the fire was stopped, honoring you and your crews for your defense of our town."

The room exploded into cheers.

Eric didn't know what to say, a part of him objecting to all of it. He'd only done his job, after all. But as he glanced around at his friends, old and new, a sense of peace settled over him.

His worst nightmare had come to life. A raging wildfire had made a run for his town. But no lives had been lost. Scarlet Springs was recovering, its spirit undimmed. People had pulled together and were rebuilding. All would soon be put right again.

Yeah, he supposed he *had* had something to do with that.

Eric waved a hand for silence. "Okay, okay, everybody. I'm honored beyond words. Thank you so much. But can you cut it out now? Where's the band? Hey, guys, play something, distract these people."

Laughter.

He sat again, warmth in his chest.

"This town loves you, Eric." Vicki kissed him, tears in her eyes. "But no one loves you more than I do."

# Thank You

Thanks for reading *Chasing Fire*. I hope you enjoyed this I-Team/Colorado High Country story. Follow me on Facebook or on Twitter @Pamela_Clare. Join the Scarlet Springs and I-Team Readers Groups on Facebook to be a part of a never-ending conversation with other Scarlet Springs fans and get inside information on the series and on life in Colorado's mountains. You can also sign up to be added to my mailing list at my website to keep up to date on all my releases and to be a part of special newsletter giveaways.

# Also by Pamela Clare

## Contemporary Romance:

### Colorado High Country Series

*Barely Breathing* (Book 1)

*Slow Burn* (Book 2)

*Falling Hard* (Book 3)

*Tempting Fate* (Book 4)

*Close to Heaven* (Book 5)

*Holding On* (Book 6)

*Chasing Fire* (Book 7)

## Romantic Suspense:

### I-Team Series

*Extreme Exposure* (Book 1)

*Heaven Can't Wait* (Book 1.5)

*Hard Evidence* (Book 2)

*Unlawful Contact* (Book 3)

*Naked Edge* (Book 4)

*Breaking Point* (Book 5)

*Skin Deep: An I-Team After Hours Novella* (Book 5.5)

*First Strike: The Prequel to Striking Distance* (Book 5.9)

*Striking Distance* (Book 6)

*Soul Deep: An I-Team After Hours Novella* (Book 6.5)

## About the Author

USA Today best-selling author Pamela Clare began her writing career as a columnist and investigative reporter and eventually became the first woman editor-in-chief of two different newspapers. Along the way, she and her team won numerous state and national honors, including the National Journalism Award for Public Service. In 2011, Clare was awarded the Keeper of the Flame Lifetime Achievement Award for her body of work. A single mother with two sons, she writes historical romance and contemporary romantic suspense at the foot of the beautiful Rocky Mountains. Visit her website and join her mailing list to never miss a new release!

Scarlet Springs Readers Group
Goodreads

www.pamelaclare.com

Printed in Great Britain
by Amazon